D0048991

THE BIG STEEP

THE BIG STEEP

Sandra Balzo

SEVERN
HOUSE

First world edition published in Great Britain in 2021 and the USA in 2022
by Severn House, an imprint of Canongate Books Ltd,
14 High Street, Edinburgh EH1 1TE.

Trade paperback edition first published in Great Britain and the USA in 2023
by Severn House, an imprint of Canongate Books Ltd.

severnhouse.com

British Library Cataloguing-in-Publication Data
A CIP catalogue record for this title is available from the British Library.

ISBN-13: 978-0-7278-9058-0 (cased)
ISBN-13: 978-1-4483-0625-1 (trade paper)
ISBN-13: 978-1-4483-0624-4 (e-book)

All Severn House titles are printed on acid-free paper.

MIX
Paper from
responsible sources
FSC® C013056

Typeset by Palimpsest Book Production Ltd.,
Falkirk, Stirlingshire, Scotland.
Printed and bound in Great Britain by
TJ Books, Padstow, Cornwall.

ONE

'That's absolutely genius,' I told the man sitting across the table from me in my Brookhills, Wisconsin coffeehouse, Uncommon Grounds. 'I'm just jealous I didn't think of it.'

Philip Woodward's freckled face flushed under his reddish hair. 'You're being too kind.'

Vivian Woodward held up one hand. 'Please don't encourage him.'

'Really? You don't think a tea shop named The Big Steep is brilliant?' Since she and her husband had moved here from Boston a month ago to open the enterprise in question, I kind of assumed Vivian was onboard with the idea. Then again, their shop hadn't opened yet, so there was still time to pull out.

'Oh, I know it's clever,' Vivian said now, patting a strand of blonde hair into place. 'Assuming people get the reference. The last thing I want to do is spend my day explaining the shop's name. Not everybody is an old movie nerd.'

Old movies and books, thank you very much. In this case, *The Big Sleep* by Raymond Chandler. A classic by anybody's measure, I would have thought. But . . .

'Unfortunately, two of the nerds are sitting right here,' my business partner Sarah Kingston said to Vivian, setting two lattes on the table. 'More's the pity for you and me.'

I slid one of the lattes in front of each of our new neighbors while Sarah went back to start on our drinks. 'When do you plan on opening the shop?'

Philip Woodward took an appreciative sip of his latte and sat back. He was very much the marketer of the duo. Outgoing, energetic, positive. His wife . . . well, I was not quite sure what Vivian was at this point of our acquaintance.

'God knows,' she said now, taking her own sip and wrinkling her nose before putting the latte mug down. 'Turning my grandparents' decrepit cottage into a tea shop is challenge enough. But every time we turn around, the city or county has another paper for somebody to sign or hoop for us to jump through.'

Like Vivian, Sarah had inherited the building where we now sat – the historic Brookhills Junction train depot. No longer a long-haul train stop, the depot served the commuter trains that ran in and out of the city of Milwaukee, fifteen miles to our east.

And, since Uncommon Grounds now occupied a space in the building that already had been outfitted and permitted as a restaurant for travelers, our renovations were fairly minor. Things like retro-fitting the station's ticket windows into service counters and refurbishing the depot's clocks that had marked the time over the decades.

The Woodwards, on the other hand, were starting from scratch. Not even up to scratch, really, given the neglect of the property over the years.

Still, Philip seemed embarrassed that his wife was being such a Debbie-downer. 'It's just paperwork really. And the physical renovation will go faster now that Eric is helping us clear the property.' He turned to me. 'Thank you for suggesting him, Maggy.'

'Thank *you* for giving him gainful employment over spring break.' My son Eric went to the University of Minnesota in Minneapolis, a five-hour drive west of Brookhills. I was grateful to have him home, but also happy he had something to do away from the living-room couch for a few hours a day. And he was earning money, which pleased both of us.

'Well, we had to hire somebody to do the grunt work,' Vivian said.

Philip glanced at me uneasily. 'That's unkind, Vivian.'

'Oh, you know what I mean,' she said a little impatiently and turned to me. 'The yard is even more of a wreck, and I certainly wasn't going to touch it or the garbage dump you euphemistically call a compost pile.'

Well, that made it ever so much better. 'There's nothing dangerous or toxic, is there?'

'How ever would I know?' Vivian asked, shrugging. 'My

maternal side of the family is . . . well, let's say it's a bit of a mystery to me.'

'Vivian's mother doesn't like to talk about the past,' Philip explained. 'What little we do know about her parents is that they were hippies back in the day, living off the land here. I'm sure the only thing in Vivian's garbage dump is just harmless waste returning to the earth.'

'Accompanied by the occasional hookah pipe,' Vivian muttered.

Reassuring. I just hoped the old folks weren't into other drugs and their paraphernalia.

'The expression "hookah pipe" is actually redundant,' Philip was saying mildly, raising his eyebrows in a professorial manner. 'It's common usage, of course, but I believe a "hookah" is, by definition, a water pipe.'

'Whatever you say,' Vivian said, discounting him with a wave of her hand. 'But they were all probably high as kites.'

This last was said a little bitterly and Philip glanced uncertainly at his wife. 'Yes, well, I guess we'll never know. But from what Eric tells me, the compost heap has turned up some interesting things, steeping away for virtually decades.'

'Tea steeps,' Vivian corrected her husband in retaliation, and her nose wrinkled again. Or maybe she was stuck that way.

'As does compost,' Philip said. 'According to Eric, once the organic material breaks down into the finished compost soil, you can steep it in water for a few days and use the resultant nutrient-filled liquid as a natural fertilizer. They even call it "tea". Isn't that perfect?'

'Include it in your menu,' Sarah suggested, popping her head out of the service window to place another latte on the counter. Being post-lunch and pre-afternoon commuter traffic, the shop was quiet. Sarah was, too, though that usually meant she was listening intently, waiting for her chance to kibbitz. 'Black, green, oolong and too-long.'

Philip laughed and slapped the table, sending the Woodwards' own lattes jiggling. 'Too-long. I like that, Sarah.'

'Funny.' Vivian's face said just the opposite.

'Not to worry, my dear,' Philip assured her. 'I won't include compost tea in our promotional materials. I just think it's a fun parallel, don't you? And maybe someday we'll go all green – as in environment, not tea – and it will be a selling point.'

Vivian said nothing, but her body language screamed 'over my dead body'.

The tension between the two spouses was palpable.

'I had no idea Eric knew anything about composting,' I said. 'We don't compost at home or here, though we do recycle, of course.'

'Good thing, since it's been the law in Wisconsin for thirty years,' Sarah said, coming around to pick up the two lattes now at the window.

Had it really? 'That's longer than Eric has been alive.'

'By nearly a decade.' Sarah set one latte in front of me and sat down with the other. 'And now he's been elbow-deep in the compost heap for two days. He's probably learned through osmosis.'

Philip chuckled. 'Osmosis, another good one. But it is amazing we've been recycling for that long. Kids like Eric just take it for granted, and I guess composting would be the next logical step for dealing with organic waste.'

'Don't get too interested,' his wife warned him. 'That heap has to go.'

'In that location, certainly,' Philip said. 'The outdoor seating will be at the back of the cottage, facing the creek, and we certainly don't want to obstruct the sight line.'

The Woodwards' property was sandwiched between Poplar Creek itself, to the rear, and Poplar Creek Road to the front. Brookhill Road, the main east/west drag into downtown Milwaukee, formed the lot's northern boundary. The location was, in a word, perfect.

'That old shed must be torn down, as well.' There went that nose again.

'That'll be a little trickier,' Philip warned. 'It's built on a concrete slab, so we'll have to either break up the foundation or cover it with some sort of de—'

'I'm sure you'll figure something out,' Vivian said, tapping manicured fingernails on the table. 'Then there's what's to be done about the parking lot, if you want to call it that.'

'You mean the driveway from Poplar Creek Road?' I asked. Viewed from the front, the lot was largely overgrown weeds with a gravel drive to the right of the house paralleling Brookhill Road.

'The driveway widens out when it stops short of the creek,' Sarah said knowledgeably. 'I'd call it a gravel parking apron, if I were listing it.'

I looked at her, surprised. 'You've investigated?'

'It's a property in Brookhills. I keep up.' Sarah had owned the eponymous Kingston Realty before giving it up to turn her full attention, such as it were, to Uncommon Grounds.

'We can tidy up the *apron*,' Philip said with a nod of approval to Sarah. 'Put down new gravel or asphalt and parking blocks so we don't lose people and cars in the drink.'

He cocked his head, thinking, and then shook himself. 'And as for composting, there's no reason we can't continue the family's ecological tradition, Vivian, and compost somewhere else, away from the creek. There's plenty of space.'

'How much land do you have there?' We were just two blocks away but being situated in an historic train station, we were pretty much stuck with no green space. We did boast an expansive wraparound porch and plenty of parking though.

'Almost an acre,' Vivian said.

'A buildable acre backing up to the creek is a rare thing,' Sarah said. 'Sure you don't want to sell it and eliminate all this bother?'

'You'd like that, wouldn't you?' Philip said, with a grin. 'Assuming we let you list the property, of course.'

'Sarah isn't practicing real estate any longer,' I pointed out. 'So she wouldn't—'

'Yes, *she* would,' Sarah said, leaning forward to override whatever it was I was going to say. 'I still have my license and, if you're interested, I could give you a nice break on commission. I don't have overhead.'

'Believe me, I'd love that,' Vivian said, picking up her latte and setting it down again with the slightest of sips. 'I'd sell the whole ramshackle set-up and be done with it. But this one' – she shrugged at her husband – 'thinks it's a gold mine.'

I agreed, quite honestly.

'I know the place needs work,' Philip said, 'but it also has a history. Maybe not of my family, but of yours, Vivian. I would think you'd want to hang onto it. You're all about family.'

'I am.' Vivian said it defiantly, but her eyes seemed to be misting up. 'But the future of our own family, not my grandparents, who lived on that property for decades like squatters.'

'Not just *like* squatters,' Sarah said.

Our heads all swiveled Ms Sensitive's way.

'Pardon me?' Vivian asked her.

Sarah shrugged. 'Like I said, I keep tabs on Brookhills property. A couple of years back, I did an online search and looked up the deed hoping I could track down the owners and convince them to sell.'

'Why not just knock on the door?' After all, she'd already walked up the driveway and inspected the 'gravel parking apron'. 'Assuming you knew they were still living there.'

'The old man wasn't living, period, full stop.' My partner was in rare empathetic form today. 'I think he died back a ways, though his name was still on the deed. As for the old lady, she wouldn't answer the door. Then, what? A year ago, she goes toes up?'

This was directed to the bereaved granddaughter.

Who apparently wasn't so bereaved. 'Finally,' was all Vivian said.

Her husband did a quick glance my way, catching my reaction. 'Don't judge us too harshly.'

'I know families can be complicated,' I offered.

Vivian snorted. 'I never even met the people. Either of them.'

'Your mother had a falling out with her parents?' I asked, though it was none of my business. But . . . I just like . . . knowing stuff.

Unfortunately, Vivian just shrugged.

Philip was more helpful. 'From what I understand,' he said, glancing at his wife, 'Vivian's grandparents – the Koepplers – walled themselves off from everybody and everything in the outside world years ago. And preferred it that way.'

'Tea Man has that right,' Sarah chimed in. 'I couldn't find a phone number, car registration, nothing.'

If I didn't know Sarah, I'd have believed she was genuinely concerned about the Koepplers. 'But how did they survive? What about food?'

'They grew what they needed apparently,' Philip said. 'And raised chickens.'

'In that shed, from the smell of it,' Vivian said. 'And I can't imagine why. I don't think they even ate meat from what Mother said.'

'Eggs maybe?' I suggested. 'Or didn't they eat those either?'

'I don't think vegans eat eggs,' Sarah said. 'Or dairy products. Or anything from an animal, including honey.'

That seemed overly punitive. I like honey. Not that I judge. 'Maybe they were vegetarians, not vegans. I think they have different rules. Or maybe pescatarians.' Though I'm not sure I'd eat anything that came out of the creek.

'Who knows,' Vivian said, not seeming to care one way or the other. 'They probably just made it up as they went.'

Old and living off the land, you probably had to.

Unlike his wife, Philip seemed genuinely concerned. But not necessarily about his grandparents-in-law's well-being. 'You said you looked up the deed, Sarah. Was there a problem? Vivian's mother assured us the title for the property was clear.'

'It is now,' Sarah said, 'but apparently there was a dust-up in the late seventies between the Koeppler and Benson families about who owned the property on the Koepplers' side of Brookhill Road.'

I'd had experience with the wealthy Bensons, as had most of Brookhills. 'Owning Brookhills Manor wasn't enough for them?'

Brookhills Manor was a senior facility where some of our older clientele lived in their own small apartments. It backed onto Poplar Creek, too, but on the north side of Brookhill Road.

Sarah said. 'Old man Benson—'

'This would be Walter Benson?' I interrupted.

'Walter's father, William. The old, old man. He claimed they owned the land along the creek on both sides of Brookhill Road.'

'Including ours?' Philip asked, adding with a self-deprecating grin, 'Or Vivian's family's, I should say.'

'Ours now,' Vivian said, a little grimly.

'Thing was,' Sarah said, 'the Bensons never paid much attention to the overgrown lots until they decided senior living would be a good place to put their money as the baby-boomers aged.'

Prescient. And, as it turned out, lucrative. 'The Manor was built, when? The eighties sometime?'

'1980, exactly.' Sarah was a savant where property and real estate was concerned in Brookhills. 'The bigger parcel was on the north side of Brookhill Road, so that's where the first phase of the project was built.'

'Then why did William care about the Koepplers' land on the south side?' I asked.

Sarah snorted. 'Because he claimed it was theirs, of course, and he wasn't about to give it up. Benson Development filed plans for a second phase of Brookhills Manor to be built there – a skilled nursing facility for residents of the Manor who eventually needed more care.'

As we all would. It was a perfect business plan – one that I couldn't help but admire, even while disliking the people who hatched it. 'But the nursing home addition is on the opposite side of the Manor from that now.'

'Thanks to the Koepplers,' Sarah said. 'They apparently had been living on the lot William wanted since the late 1950s, which was more than twenty years. The cottage was already there and then the storage shed. By the time the Bensons came calling – or demanding – the Koepplers claimed adverse possession—'

'Adverse possession?' Vivian asked. 'What is that?'

I flashed her an apologetic smile. 'Basically, squatters' rights.'

'Squatters,' Vivian repeated, more entertained than aghast. 'My mother's parents actually were squatters?'

'But awarded the property, right?' For his part, Philip was more interested in the outcome than the circumstances.

'Ultimately,' Sarah said. 'From what I gathered, there was a big dust-up in the papers. The way the press played it, this was the money-grubbers versus the tree-huggers.'

'And the tree-huggers won?' I asked, surprised.

'More like they wore the money-grubbers out,' Sarah said. 'Walter, who would have been maybe mid-thirties then, brokered the deal.'

So William Benson had been a harder ass than his son Walter was. Hard to imagine. And Walter's son, Way, had been right up there in ruthlessness with his grandfather in my experience.

On the other hand, Way's son Oliver was a schoolmate of my own son Eric and had broken the Benson mold both by being a good kid and by refusing to use his given name of Wendell. So, it was William, Walter, Way and . . . Oliver.

'Walter settling the dispute probably didn't sit well with his old man,' Sarah was saying, 'but the Bensons had all the land they needed on the north side of Brookhill Road for the Manor as well as the nursing home, which they added fifteen years later.'

'All a person needs isn't necessarily all they want,' Vivian said. 'Though I guess my grandparents were the exception to that. They must have been happy with what they had.'

'And the Bensons should have been happy with what they had,' I said. 'They're adding a phase three now – luxury condominiums.'

'On that same piece of land?' Philip asked. 'It must be huge.'

'It is,' Sarah said. 'They're building the condos to the north on the far side of the nursing home. They'll be free-standing to make sure people don't feel part of the Manor's circle of life.'

'Circle of life?' Philip had to ask.

And Sarah was delighted to answer. 'The nursing home is physically connected to the original Manor so they can just wheel the old farts over when the time comes. I'm surprised the next phase wasn't a funeral home.'

'That's down the block,' I reminded her. Though admittedly not owned by the Bensons.

'Old farts?' This, Vivian thought, was funny.

'You'll have to forgive my partner,' I said. 'It's true that the nursing home was built as an addition to the original retirement home. But I suspect it was because it was cheaper to add on than build a whole new structure. That would appeal to the Bensons.'

'You've had dealings with them?' Philip asked.

'Walter's son Way terminated our lease in Benson Plaza to make way for more lucrative tenants.'

'That's why you moved here to the depot?' Philip asked. 'If so, I'd say this Way did you a favor. This is a wonderful spot.'

Not quite as picturesque as their acre on the creek, but the depot did have a certain character.

'I agree,' Sarah said. 'And the shopping mall collapsed before Way could kick Maggy out, anyway.'

'Served him right,' I said.

'This collapse – was it an accident?' Vivian asked, eyes wide.

'Maggy didn't do it,' Sarah said. 'If that's what you're asking. As for Way, he didn't do it either. There are better ways to commit insurance fraud.'

'Arson for one,' I said. 'But in this case the weight of snow on the flat roof collapsed the mall.'

'If you want to burn down the structures on your property, though, I know somebody who can do it,' Sarah said. 'Then we can list it as a buildable lot.'

'You *know* an arsonist?' I was getting married to the county sheriff. I had a responsibility to keep the guest list free of arsonists and the people who hire them. Even if she was my best friend. God help me.

'Slow your roll, Maggy,' Sarah said. 'I meant the Brookhills fire chief. The department would probably love to burn down the Koepplers' cottage as a training exercise.'

'Oh.'

'No insurance settlement, of course,' Sarah continued. 'That's the downside. But the house is gone, and you don't have to pay the arsonist. So it's kind of lose, win, win.'

'I think we'll pass for now,' Vivian said. 'But just for my own information, does this "adverse possession" application appear on the deed? And affect the future salability?' She glanced at her husband. 'If we were to consider it.'

'Which we're not,' Philip said a little tersely before he seemed to catch himself and consciously relax his face.

'Right,' Sarah said, glancing at him. 'But no worries either way. A quit claim deed was filed in 1979 transferring ownership from the Bensons to the Koepplers for "consideration," which was probably a buck.'

'Good to know we're all legal,' Philip said. 'And I admit the slightly shady history makes the place even more intriguing.'

'Of course you would think so,' Vivian said.

'I do, because it ties nicely into our noir theme,' Philip said. 'Use your imagination, my dear. You've already done wonders with the cottage. And with the creek behind us, the picturesque Brookhill Road bridge next to us—'

'And the junk-strewn yard and the compost heap in between, it's heaven.' But Vivian was smiling. 'I honestly don't think my grandparents threw away anything.'

'At least not farther than the backyard, where they could reclaim it if necessary,' her husband said.

'The location will be prime once you have it cleaned up,' I assured them, still trying to get a bead on the two of them. Philip was all in, but Vivian seemed to feel she had to counter her husband's unbridled enthusiasm.

'Do you think so?' she asked now. 'Here you have the commuter traffic. People taking trains into the city. That must provide a built-in customer base.'

'It does,' I said, 'but the only reason we need it is because we're not directly on Brookhill Road now.' I pointed out the window to the street that fronts the shop. 'Junction Road is set at an angle and intersects with Poplar Creek a block north of Brookhill Road.'

'But what's a block?' Philip asked.

'A mile, if you're running late,' Sarah said.

'It's true,' I confirmed ruefully. 'People who drive into Milwaukee blast down Brookhill Road and they'll stop anywhere along the way – your location or our former location in Benson Plaza – to grab a quick cup. A detour, even of a block, isn't on their morning schedule. But you're right on Brookhill, plus you'll get customers from Brookhills Manor right across the street.'

Vivian was studying me. 'You're too nice to be for real.'

'Don't let Maggy fool you,' Sarah said. 'She's really not.'

'Oh, is there something we don't know about Maggy?' Philip asked, rubbing his hands together theatrically. 'Skeletons in the closet perhaps?'

As it turned out, they weren't my skeletons. And not my closet, either.

TWO

'It's true,' I confessed to Philip Woodward. 'I was even suspected of murder once.'

Sarah wrinkled her nose. 'Was it just the once? I lose count.'

Me, too.

'But you were saying Maggy is faux-nice, Vivian?'

Vivian Woodward seemed discomfited but plunged on. 'I just mean that we're potential competition. We've said we're only doing tea, but how can you be sure we won't expand to espresso at some point?'

'She'll kill us if we do, apparently,' Philip said with a laugh. 'Besides, I've given Maggy and Sarah my word that we are a teahouse and teahouse only.'

'Of course, of course.' Vivian was waving her hand. 'But we all hardly know each other.'

'That's what I said.' Sarah shrugged. 'But Maggy is the trusting sort, despite the criminal record.'

'Please don't listen to her,' I said, shaking my head. 'I have no criminal record and the fact is that anything that draws people to this area will benefit all of us. Besides, as you said, our location has a built-in clientele. People park their cars at the depot and pick up a coffee for the train. After work, they grab a quick cup or something that our chef Tien Romano has baked or cooked up for their dinner. It works.'

'You mentioned the people at Brookhills Manor,' Philip said. 'Are they really potential customers? They haven't been very welcoming.'

'That's just their way,' I said.

'They'll come,' Sarah said, 'but they'll piss and moan about how expensive everything is and how they can get coffee – or tea, in your case – free at the Manor.'

'That would be an improvement,' Vivian said. 'So far all they do is stand across the street and stare. It gives me the creeps.'

'That one couple came over,' Philip pointed out.

'Who?'

'You know, the soldierly gentleman with the hat and the lady.'

'Lady,' Vivian repeated, turning to us. 'She has fluffy white hair and the sweetest face, but once she opened her mouth—'

'That would be Sophie Daystrom,' Sarah said. 'You should have heard her when she used real swear words.'

Philip grinned. 'I believe her first words to us were: "It's gol-dang time some donkey-butt cleaned up that fricking poopshow of yours."'

'Vintage Sophie, indeed,' I confirmed.

'And there was that other woman, the redhead whose face didn't move,' Vivian said to her husband.

'Botox Vickie,' Sarah supplied.

Vickie LaTour was dubbed Botox Vickie by friends and enemies alike – not just because of her use of cosmetic procedures herself, but because she regularly hosted Botox and collagen parties. In fact, I suspected she'd come up with the name herself, since branding never hurts anyone.

'Yes, that's it,' Philip said. 'And the man was . . . Henry?'

'Henry Wested. He and Sophie are a couple,' I told him.

'Well, they all seemed very nice.' Philip laid his hand on Vivian's before she could counter him. 'Henry said he remembered when Vana was a little girl.'

'Vana?' I asked.

'My mother,' Vivian said.

'Oh, does she still live here?' I asked.

'Mother? Heavens, no. She left a long time ago.'

'Vivian's mother is the antithesis of pausing harmony,' Philip explained.

I didn't know what that meant. So I just said, 'Oh.'

Sarah glanced over at me. 'That was their names.'

'Whose names?'

'Vivian's Grandma and Grandpa Koeppler,' Sarah said. 'Paz and Harmony.'

Ahh, Paz and Harmony, not pausing harmony. Though it didn't make much more sense. 'This was back in the sixties?'

'Bingo,' Philip said. 'Vana's given name is Nirvana.'

Of course it was.

'Hippies. But as I said, I never knew them,' Vivian said, holding up her hands. 'And, before you ask, my mother never even talked about them.'

Philip was grinning. 'Vana apparently ran away to New York when she was eighteen to marry above her station.'

A grin threatened to break out on Vivian's face. 'For God's sake, don't let her hear you say that when she gets here.'

'You know full well that Vana has heard me say it many times,' Philip said. 'It endears me to her, I think. And you, my dear, love it.'

'Your mother is visiting?' I asked Vivian.

'Any minute now.' Philip glanced out the window feigning nervousness. 'She'll tip-tap her size six Louboutins right up the porch steps and through that—'

The door opened on cue, sleighbells jangling against the plate-glass window, but it was my son Eric who pushed his way in. Tousled brown hair and half a foot taller than me, Eric is the best thing I ever did. 'Hey, Mom. Can I get an iced tea for me and some water for Frank?'

Frank is Eric's sheepdog. Or was. I'd inherited the giant fur ball when Eric left home for college now nearly four years ago. When Eric's father, Ted, left me mere days later for another woman, Frank and I drowned our mutual sorrows with copious amounts of pepperoni pizza, red wine and old movies. (Us/me/us respectively.) Now I couldn't imagine my life without him.

I could, however, imagine my coffeehouse sans Frank. 'Fuzzy wuzzy,' I ordered. 'Out!'

Frank had started to follow Eric in. Now he stopped, two paws in and two paws out, and cocked his head at me. A grimy rag undoubtedly foraged from the garbage heap across the street dangled from his mouth.

'Health department orders,' I explained. 'If it was up to me, I'd let you in.'

It was always hard to know what the sheepdog was thinking under his bangs, but his demeanor drooped visibly as he turned and padded back out onto the porch with his prize.

'You hurt his feelings, Mom,' Eric said.

'I know,' I said with a twinge of regret. My sheepdog had been so proud of his filthy find. 'But for now, Frank stays out and you take your shoes off. They're covered in dirt, too.'

'Compost soil,' Eric corrected me, using the toe of one shoe to dislodge the heel of the other. It went flying across the room, shedding said compost as it skidded to a stop next to Sarah's chair.

'Yeah, Maggy,' Sarah said, glancing down at the shoe with her lip curled. 'Don't confuse nice clean dirt with the decayed organic matter that's now all over our floor.'

'Sorry,' Eric said, removing the other shoe before padding over dirty-sock-footed to retrieve the shoe and set it on the mat. 'You want me to get the broom?'

'No, that's OK,' Sarah said. 'Your mother will take care of it later.'

Eric glanced toward me and I gave him a nod. I'd kind of missed cleaning up after the kid. But then it hadn't even been two weeks.

'How's the work going, Eric?' Philip asked. 'Making progress?'

'There's layer after layer of stuff there,' Eric told him. 'Did my friend Oliver ask you if he could help? He was going to.'

'Oliver?' Philip glanced at Vivian to see if she knew.

'Oliver Benson,' I supplied. 'Way's son. But not at all like his father.' Or grandfather. Or great-grandfather.

'Oliver Benson, yes,' Vivian said now, and I could have sworn I saw her flush. 'Nice-looking young man. He came to the door this morning. You were in the shower, Philip.'

Oliver was two years younger than Eric – a sophomore at the University of Minnesota to Eric's senior status. The two had gotten closer after Oliver's parents were killed and he started school at the U. They'd driven down from Minneapolis together, having chosen to spend spring break at home rather than Cancun or the equivalent. Good boys.

'You wouldn't have to pay him or anything,' Eric explained to Philip now. 'Oliver's just kind of a history nerd and his family has been here forever. He thinks this old stuff is cool.'

'Well, if your friend wants to help excavate our compost

heap, that's fine by me,' Philip said, glancing to his wife for confirmation. 'Did you tell him it was all right, Vivian?'

'Absolutely,' she said. 'The more strangers digging around in our family garbage the better. My mother will have fits.' The idea didn't seem to displease her, though.

Eric was at the fridge making his drink choices. 'It's actually like an archaeological dig. Yesterday I got down to the nineteen eighties.'

Ancient history, indeed.

'How can you tell?' I asked. 'I thought the whole idea of composting was that the stuff degraded.'

'Not plastic,' Eric said. 'I found a Transformer – not the new Transformers, but like *original*.'

I'd take his word for it, not being an aficionado of action figures.

'There's pretty much everything in this pile,' Eric continued, glancing apologetically at Vivian. 'I don't think your grand-parents knew that much about the science of composting.'

'The science of anything, most likely,' Vivian said. 'They were probably more "go with the flow." No need to spare my feelings.'

'From what I've been able to discern, Harmony and Paz waffled over the years between composting and just plain piling up trash there,' Philip said. 'I removed an old tricycle and a truck tire before we called Eric in to help.'

'I thought they didn't drive,' I said.

'They would have needed three more to even make a start at it,' Sarah pointed out.

'I think it might have been a swing,' Philip said. 'There was a rope, too, and I could see where it dug into the limb of the tree by the shed. Must have been there for years.'

'It's stuff like that, the stuff that didn't disintegrate, that makes it so cool,' Eric said, as the sleighbells on the door jangled again. 'Just now, I found this vintage box for a Babs doll? It—'

'Barbie, I think you mean,' I said.

'Babs,' the woman who'd just entered said. 'The boy had it right.'

'Vana,' Philip said, getting up to give the elegant woman a

hug. She looked to be touching seventy and, yes, the lacquered red soles of her stilettos marked them as Christian Louboutins. 'Come in and meet our neighbors, Maggy and Sarah. They own Uncommon Grounds here.'

'You're mussing me,' she said, smoothing imaginary wrinkles on her elegant skirt before turning to her daughter. 'Hello, Vivian.'

'Mother.' Vivian didn't stand but turned her cheek to receive a kiss from the older woman.

'Gotta go,' Eric said, with the good sense he was born with.

'You have the water for Frank?' I asked as my son retrieved his shoes and sock-footed it to the door.

'Yup.' He patted his jacket pocket.

'And don't let Frank have the empty water bottle – he'll eat it. You can throw it in the recycle bin out front – they don't pick up until Monday. And those socks are going to get even dirtier if you don't put on—' The door jangled closed behind him.

Sigh. At least Eric could *pretend* to listen to me when I talked to him like he was still five years old.

'Frank? Would that be that gigantic creature on the porch?' Vana asked, taking the chair Philip was holding for her. He dragged another over for himself. 'He's filthy.'

'He's been helping my son remove your parents' trash,' I said, giving her a big ol' smile. Don't mess with my sheepdog. Or my son. 'Including the detritus of your childhood, apparently.'

Philip stifled a grin and turned to his mother-in-law. 'Will you have a coffee, Vana?'

'If we're staying, I suppose I must,' Vana said. 'Cappuccino. Dry.'

I remained seated, as did Sarah.

'Was the Babs doll yours then?' Sarah asked, leaning forward to regard Vana as if she were a zoo animal.

'Oh, and oat milk, please,' Vana called to the imaginary barista, before turning her attention to Sarah. 'Yes, sadly. I'd asked for a Barbie for Christmas.'

'Babs was a knock-off of Barbie?' I asked and got a curt nod.

'Maybe your parents didn't know the difference,' Philip said charitably.

'More didn't care,' his mother-in-law said, lifting her chin. 'I was humiliated. It was in a battered box – most likely the one your son found . . . Maggy, is it?'

This time I nodded.

'Anyway, the thing's hair was chopped off and face smudged like it had belonged to a careless child who sold it at a yard sale.' She shuddered. 'I swore I'd never have anything used or fake ever again and threw it away under the trash when my parents weren't looking.'

Which meant Eric could look forward to finding the vintage doll to go with the vintage box.

'Mother is one-hundred-percent genuine,' Vivian said dryly. 'From her Louboutins to her Rolex and beyond.'

'Really?' Sarah was studying Vana's chin-length chestnut coif. 'I mean, you have to have some gray hair at your age. A few wrinkles, maybe?'

Vana's chin went up. 'I'll have you know, I do not—'

'It must have been hard, living off the grid like that,' Philip said, steering the discussion back to a not necessarily safer harbor. 'But you must admit there was a certain romance to the sixties.'

'Romance,' Vana repeated, seeming to muse now. 'The old hippies might remember it that way, an innocent time.'

'But try being the child of children,' Sarah said. 'Flower children, in this case.'

'Exactly,' Vana said, seeming surprised at this insight from the woman who not thirty seconds ago accused her of having work done.

'Well, this has been nice,' Vivian said, standing before things got so deep we'd have to shovel. 'Shouldn't we be going?'

'Are you staying at the cottage?' I asked Vana.

She cringed. 'Heavens, no.'

'We've made a reservation at the Morrison for her,' Vivian said as her mother stood, too.

The Hotel Morrison was just a few blocks east of us on Brookhill Road.

'Nice,' Sarah said. 'The Morrison is *the* place to stay in Brookhills.'

Sarah enjoyed putting it that way because the Morrison was literally the only hotel in Brookhills. But it also was a great old building. 'Caron Egan, my former partner – before Sarah – owns it. It's very comfortable. All the rooms are mini-suites with kitchenettes.'

'Then' – Vana wiggled her fingers at Sarah and me – 'you two are a . . . couple?'

'Couple of idiots,' Sarah said. 'Want this in a to-go cup or down the drain?' Sarah lifted Vivian's mostly untouched latte.

'We're business partners,' I told Vana as Vivian shook her head in answer to Sarah's question. 'As were Caron and myself.'

'Oh, good.' She held up her hands. 'I was hoping you weren't raising your son in such . . . unorthodox circumstances.'

'Not that it would be any of your business if she were,' Sarah said pleasantly.

'No, no. Quite so,' Vana said. 'I—'

'Where's your luggage, Vana?' Philip asked, standing now, too.

'Oh, on the porch,' Vana directed him, then her expression changed. 'I hope that dog didn't—'

'Eric took Frank with him,' I told her. 'Besides, he wouldn't damage your suitcase.'

'You don't know, Maggy,' Sarah said helpfully. 'He might pee on it.'

'Only in a fit of pique,' I assured Vana, going to the door. 'Besides, since Mocha joined the family, Frank seems to have forgotten how to lift his leg on anything.'

'Mocha?' Vivian asked.

'Alpha female chihuahua,' Sarah said.

'She's teaching Frank to squat.' I went to open the door. It stuck.

I put my eye to the crack. 'What are you doing back?'

Frank was laying down in front of the door, snuffling at something.

I certainly hoped it wasn't the handle off Vana's luggage. I shoved the door again. 'C'mon, Frank – move.'

The sound of Eric's shoes came pounding up the steps. 'Sorry, Mom. He dug up something and ran over here when I tried to get it away from him. I think it might be a chicken or turkey bone.'

My heart seized. Eating bones from fowls – the cooked kind, rather than the feathered and on-foot version – can kill a dog.

Eric was tugging on Frank's collar to turn his head toward him. 'C'mon, Frank, give it to me.'

'Leave it, Frank!' I put my weight behind the door, hoping to slide him so I could slip out and help. But when a hundred plus pounds of sheepdog doesn't want to move, he just doesn't.

Behind me, Vana's stiletto toe started to tap.

'Can I help?' Philip asked.

'If you just help me push,' I said, gratefully, moving over. 'Maybe Eric can pull—'

Outside, someone whistled and suddenly the logjam gave way, spilling Philip and me onto the porch and nearly toppling Eric. Frank was bounding down the porch steps to Brookhills County Sheriff Jake Pavlik who was standing on the sidewalk.

'*That* is Maggy's "partner,"' Sarah said, leading the others out onto the porch.

'Nice,' was all Vana had to say.

And she was right. Pavlik was nice, when he wasn't accusing you of murder. But I'd obviously gotten over that. 'Take that bone away from him, Pavlik. Before he chokes on it.'

Pavlik dislodged Frank's offering and straightened, the sun playing on his dark hair as he smiled at Eric and me. 'You having trouble with the big guy here?'

'Not anymore,' I told him, heart reverting to a normal rhythm now that my man had saved my dog. 'Have you met Philip and Vivian Woodward? They're opening a tea shop in the old place on the corner of Brookhill and Poplar Creek roads. And this is Vivian's mother, Vana . . .'

'Shropshire,' Vana filled in, mincing down the steps. 'And you are?'

'Jake Pavlik.' Pavlik gestured with Frank's gift. 'I'd shake hands, but . . .'

He stopped, only now really looking at the object he was holding. 'What the hell is this?'

I peered at it. 'A turkey or chicken bone, we thought.'

Eric nodded. 'He dug it out of the compost pile and took off with it.'

'Eric is helping us clear the old compost heap,' Vivian explained. 'It's revealing all sorts of things. That my mother had a Babs doll for one thing, and now that my grandparents weren't the vegetarians they claimed to be.'

She was chattering away in a fashion that seemed unnatural from what I'd seen of her so far. But that was Pavlik's effect on people. Women people.

'The sheriff isn't interested in your grandparents' dietary habits, Vivian,' Vana told her daughter severely, before gesturing toward her suitcase. 'Can you collect that, Philip?'

Her son-in-law lifted the bag down the steps to the sidewalk where Pavlik was still examining the bone in his hand. 'What was the Koeppelers' secret pleasure, Sheriff? Turkey wing? Chicken drumstick?'

Pavlik held up a slim bone just a few inches long. 'Human femur.'

THREE

And the news only got worse that night.

'An infant?' I repeated when Pavlik told me the county coroner's initial assessment. 'How old?'

Pavlik shrugged out of his jacket. 'The femur or the child when he died?'

I shook my head and took the jacket. 'This isn't funny.'

'Believe me, I know.' He sank onto the couch, his blue eyes a muddy gray as they tend to be when he's troubled. 'Come here, Mocha.'

Mocha – a one-person chihuahua, that person being Pavlik – hopped up next to him and laid her little head on his leg.

Pavlik scratched the pup behind her right ear.

'You said "he"? It's a boy?' My voice cracked a little.

'To be honest, we don't know yet,' Pavlik said, signaling for me to come sit. 'It just seems wrong to call him or her an "it". So for now, he's Baby Doe and likely only a few months old, going by the bone.'

I slipped onto the couch next to him. 'Poor little thing.'

Frank, who was sleeping in front of the unlighted fireplace, raised his head at my tone. Then he got up one limb at a time, stretched and staggered over to collapse in front of the couch, his head on my feet. Giving sheepdog comfort, best he could. I wiggled my toes. 'It creeps me out that Frank had that bone.'

'I had it, too,' Pavlik said.

'But you weren't chewing on it.'

'It can't hurt him now – Baby Doe, I mean.'

'I know, but . . .' I couldn't quite say it.

So Pavlik did. 'You're afraid Frank will get a taste for human?' He studied my face with just the ghost of a grin. 'We'll know when the pizza comes. Does he eat the pie or the delivery guy? I know which my money is on.'

Comic.

Pavlik slid an arm around me and pulled me close. Squished,

Mocha got up with a long-suffering sigh and hopped down to curl up next to Frank. 'I know this is hard. But remember that the bone may have been there for fifty or sixty years.'

'How can we know that?'

'It's just a guess for now, based on the condition of the bone and the deterioration of the tissue on the bone.'

Lack of tissue on the bone, more like it. But that could have been due to animals as well. I shivered.

Pavlik felt it. 'There are also artifacts, though.'

Way to divert me. 'Artifacts? Like pottery at an ancient grave site?'

'Artifacts don't have to be ancient.'

Ahh, which brought up my son the archeologist. 'Like the Transformer figures and old doll boxes Eric found.'

'Not to mention a magazine with a date, which is even more helpful.'

'What date?' I was intrigued. Maybe the Koeppelers hadn't unplugged from society completely. At least not early on. 'And publication?'

'Not sure on the particular magazine, but it dated back to 1967.'

I frowned. 'But Frank moved the bone. Do we even know it was in the vicinity of the magazine and other artifacts, as you put it?'

'Only Eric's recollection that Frank was nosing around in the area.'

'But—'

Pavlik held up a hand. 'Believe me, I know none of this is definitive. We'll have a forensic anthropologist examine the bone and my people won't stop until that trash heap is bagged and tagged. But what I *can* say now is that whatever happened to Baby Doe was a long time ago.'

There was something in his voice. Something he wasn't saying.

I pulled back to see the sheriff's face. 'Do you have any idea what did happen to him? How he died?'

Pavlik met my eyes. 'We'll know more if we find more bones. And the pathologist, of course, will have to examine those, as well.'

'But . . .'

'But . . .' He took a deep breath. 'I thought I saw a fracture and the pathology confirms it. At least one.'

At least. 'It – they – couldn't have been sustained post-mortem?' I asked, using forensics TV lingo to distance myself.

He shook his head. 'It's apparently a spiral break, which would indicate pre-mortem. Desiccated bones usually break cleanly across or crumble.'

The sheriff was keeping it technical, as well.

It wasn't like Baby Doe grew up to fall off his bike. Or climb a tree in the backyard. Or run to catch a ball. 'Somebody hit him? Or dropped him? Or shook him until . . .' My voice was getting louder with each possibility.

Pavlik's, on the other hand, was quiet. 'Maybe.'

We both let that sink in.

'I guess . . . I guess I thought maybe the baby had been stillborn, you know?'

Pavlik nodded.

'Or maybe he'd died at birth and the mother had panicked.' A young mother, in my imagination. Frightened and alone. 'Something sad and wrong, but not . . .'

'Murder,' Pavlik finished for me. 'I know. Me, too.'

'But years ago.' I was trying to remind myself that, like Pavlik had said, whatever had happened to Baby Doe, it was over now. He wasn't hurting anymore. It didn't help. 'According to Sarah, Vivian's grandparents had lived on that property doing their hippy thing since the late fifties.'

'Assuming we find the rest of the body there, we'll—'

'But where else would it be? Eric saw Frank dig up the femur in the compost heap.'

'But we don't know the baby was buried there. The bone could easily have been dropped by a roving animal, maybe decades ago.'

As horrible as that sounded, Pavlik was right. Frank, after all, had brought it to the front porch of the coffeehouse and dropped it there. 'Were Vana, Vivian and Philip able to tell you anything?'

Pavlik had called in Forensics immediately and asked the trio to come to the station to make statements.

'Philip and Vivian Woodward had never even stepped foot on the property until after Mrs Woodward's grandmother died about a year ago,' Pavlik said. 'Mrs Shropshire, likewise, after decades of estrangement.'

Happy families. 'If the bone does date back to the sixties, Philip and Vivian wouldn't have been alive. What about Vana?'

'Born in 1962,' Pavlik said.

So maybe old enough. 'Does she remember a brother or sister? Or maybe a playmate who . . .'

'Disappeared?' Pavlik asked, sitting back. 'Not that she can recall.'

This last was said a little dryly. 'Those were her words?'

'I got the impression she put her childhood behind her a long time ago and has no intention of revisiting the period.' Pavlik rolled his head around on his shoulders, trying to loosen up muscles that got particularly tense with these kinds of cases. Which weren't many, happily. Mostly it was grown-ups killing each other.

I hiked myself up so I could knead his shoulders. 'Maybe for good reason. If they abused and killed one child, who's to say they didn't abuse the other?'

'If so, Vana Koeppler Shropshire is not saying. And unless we find the rest of the body on the family's property, there's no reason to press her.'

But I so wanted to press the perfectly coiffed grand dame. 'No?'

'No.' Pavlik rolled his head again and patted my hand in thanks. 'It may have nothing to do with their family.'

'You're right,' I said. 'The Bensons were around then, too.'

'More of your favorite people,' Pavlik said with a grin. 'Also remember gangsters used to hide in the room beneath your train station. And the old slaughterhouse down the block has a shady past. Not to mention Romano's.'

Owned by our Tien Romano's grandfather, the slaughter-house-adjacent restaurant had hosted a few gangsters and at least one legendary mob killing. Which probably explained why Tien's father Luc had chosen to name his new restaurant simply Luc's. Though Philip Woodward probably would have taken the mob connection and marketed the hell out of it.

Anyway. 'You're saying our glass neighborhood shouldn't throw stones?' I settled down next to Pavlik again, only to have him get up.

'At least not yet. Want a glass of wine?'

'Please,' I said, willing to give him up for a minute to get him *and* the wine back. 'Are your people staying out there tonight?'

'At the Koeppler – now Woodward – place? No. We'll start up again tomorrow morning.' He went into the kitchen and then his head reappeared from around the corner. 'Red or white?'

'Red, please. I ordered pepperoni.' I got up and stepped over Frank to follow Pavlik into the kitchen. We'd need plates and napkins, too. 'I guess this is the end of Eric's spring break job.'

'It is for now,' Pavlik said, taking two wine glasses out of the cabinet. 'Is he doing OK? I didn't get a chance to talk to him after.'

'After his dog retrieved a human bone and he was grilled by your detectives? I think so.'

Pavlik let the 'grilled' go. 'He seemed to get a kick out of being interviewed.'

'I'm sure he did,' I said, handing the sheriff a bottle of Pinot Noir. 'But when he finds out it's a child—'

'He already knows.' Pavlik removed the foil from the bottle and picked up the corkscrew. 'He stayed at the site with us and was very helpful, actually. You have a smart kid.'

'I do,' I said, taking four plates – three large and one chihuahua-size – from the cabinet. 'You know, he was fascinated digging through the decades in that pile. And that was before we realized it could provide clues to the baby's identity. Just naturally inquisitive I guess.'

'Wonder where he got that from,' Pavlik said with a grin. 'He's not eating with us tonight?'

'Out with friends. The five of them have been close since grade school. Erin went to college out east, Matt to Cal State, I think, Liz and Colleen to . . . I can't remember where. They used to fingerpaint at my kitchen table and now . . .' I sighed.

'They're all grown up,' Pavlik said, with a smile.

'You laugh,' I said, retrieving a stack of napkins and fork and knife. Sometimes Pavlik cut up his pizza. Takes all kinds. 'But I'm sure it was the same with Tracey. One day they're playing in the sandbox, the next day they're gone off to college.'

Tracey was Pavlik's daughter with his ex, Susan, who had remarried and was living in nearby Milwaukee.

'Tracey is only fourteen,' he said now. 'She's not running off to college. I haven't even taught her to drive yet.'

'Don't do it,' I warned. 'Eventually she'll drive herself right out of your and Susan's lives.'

'My, my, my,' Pavlik said, pouring the Pinot. 'Aren't we feeling morose? Or is it just that spring break is coming to an end?'

He was right, of course. It was Tuesday today and school started next Monday.

Pavlik handed me a glass. 'You could make Eric spend every waking minute with you until Sunday, so you won't miss him so much.'

'It won't work. I'll still miss him.' I clinked glasses with him. 'But to be honest, I'm also a little relieved. I didn't know how this break would go.'

'Why's that?' He was leading the way back to the living room.

'You.'

Pavlik stopped short, nearly causing a collision and loss of wine. 'Me?'

I squeezed by him to set my glass down. 'Yes, but don't worry. He likes you better than he does me most days.'

'You do nag him about dirty socks.'

It was true.

'But I understand,' he said, stepping back over the dogs to settle on the couch before pulling me down next to him. 'It's the first school holiday Eric has spent here since I moved in.'

My son had gone skiing and then stayed at his father's house for Christmas break, to bond with his little sister. 'Mocha is new to the scene, too, don't forget.'

Pavlik and I had adopted the stray not a year together. 'Five pounds of trouble, that one. But I get it. Mocha and I bring new dynamics.'

Mocha lifted her head at the mention of her name and now set it back down, using Frank's paw as a pillow.

'It used to be just me and Frank when Eric came home on break,' I explained. 'It's important to me that he still feels totally comfortable here. Not like a third – or fifth – wheel.' So that my son would prefer my house to his dad's. Which was bigger. And better. And had a baby sister in it.

'And?'

'He does. And now that you have an investigation he's tangentially involved in, he's hooked, I think.'

'Me and the mini-mutt can stay?' Pavlik nuzzled into my neck.

'You bet.'

I opened with Amy the next morning.

Amy Caprese was our sole paid employee. She made more money than Sarah and I had ever been able to take out of the business in the form of salary, but Amy was worth every penny. She didn't even charge extra for the multiple piercings and this week's blue, purple, yellow and pink-striped hair.

'Was this in honor of Easter on Sunday?' I asked, not having seen her since then.

'Do you think it's too literal?' she asked, going to catch her reflection in the front window. 'I was trying to suggest the straw in kids' Easter baskets. And Peeps, of course.'

Peeps being the sugar-covered marshmallow chicks, also in yellow, pink, blue and purple. 'Eric used to microwave Peeps and they'd inflate as they cooked. Then, when they cool off, they collapse all crusty and delicious.'

'Do they taste like when they're stale?' Amy asked. 'That's when they're the best.'

'Absolutely. And as for your hair, it screams Easter,' I said, coming over to touch her do. 'I hope you're conditioning.'

'Not to worry. Deep-conditioning and the color is semi-permanent,' she said, running her own fingers down a strand of purple. 'Only thing is, I had to bleach it first to get good color and now it feels a little' – she frowned – 'strawy.'

'Nailed Easter basket straw then,' I said, smiling. 'The

customers love seeing what you're going to do next, but don't ruin your hair.'

'I really do it more for me,' she said. 'And Jacque gets a kick out of it, too.'

Jacque Oui was Amy's on-again, off-again boyfriend. Or more man-friend, since he was considerably older than her. Jacque owned Schultz's Market, which apparently resonated better than Oui's Market. 'Having a rainbow-striped beauty on his arm makes him feel young, I'm sure.'

Amy's reflection in the window grinned. 'He likes *you*, Maggy.'

'And I like him.' Now we were both lying. I love an even playing field. 'Another crime scene van is arriving,' I said nodding toward the white Brookhills County van which was passing out of sight.

'Strange doings at the old Koeppler place,' Amy said, craning her neck to see the truck rumble over our railroad tracks and turn left on Poplar Creek Road to the Koeppler/Woodward property. 'I was scared to death of that place when I was a kid and maybe rightly so. They say you should trust your instincts.'

'Yes, they do,' I said.

'I mean, who knows how many other bodies they'll find buried there?' She shivered. 'Maybe kids just like me back then, innocently nosing around.'

'Pavlik says it's possible the bone was dropped there by an animal. There may not be anything more to find there.'

'If not there, where?' she asked.

I had moved to Brookhills when Ted and I got married. After the divorce, I found a small house on the north end of Poplar Creek Road, which was less desirable than the south end. Meaning I could afford it. 'I have no idea what was here in the sixties. Except for the train station, of course. And the slaughterhouse.'

Amy gave another shiver. 'Now there would be a place to hide a body. Just tuck it in under a cow carcass.'

'Yes, but the slaughterhouse was shut down decades ago and the property completely cleared out a couple of years ago.' After an unfortunate incident. Which involved me.

'But you said the bone could have been moved by an animal.

Who is to say it wasn't taken from the slaughterhouse a long time ago?'

'Nothing, I guess,' I said, doubtfully. Did it say something about me that I believed even gangsters didn't go around killing babies? There were plenty of adults to put hits out on. Besides, the gangster glory years were more in the 1930s, not the 1960s. 'You say you knew the Koepplers?'

'Knew? No,' Amy said. 'We'd just see Mrs Koeppler outside or in the front window. Long gray hair, flowy clothes and wrinkled face. We were sure she was a witch.'

Older women who didn't color their hair, use Botox or have 'work' done, did tend to stand out in Brookhills.

'From what I understand, three generations ago she wasn't much different than you.'

'Me?' Amy was surprised.

'Sure. Young, nature-loving, nonconformist.' I shrugged. 'Take a flower child of the sixties and age her sixty years and you've got the long gray hair, flowy clothes and face that comes naturally with being eighty. Not a witch.'

'She shook a broom at me.'

'Cleanliness before godliness.'

Amy grinned. 'Bet she didn't own a vacuum cleaner. Probably didn't even have electricity.'

I had turned my attention back to the window. 'Is that Philip Woodward coming this way?'

Amy's gaze followed my pointing finger out the window and down the street. 'It is, though I don't know why you're surprised. He likes you.'

I felt myself blush. 'He does not.'

'Why is he always in here by himself then?'

'Because he likes coffee and Vivian doesn't,' I said. 'Besides, that's not true. They were both here just yesterday afternoon. You missed them. Vivian's mother Vana, too.'

'All I know,' Amy said, turning away from the window, 'is that when Philip Woodward comes in the two of you chatter away like old friends. The sheriff should be careful.'

'Philip is a marketer,' I said, as the man in question bounded up the steps. 'Which you should appreciate, being creative that way yourself.'

'As are you, doing corporate marketing for years and years before opening Uncommon Grounds.'

Why did that make me sound ancient? 'I like hearing the Woodwards' plans for the new place. Philip's not afraid to get a little out there.' I waggled my fingers at wherever 'out there' was.

The door opened. 'Hello, ladies. What are you two up to this morning?'

'Talking about you, in fact,' Amy said, flashing me a grin as she moved toward the counter. 'And your big marketing brain. Maggy admires it.'

'Is that true?' Philip asked, approaching the counter.

'Absolutely,' I said. 'As I was about to tell Amy, I'm jealous because my career was spent marketing financial products. Hard to get too creative with a checking account.'

'I think it's The Big Steep name that you're jealous of,' Philip said. 'But Uncommon Grounds is every bit as good.'

'Coffee puns are a dime a dozen these days,' I said. 'But it takes real talent to combine classic noir and tea. Did you hear about Philip's brilliant idea for a tea infuser in the shape of a car, Amy?'

Amy had rounded the corner into the service area and now popped back out at the window. 'No. Tell me.'

'Maggy is overselling it,' Philip said, his freckled face tinging pink. 'The idea is not brilliant – it is, in fact, a bit of a stretch.'

'But you still love it,' I said.

'I do,' he admitted, turning to Amy. 'It's a novelty tie-in to *The Big Sleep*, which of course is the 1939 book that inspired our name. In it, Sternwood's—'

'Sternwood is the client of private investigator, Philip Marlowe,' I supplied. 'Played by Humphrey Bogart in the 1946 movie version and Robert Mitchum in 1978. Bogart being my preference.'

'And mine,' Philip said. 'Anyway, Sternwood's 1938 Packard has been driven off a pier. When they pull the Packard out – great scene in the movie, with the water cascading from it – they find the body of Sternwood's chauffeur in it.'

'Obviously, since he must have been driving,' Amy said.

'But' – Philip raised a finger – 'was the death of chauffeur Owen Taylor suicide or murder? And, if it was murder, at whose hand?'

'And the answer?' Amy said, lifting her head expectantly.

Philip and I exchanged smiles.

'I know. You don't want to ruin it in case I see the movie?' Amy's face said that would never happen.

'It's not that,' Philip said. 'Even if you read the book the movie was based on, you wouldn't know who, if anybody, killed Owen Taylor.'

'Really?' Amy asked, and then her face changed like she'd gotten it. 'It's one of those eternal mysteries, right? The kind the author wants the reader or audience to ponder?'

'You'd think so,' I said. 'But as the story goes, during production of the movie the screenwriters decided to ask Raymond Chandler—'

'Author,' Amy said, before I could tell her.

'Good for you,' Philip said. 'Yes, the screenwriters sent Chandler a telegram asking who killed Taylor—'

'Chauffeur,' I reminded her, just in case she was getting lost.

'Got it.' Apparently not lost.

'Chandler replied that he had no idea.'

Philip and I beamed at each other.

Amy pursed her lips and closed one eye. 'Sooooo, this all ties in with tea because . . .'

'No idea,' Philip said.

'Very funny,' I told him. 'It's perfect. The place being called The Big Steep and all.'

'And the tea infuser?' Amy prompted.

'Is in the shape of the Packard,' I said delightedly. 'Put tea in it, submerge it in the cup and when you pull it out by the string—'

'Strings, plural, braided to look like a chain,' Philip augmented.

'Nice touch,' I told him. 'So when you lift it from the cup, the tea pours out of the infuser just like water from the car in the movie.'

'And I suppose there's a chauffeur inside?' Amy asked, elbows now on the pass-through, head on hands.

'I'm afraid not,' Philip said. 'There seemed no room what with the tea and all. I also didn't know if it would be a little too macabre to have a body fall out.'

'Unlike the whole idea,' Amy said.

'I wonder if you could have special teabags made,' I said.

'In the shape of a body?' Philip asked. 'Now *that* is brilliant.'

'And macabre,' Amy said. 'Which is what everyone wants at teatime.'

'There is that.'

Silence.

'Though it is cool your name is Philip,' Amy offered as an olive branch.

'My name?' Philip asked.

'Philip? As in Marlowe?'

Philip blinked. 'That never occurred to me.'

'Brilliant,' Amy said, straightening up.

'She's humoring us, isn't she?' he said, glancing sideways at me.

'Mocking, more like it. I can't believe you're not into this, Amy. You have a "brilliant" marketing brain yourself and you love pop culture references.'

'Preferably pop culture references from the current millennium.' Amy straightened to dispense espresso into a portafilter and twist it onto the espresso machine. 'So more living people recognize them.'

'Child,' Philip said with a smile. 'I suppose we shouldn't tell her they cut two versions of the Bogart film.'

'1945 and 1946,' I said. 'But no.'

Amy just rolled her eyes and disappeared from the window.

'Vivian says I'm an old soul,' Philip said, taking a chair at the table by the window. 'Not necessarily in complimentary terms.'

'Where is Vivian this morning?' I asked, mindful of what Amy had said about Philip and me. 'Visiting with her mom?'

'More like escaping with her.' Philip went to stand back up politely as I pulled out the chair across from him. 'Can I get you something?'

'No need,' Amy said, appearing at his elbow with an espresso for him and a latte for me. 'I have it.'

I smiled my thanks and sat down, wrapping my hands around the latte mug. 'Do you mean they're escaping the county forensics people?'

'And the reporters. Though at least they're required to stay on the sidewalk.'

'Do you believe there's no such thing as bad publicity? I've never been sure.' Amy tossed the question over her shoulder as she disappeared around the corner.

'One of those questions for us to ponder, I guess,' I said to Philip.

He glanced up a little sheepishly. 'I have to admit, it did occur to me that the publicity wouldn't be all bad, as long as our work on the tea shop and grounds isn't shut down as a result. Ancient burial ground, or some such thing.'

I grimaced. 'You know it's a baby's leg bone, right?'

'No. No, I didn't. That's awful.' He'd turned a little green.

I wasn't feeling great myself, especially because I wasn't absolutely sure Pavlik would be OK with my giving Philip this information. 'Please don't say anything to the reporters or anybody, would you? Pavlik may have told me that in confidence.'

'I understand, though does Eric know? He was speaking with a reporter when I left.'

Uh-oh. I should have assumed Eric would be back at the Woodwards' this morning. He'd still been sleeping when I left for work. 'What reporter?'

'Dark hair? Irish name, I think. She interviewed us when we unveiled our plans for the tea shop.'

'Kate McNamara.' Kate and I met in school and, unfortunately, reconnected decades later when she was editor of Brookhills' weekly newspaper. Since then, I had left corporate public relations and opened a coffeehouse. Kate had gone on to cable and then broadcast news. Our relationship, though, had stayed at about the fifth-grade level.

'Yes, that's her.' He leaned forward. 'But about this baby.' He ran a hand over his face. 'I guess I should have realized from the size of the bone, but I've never had a child of my own. Whose baby is it? From where? When?'

'Those are all the questions forensics and the crime scene technicians are hoping to answer, but first they have to find the rest of the skeleton.'

'Crime scene. In our compost pile.' Philip wasn't looking so pleased about the publicity now. 'The sheriff didn't say anything about a baby.'

And yet I had. 'Pavlik said the bone could have been left in your yard by a roving animal years ago. The skeleton isn't ancient, as you said, but it had been there – wherever "there" turns out to be – for a long time. Half a century or likely more. This area has a bit of a checkered past where the law is concerned.'

The green had deepened as I'd talked 'roving animals' but now some normal color had come back. 'But Vivian's grandparents apparently date back to the late fifties, early sixties on that property, legally or not.'

'Do you know if it was just the two of them?'

Philip blinked. 'And Vana, of course, when she came along. Why?'

'I just wondered if they might have been part of a larger group who lived on the land there.'

'You're talking about a' – he smiled now – 'commune?'

'Not necessarily, but they did exist back then, right?'

'Well, now.' Philip had pushed back his chair a bit and crossed his arms. 'Wouldn't that be something to think about? Vana growing up in a commune.'

'She never said anything about having a lot of aunts and uncles maybe?'

'Aunts and uncles who really weren't aunts and uncles?'

'Well, yes,' I said. 'Not that I'm suggesting anything. My ex and I told Eric he could call our friends Aunt Wendy, Uncle Bob or whatever, even though they weren't any relation. It just seemed easier than Mr or Mrs.'

'And better than having a little kid call an adult by their first name.'

'Exactly.'

'In a commune, though, you could call everybody Mom

and Dad, since you might not know whose was whose.' Philip was starting to enjoy this.

Now I folded my own arms. 'Let's not make assumptions. Just because they lived in a commune doesn't necessarily mean they were sleeping around.'

'You've heard about the sixties, right?' Philip asked with a full-blown grin. 'Free love and all that jazz?'

'You're just practicing those lines in preparation for torturing your mother-in-law,' I told him. 'But please don't. And please don't tell her and Vivian about the baby just yet. Like I said, I may have spoken out of turn.'

'You want me to keep something from my wife?'

'No, no, I—'

He held up both hands. 'I'm just messing with you. I won't even see Vivian until tonight and hopefully not Vana until tomorrow.'

'You don't like your mother-in-law?'

He grinned. 'You keep that secret, I'll keep yours.'

'Deal,' I said, 'but you put up a surprisingly good front. I thought she at least' – I was casting about for a word – 'entertained you.'

'Entertained, that's a very good way of putting it,' he said. 'I find Vana interesting as a study, I guess.'

Now I felt slightly uncomfortable. 'A study of what?'

'A phony, perhaps?' He shook his head. 'No, not really that. Just somebody who reinvented herself.'

'You do kind of admire her,' I said, studying him now. 'Don't you?'

He shrugged. 'She is a true self-made woman. I kid about her marrying well, but she is responsible for a lot of what she and Gilbert built.'

'Gilbert is Vivian's father?'

'Was.'

'Oh, he's dead,' I said. 'I didn't know.'

'Years ago. He was much older than Vana. Fifty-two to her eighteen and they married within weeks of meeting.' Philip put his finger to his lips. 'Don't tell anybody, but I think it was a shotgun wedding.'

'Haven't heard that term in a lot of years,' I said. 'The age difference of thirty-four years is more shocking than the fact Vana got pregnant before they got married.'

'But remember this is Vana we're talking about,' Philip reminded me. 'She told Vivian she was born prematurely to cover up the discrepancy.'

'And Vivian believed it?' Not that it was any of my business. Again.

He shrugged. 'Sure. Anything else would reflect poorly on the family.'

I studied his face. 'It's usually best not to pick at scabs. Especially other people's scabs.'

He laughed. 'That's disgusting.'

'But very true.'

'I know,' he said and then leaned forward. 'I do love hazing Vana when I see her, but I truly want Vivian to be happy here.'

'She's not?' As if I couldn't tell.

He shrugged. 'We never had kids, so Vivian has had to satisfy herself teaching other people's. Now I've taken her away from even that.'

So Vivian was a teacher. I hadn't known. 'We don't have the same number of schools per capita that Boston does, but there are teaching jobs here,' I told him. 'What grade?'

'First.' He shook his head as Amy came around the corner from the service area. 'It's going to break her heart to hear that bone belonged to a child.'

'Can I get you fresh drinks?' Amy stood back a bit, so as not to intrude.

'I think I'm OK, but . . .' I looked toward Philip.

'I'm fine, too,' Philip said, flashing Amy a smile and waving her over. 'Now you two tell me about Brookhills' checkered past. What have I gotten myself into by moving here?'

Amy recognized the change of subject and obliged. 'Maggy may know more, but I understand there were some mafia figures who lived or vacationed hereabouts. People like Baby Face Nelson, John Dillon and Al Capone.'

'I have done a bit of research,' I admitted. 'Obviously back then, suburban sprawl hadn't gotten this far west of Milwaukee. This area – just fifteen miles west of Milwaukee and about a hundred north of Chicago – was essentially lake country with large, wooded areas and just a few homes spotted around the lakes. The train station was already here, meaning it was an easy ride for people who wanted to be off the . . . well, I guess the radar, rather than the grid.'

'And these gangsters commuted into Chicago?' Philip asked, obviously intrigued.

'Chicago and Milwaukee,' I said. 'Milwaukee had organized crime, too, not that the city fathers liked to admit it.'

'It all sounds like something out of *The Untouchables*,' Philip said.

Real life treasury agent Elliot Ness and the officers he recruited, dubbed 'untouchable' because they were uncorruptible, had become the stuff of legend. And television and movies.

'Of course, all this pre-dated Vivian's grandparents,' I said. 'It was during the Prohibition era – late twenties and early thirties.'

'Too bad, but it does all play into our noir theme.' Philip probably was already entertaining visions of Tommy Gun tea cozies.

'But as I was saying,' I continued, 'the bone that Frank picked up on your property didn't necessarily come from there. There are other buildings – this station, a slaughterhouse and a mobbed-up restaurant, for three – that might have attracted an unsavory element over the years. People who did bad things and didn't want to be found.'

'It wasn't all shady, there was also the college,' Amy said. 'Brookhills College drew people here for nearly a century before it closed.'

'That's true,' I said. 'Maybe Paz and Harmony met in school and just stayed.'

'Under the radar, like the mobsters,' Amy said, sitting down. 'Paz could have been evading the draft.'

'You're too young to know about the draft.' The draft – or Selective Service System – had inducted young men into the US military from 1940 to 1973, ending well before Amy was born.

'My father was a conscientious objector,' Amy said. 'But it makes sense. Look at Mr Koeppler's name – Paz.'

'Meaning peace.' Duh. 'What were their real names, Philip? Do you know?'

'Ray and Matilda.'

'Not good flower power names,' I admitted.

'No.' But Philip was looking past Amy and me and out the front window. 'Something's happening.'

I craned my head around in time to see a squad car and the coroner's van speed by, lights on sirens off. 'They must have found something else.'

FOUR

'Go forth and detect, as is your calling,' Amy said breezily, standing to gather our cups. 'I'll take care of these.'

'Thank you,' I said grabbing a light jacket and opening the door. 'Shall we?'

'Shall we detect, you mean?' Philip stepped out onto the porch. 'Is there something I should know about you?'

'About me?' I led the way down Junction Road to Poplar Creek as a helicopter buzzed by. 'I'm just nosy.'

'Anything to do with the fact you're marrying the sheriff?' Philip asked, on my heels.

'Absolutely not. I was nosy well before I met Pavlik.'

As Philip and I crossed Brookhill Road to the Woodwards' property, I caught sight of Eric and his friend Oliver and waved them over.

'Hey, Ms T,' Oliver greeted me a little breathlessly as they jogged up.

'Hi, Oliver.' Oliver had a respectful manner about him. Not a slimy Eddie Haskell kind of cordiality, but that of a child who has grown up around adults. Oliver's mother, Aurora, had divorced Way early on and Oliver had spent his adolescence reading comic books in Goddard's Pharmacy in Benson Plaza. That might have been a bad start if it hadn't been for Gloria Goddard – or Mrs G, as Oliver called her – who had practically adopted the boy. 'Have you met Philip Woodward? Philip, this is Oliver Benson.'

'Who is also helping Eric out, right?' Philip said, extending his hand to shake Oliver's. 'My wife said you'd stopped by yesterday.'

'I hope that's OK.' Oliver pushed back the dark curly locks he kept just a bit shaggy.

'Of course,' Philip said. 'Any friend of Eric's is a friend of ours. And I'll be happy to pay you.'

'You don't have to,' Oliver said. 'Eric has been telling me about all the great things he's come up with—' Realizing that the most recent findings couldn't be termed 'great', he ducked his head. 'Sorry. This is horrible, really.'

'The crime scene techs have found something else?' I asked.

'More bones,' Eric said.

We followed the boys down the rutted gravel driveway past the cottage to the creek where the gravel and weeds widened into Sarah's 'parking apron'. A crime scene truck and the coroner's van were parked there, noses to the creek, as was Eric's blue Dodge Caravan, which had been a hand-me-down from me.

'I hope you set the brake,' I told him, nodding toward the Caravan.

'I did,' he said, exchanging a grin with Oliver. 'Though if it rolled into the creek, I could take the insurance and buy something sportier.'

Sportier than a faux wood-sided minivan? My son jests.

'There's room on the street behind mine,' Philip said, nodding back toward a black Land Rover. Vivian must have taken their Lexus. 'I moved the vehicles out of the way in case they needed the space.'

And to keep them safe from the goings and comings of the crime scene team, I'd have thought.

As we got closer, I could see that yellow crime scene tape had been strung from the door of the ramshackle shed standing between where we were in the parking area and the spikes driven in the ground to cordon off the compost heap on the far side of it. All three – the parking apron, the shed and the compost heap – ran along the creek.

As Vivian had said, the shed was both stinky and obscured the view, its battered door hanging open on one hinge. Inside a child's handprint had been pressed into the concrete floor.

'NK for Nirvana Koeppler,' I said, squatting to trace the initials that were punctuated by a small peace sign.

But the rest of my group's attention was focused beyond the shed.

I shielded my eyes against the sun. 'Under the blue tarp?'

'On top of it,' Eric said in a hoarse voice.

Rocking up on my toes to get what elevation I could, I just made out a tiny skull on the tarp. Below it, a skeletal shape was taking form as more remains were uncovered and arranged.

'Oh, my God.' I instinctively reached out and pulled my son close.

The four of us stood in silence watching until we gradually became aware of a helicopter throbbing closer.

'Who the hell?' Philip said, looking up.

'News5,' Eric said, giving my shoulder a reassuring squeeze before extricating himself.

'Five,' I said. 'That means—'

'Me,' a female voice behind us said.

I turned to see Kate McNamara. 'Fall off your chopper, Kate?'

And by chopper, I meant broom.

'My camera operator is in the chopper,' she said sweetly. 'You remember Jerome?'

As if he'd heard her, a blond, bespectacled young man hung himself out of the helicopter, camera on his shoulder.

'Be careful!' I called up.

'He can't hear you, you know,' Kate said. 'And he is a grown man. And an excellent camera operator.'

'Under your tutelage,' I said dryly, turning back to the reporter.

'I'm not banging him, Maggy,' Kate said, her nose tinging red. 'If that's what you mean.'

It wasn't, but her blush reminded me of Vivian's yesterday when she mentioned Oliver's visit. I glanced around to see that he, Eric and Philip had abandoned me upon Kate's arrival.

Freed to be me, I turned back to the reporter. 'I didn't say you were banging him. Jerome is young enough to be your son.'

'Actually, Jerome could be *your* son. You'll recall I'm a bit younger than you are.' Kate had always done 'snide' exceptionally well.

'A year younger,' I said, holding up a finger. 'As in one.'

But Kate wasn't listening to me. She was on the trail of new quarry.

'Mr Woodward,' she called, mincing over the gravel toward him and the boys.

Philip turned politely. 'Ms McNamara.'

'Yes, hello,' she said, digging into her purse for her phone to record. 'Kate McNamara, News5. Can you tell me about what the sheriff's department has discovered on your land?'

'Not really, I'm afraid,' Philip said with a tone and expression that managed to perfectly balance concern with ruefulness over not being able to help more.

'Was it a surprise?' she asked as Eric and Oliver scattered in opposite directions, leaving Philip to it. 'This discovery, I mean.'

'She doesn't know what's been found, does she?' I said in a low tone to Eric as he passed by.

'I don't think so,' he said. 'I sure didn't tell her.'

'Good boy.' But I still had to hope Philip wouldn't blab what I'd shared in confidence.

I needn't have worried.

'As you may know, my wife and I are opening a teahouse called The Big Steep here,' he said, being sure to get the name in.

'And?' Kate said encouragingly.

'And as for anything involving the sheriff, I'm advised that the county's public affairs division would be the best place to direct any questions—'

'Psst, Maggy.' A bony finger was poking my shoulder.

I turned to see Sophie Daystrom and Henry Wested, my octogenarian friends from across the way at Brookhills Manor.

It was Sophie's finger doing the poking. 'We were watching from across Brookhill Road,' she said, now using the finger to shove a fluffy strand of white hair behind her ear. 'Dang shed was in the way.'

Henry, a courtly man who always wore a fedora with a small red feather tucked in the band, swept it off his head. 'Good morning, Maggy.'

'Good morning, Henry,' I said, raising my voice to be heard above the helicopter. 'Sophie.'

'We heard they found a body,' Sophie said, loudly, causing Kate's head to swivel our way.

I motioned them to step closer to me. 'We should keep our voices down.'

Sophie glanced toward where Philip and Kate were talking, heads bowed, and whispered, 'Then you do know something.'

I shook my head and fibbed just a little. 'Less than you do, apparently. I only heard a bone was found.'

'That was as of yesterday evening, Maggy,' Henry said in his careful way. 'We believe the rest of the body may just have been discovered.'

'Skeletal remains, I heard.' Sophie was rocking up onto her toes to try to see into the taped-off area. She was a couple inches shorter than me. 'That means the body has been here for a while. Maybe you knew them, Henry.'

'Maybe,' Henry said with an indulgent smile.

Their exchange reminded me that Henry was, indeed, a local. 'Did you know the Koepplers, Henry?'

'Paz and Harmony or whatever the hell they called themselves, you mean?' Sophie demanded.

'Oh, yes,' Henry told me. 'An exceedingly long time ago, granted. When I was in school.'

'Then they were local, too?'

'No, not that I recall. I was going to Brookhills College when I first met them.'

'I didn't know you went to BC before you served.'

'Oh, yes,' he said. 'I had a college deferral from the draft. But when I graduated in 1965, off I went to fight in Vietnam.' He shook his head. 'It didn't sit well with some people, but I saw it as my duty.'

'That's right,' I said, remembering my history. 'The anti-war protests were underway. Were Paz and Harmony active?'

'Them and others. This being a college town back then, the sentiment was—'

'Shameful, if you ask me,' Sophie interrupted. 'Henry served his country honorably and was villainized for it.'

'You knew each other then?' I asked, surprised. Sophie and Henry had only been together for three years or so, so far as I knew. But maybe they were one of those couples who had been high school sweethearts and then reconnected fifty years later.

'No way,' Sophie said. 'I'm a helluva lot younger than Henry.'

'Always has preferred older men, she tells me,' Henry said fondly, slipping an arm around her. 'I told her that if she keeps going for older men after me, she'll be grave-robbing not cradle-robbing.'

'Oh, stop,' Sophie said, giving his shoulder a shove and nearly knocking him over. 'It's just nine years between us. But I do remember how disgracefully returning soldiers were treated after the war. All those protestors.'

Henry put his arm back around her. 'They were against the war, Sophie, not the soldiers. We just got in the middle of it.'

'Took the brunt of it, you mean,' Sophie said.

'Water over the dam,' Henry said, and then turned the discussion toward a subject he knew Sophie would embrace; information she could lord over her friends when she got back to the Manor. 'Now what were you saying, Maggy? About the bones?'

'I'm afraid we just got here,' I said.

'But we saw you walk over with this Philip.' Nothing got past Sophie. 'I can't believe you didn't worm something out of him. And your Eric and Oliver Benson have been working here and came out to meet you. One of them must know something.' Her head was swiveling. 'And where's that nasty wife of his?'

His being Philip, I assumed. 'With her mother,' I told her. 'Vana just arrived yesterday afternoon.'

'While the rats are away the mice will play, huh?' Sophie winked at me.

I frowned. 'Meaning Philip? Who's he playing with?'

'You, of course,' Sophie said. 'You can't think people don't see how much he's over at your place.'

'*They* were at Uncommon Grounds yesterday, in fact,' I said pointedly. 'When Vivian's mother, Vana, arrived.'

'Vana,' Henry said, picking up on my shift of subject. 'Was that the Koeppler girl's name?'

'Short for Nirvana,' I said.

Henry raised a hand in acknowledgment. 'That I do remember. Seemed odd, but then it was a different time.'

'A time well past, thank the lord,' Sophie said, as Kate left Philip's side and came to join us. 'What did you find out, Ms Newswoman?'

'That Philip Woodward is a charming man and a great schmoozer,' Kate said. 'He gave me nothing and made it seem quite the opposite. Reminded me of you, Maggy, in your public relations days.'

'I knew I liked the man,' I said.

'So I understand,' she said, as her phone signaled a text message. She punched it up. 'Oh, God.'

'What?' I asked as the rest of us exchanged glances.

'Please, God. No.' Kate was tap-tapping frantically on her phone. 'Don't let him have put that out.'

'Put what out where?' I asked, trying to see over her shoulder.

'This.' Eric had reappeared and he thrust his own phone at me. The station's Twitter feed.

And on it was an aerial photo of the scene in front of us, including the blue tarp.

And on that were the carefully laid out segments of a tiny skeleton.

FIVE

'It's gone.' I clicked off and then back onto the News5 Twitter feed on my own phone. 'Hopefully, nobody saw it before Kate had it taken down.'

The 'it' being the aerial photo of Baby Doe's skeleton. A half-century or more after the baby's death, one more indignity to be suffered. At least Frank hadn't known any better when the sheepdog showed off his find to Pavlik.

'Maybe nobody saw it except us,' Eric said, 'and Sophie and Henry.'

'Which means Sophie will tell everybody at the Manor,' I said, woefully. 'I think she screen-shotted it.'

'You'd think she would be especially sensitive,' Eric said, running his hand through his sandy hair. 'Being that old and . . .'

'Close to being a skeleton herself,' I said wryly.

'Speaking of insensitive, Mom,' Eric started. 'You—'

'Have been hanging around with Sarah too long, I know.'

'You realize you're as bad as she is,' my son said. 'You just don't say it aloud.'

No, I didn't. Mostly. 'Where did Oliver go?' I asked, looking around.

'Kind of vanished when the Manor contingent showed up,' Eric said. 'Sophie and Henry are great, but I think Oliver gets enough advice and stuff from them and everybody else over there when he stays with Mrs G.'

Gloria Goddard had lived at the Manor since having a stroke about a year ago. Hadn't slowed her down much, though. Either physically or presumably opinion-wise.

'Must be like having fifty grandparents,' I said, getting it. 'None of them yours.'

'But they all know what's best for you,' Eric said. 'Do you suppose Jerome is going to get into trouble?' Brookhills was a small place and Jerome had gone to the same high school as both Eric and Oliver, albeit a few years earlier.

'If he was the one who tweeted the photo, probably.' Kate had called the station and then taken off like a shot. There might be a public outcry regarding the insensitivity of posting the picture, but poor Baby Doe had no family to object to the violation of privacy. 'Though it's really the station's fault if they encourage journalists to post this stuff immediately without any oversight.'

'If it bleeds, it leads,' Philip said, rejoining us. He had gone into the house to pull on a light jacket against the spring winds.

'Especially now with social media,' Eric said. 'If the professionals don't post it, somebody else with a cell phone will.'

'In this case they'd need a cell phone and a helicopter,' I pointed out.

'Or an apartment on the upper floors.' Eric nodded toward the south-facing windows of Brookhills Manor across the street.

Philip was shaking his head. 'I think this is proof positive that there is such a thing as bad publicity.' His gaze followed the gurney carrying the tiny bones to the coroner's van.

A car engine revved once before shutting off and I turned to see Vivian climbing out of the driver side of her dark green Lexus in the driveway. Her mother was already out of the passenger side, reaching into the back to retrieve bags from a local boutique.

'I had a news notification on my phone,' Vivian said, slamming the car door and coming down the drive to join us. 'That photo.'

Then it *had* been widely disseminated.

'It's the skeleton of a baby?' she asked, then shook her head. 'Stupid question. It was so tiny.' Her voice cracked.

'I'm afraid so,' Philip said, putting his arm around her.

She shook it off as she turned to her mother, who had a shopping bag in each hand. 'Who could it be?'

'Why are you asking me?' Vana said. 'It's been over forty years since I left. I have no idea what went on after that.'

The bones likely dated back a good ten or twenty years before she had left. 'But when you were a kid, Vana, do you remember a baby boy or girl? One who was stillborn or died—'

'And was dumped in the garbage heap?' Her voice rose, and she lowered it as the knot of seniors across the way started to take notice and chatter rose. 'I think I'd remember that, don't you?'

'Of course.' Her daughter took the shopping bags from her. 'Should we take these in the house and then you and I go out again?'

Vana nodded. 'Yes, no need to be around all this unpleas—'

'Nirvana? Is that little Nirvana?' A tall, elderly man with gray hair and an unnaturally black mustache was crossing the road toward us.

'Vana,' she corrected him, cocking her head to watch him come. 'Do I know you?'

'Walter Benson,' the man said, handing her a business card. 'I knew your parents. You were probably too young to remember, but I do remember you.'

'You're Way's father,' I said, referring to our former landlord.

It was Walter's turn to correct. 'I was. He's dead, you know. Couple years now.'

Yes, I did know, as I'd discovered his son's body. But no need to go into that. 'Are you living at the Manor now?'

'And why wouldn't I?' he said, smoothing his mustache. 'I built the place after all. Deserve the best damned apartment they have.'

Yup, Way's dad. 'Oliver was just here,' I told him.

'My grandson never even calls. But what do you expect from kids these days?' As he spoke, he was getting closer and now he stood so near to Vana that she stepped back.

For a second I thought he was going to sniff her.

Which reminded me. 'Where is Frank?' I asked Eric, glancing around for our sheepdog.

'Went to the office with Pavlik,' Eric said. 'Maybe they need to exclude his teeth and stuff. You know, any marks he made on the evidence?'

I thought I got it, but it was kind of creepy. 'Really?'

Eric shrugged. 'Either that or Frank just wanted to go.'

That sounded more likely. The sheepdog could be persuasive. And if he jumped into the car, it wasn't easy to get him back out.

'—the image of your mother,' the old man was saying into Vana's ear. 'And don't tell me. This must be your daughter?'

Vivian hadn't gone to stash the bags in the house yet and was regarding the man with distaste. 'Yes, Vivian. And you—'

'Walter Benson.' He smiled to reveal tobacco-stained teeth and a missing canine of his own.

You'd think somebody with so much money would invest in dental work. And mustache dye that didn't look like shoe polish.

'I'm the man your grandparents stole this land from,' he continued.

'That's an interesting way of putting it,' Vivian said. 'I was told—'

The old man burst out in a sputtering laugh, causing Vana to move back even more. 'Aww, I'm just messing with you. Trouble long past.' He was surveying both Vivian and Vana. 'Classy ladies, the pair of you. Your mother would have been proud, Nirvana.'

Vana had taken a tissue from her pocket and dabbed her face. 'I'm so glad. Now if you'll excuse us?' She raised her eyebrows at her daughter. 'We should get back to the Morrison.'

'Absolutely,' Vivian said, still holding the bags as Vana tip-tapped her heels to the Lexus.

'Why don't you and your mother have dinner out?' Philip suggested to Vivian, taking the bags from her as Walter, finally seeming to get the hint, moved away.

'We do need to talk,' Vivian said, biting her lip.

'Good. Catch up, the two of you. There's no need for you to be bothered with all this.' He nodded at the crime scene, toward which Walter Benson was now toddling.

'All this is a dead *child*,' Vivian snapped. 'I wish we'd never come here.'

'I guess I can't blame her,' Philip said as we watched his wife back the Lexus unsteadily down the gravel driveway.

'No?' In my book, Vivian was a bit of a whiner. And a crappy driver.

'No.' Philip held up the bags. 'Come with me while I take these in?'

Eric had drifted over to where Walter had one of the deputies cornered, so why not?

'Vana must have bought these things for Vivian,' Philip continued as we moved toward the house. 'Designer labels.'

'*Genuine* designer,' I said with a grin. 'No knock-offs need apply.'

'No, indeed,' Philip said, also grinning, and then sobered. 'I think Vivian is embarrassed to be living in a cottage.'

'But it's lovely.' While the cottage had stood for years with its wood rotting and paint peeling, the exterior and deck of the structure were now repaired and painted ivory. The door and trim were a sweet shade of soft green. 'It's not your fault there's a skeleton in her grandparents' backyard.'

'No, but I did convince Vivian to leave Boston and come here in the first place. Starting the tea shop was my dream, not hers.'

'Maybe,' I said, trailing him and the boutique bags up the front porch steps, 'but Vivian agreed. And the tea shop is going to be a gold mine once you have it up and running.'

'It could be just as lucrative to sell it, according to your friend Sarah.' He swung open the door. 'Without our needing to stay here.'

I was getting a little defensive about 'here'. Brookhills was not exactly hell on earth. 'If you agreed to let Sarah list the property,' I said, following him in, 'do you know what she'd do?'

'Sell it?'

'No, she'd—' I broke off and looked around. 'You know, this is really charming.'

The front door opened into what would be the dining room of the tea shop, a corridor opposite us leading to the back door and, presumably, the living space. It was a shame there was no view of the creek from this room, so I could understand the Woodwards' desire to clear the yard for a deck and do it quickly.

Still, the main room was airy with windows on both the north and south walls. A counter and display case had been installed in one corner and tables were stacked in another.

One of the tables had been moved to the center of the room along with two folding chairs, a makeshift dining area for now.

'Gorgeous table,' I said, running my hand along the live edge of the wooden top.

'Black walnut,' Philip told me, unloading his wallet and keys onto it. 'Vivian has chosen simple chairs to go with them. They'll be here next week.'

'Vivian has good taste.' In men, too, though I was starting to think she didn't deserve Philip if she couldn't stand up to her mother. 'Anyway, I was saying that if you gave Sarah the chance, she wouldn't sell this place. She'd buy it.'

'She would what?' Philip had moved toward the hallway and stopped. 'I thought she wanted to list it. Help us sell it to somebody else.'

'She's saying that because she needs to be sure you want to sell it. If you do, I think she'll make you a fair offer.'

'She told you this?'

'No,' I said. 'But I know Sarah and how valuable she believes this location is. You'd make a lot of money if you sell, but not as much as if you develop it yourself into a money-making business. If that weren't true, Sarah wouldn't be interested.'

'Making money would be a good thing,' Philip said, raising the chic boutique bags. 'Want to see the rest of the place?'

'Please. I peeked in once, but it was before you were here.' I ducked my head. 'Sorry.'

'Don't apologize. I'm sure you weren't the only one to investigate while the place was vacant.' He nodded out the north windows toward the Manor.

It was true that after Harmony's death, people took the opportunity to tour what was a true open house. In fact, I wasn't sure there had ever been locks on the front or back doors when the Koepplers – or even Harmony alone – had lived there. Eventually, though, the city had installed padlocks to keep vandals, and snoopers, out until the Woodwards arrived.

Now Philip swung open one of the three interior doors that opened off the hallway. 'This is the kitchen, as it is. We'll have to expand it, of course, if we're going to do anything beyond serving tea and selling other people's baked goods. We couldn't get a permit from the health department to cook in here.'

I bit my tongue as I surveyed the galley kitchen, with its

linoleum-topped counter and avocado green appliances. It obviously hadn't been updated since the sixties. On the other hand, Uncommon Grounds had a full commercial kitchen.

I almost offered Philip the use of it. Or, alternatively, suggested he contact Tien, who used our kitchen for her catering and baking business. But as Vivian had said, The Big Steep and the Woodwards were still competitors.

'I know, it's awful,' Philip said, closing the kitchen door and moving to the next. 'This is worse. The single bathroom we'll have to use for the public – and for Vivian and myself – until we can remodel it.'

I stuck my head in to survey the harvest gold toilet, sink, tub/shower, countertop and floor. In fact, the only thing that wasn't gold was the poorly frosted window that blocked what would have been the view to and from the creek. 'Retro. People will love it.'

'Sure they will,' Philip said, crossing the corridor to open the third door. 'And this is the bedroom. There's just the one.'

'But it's big,' I said as he set the shopping bags on the low wooden dresser. 'Is this the original furniture? It looks hand-made.'

'I believe it is hickory,' Philip said, pulling out a drawer to show me the dovetailing. 'Probably hand-built by Paz and Harmony themselves.'

Probably? 'Have you asked Vana?'

'Of course, and she made a face. You may have noticed my mother-in-law doesn't recall her childhood fondly and, in my experience, prefers not to talk about it.'

'But her parents are dead now.' If the only thing that the two of them did wrong was give Vana a Babs instead of a Barbie, I didn't see the reason for all the resentment. But then there was a dead baby outside. A shiver crawled up my spine. 'They can't hurt anybody now.'

Philip stiffened. 'Do you think they had something to do with that baby dying?'

'I don't know,' I said. 'But maybe Vana has a good reason for not wanting to remember her life here.'

SIX

'Was there . . . I mean, did you find all of him?' I asked Pavlik that night.

'Yes. Though we still don't know whether Baby Doe is a him or her. In an adult, they can use the skull and, particularly, the pelvis to determine sex. In an infant it's more difficult and the age and condition of this particular skeleton poses even more challenges.'

I guess we'd stick with 'he' until we found out otherwise. And from the sounds of it, that meant actually identifying him. Or her. 'Since the entire skeleton was there, he must have died – or at least was buried – on the Koeppler property.' I picked up a piece of cheddar and set it back down again.

Eric had gone to his dad's, so it was only Pavlik and me at what passed as the dinner table in our house. I was fairly proud of the spread on the coffee table. I'd sliced up white cheddar and Manchego cheese and paired them with half a baguette and the lone apple I had found in the fruit and vegetable drawer. I didn't remember buying the apple, but it seemed fine despite browning a bit as I waited for Pavlik to get home.

'And buried, such as it was,' Pavlik said, and I could tell he was angry. 'You lose a dog or cat, a parakeet, for God's sake, you'd put them in a box and bury them properly. Not just dump them into a garbage heap with the other stuff you no longer need.'

I was sitting on an overstuffed chair perpendicular to the couch where Pavlik sat – the better to reach the food – and now I leaned forward and touched his shoulder. 'You said you thought the baby's leg was broken. What about the rest of the body? Could the coroner tell what the cause of death was?'

Pavlik took my hand and kissed the palm, before tugging me onto the couch with him. 'Not definitively, but . . .'

'But what?' I asked when he didn't go on.

'There were more broken bones,' he said, into my hair. 'His upper arm and clavicle. A rib.'

I said what I thought Pavlik couldn't bring himself to say to me. 'The poor little thing was beaten or shaken to death.'

'Maybe.' He wrapped his arms around me. 'But the leg break wasn't new. It had mended. Another was starting to mend, but improperly. It suggests a pattern.'

'He was so young,' I said, my voice barely a whisper. 'You said he was maybe a few months old.'

'Kids heal fast.'

Not when they're dead. 'He was abused and then he was killed.' All in the space of 'a few' months.

'That's what it looks like, I'm afraid.'

There was silence between us. 'I was talking to Philip. He says his mother-in-law doesn't like to talk about her childhood.'

'Maybe there's good reason for that.'

'I know,' I said. 'If Baby Doe was Vana's brother, she might have been abused too.'

'Or, conversely, she might feel guilty because he was hurt and she wasn't.'

I started to ask if that sort of 'survivor guilt' was common in families with abuse, but I wasn't sure I was ready to delve into those dark depths right now. 'Or she might have been the younger child and not even alive at the time. She didn't remember a child this afternoon when I asked her.'

'You asked her, huh?'

I ducked my head. 'I did, I'm afraid. She'd just learned about the skeleton and it seemed a natural question.'

'It was,' Pavlik said. 'Anthony is talking to Mrs Shropshire again tomorrow. We'll see if she's remembered anything more.'

Kelly Anthony was one of the sheriff's deputies. 'Does Vana know about the broken bones?'

'We didn't tell her,' Pavlik said. 'Or release it to the media.'

I'd been leaning back against Pavlik and now I turned. 'Did you see what News5 did?'

'The photo of the remains?' he said. 'Yes.'

'I'm sure the station is getting criticism.'

'It is.' Pavlik rubbed the back of his neck. 'But to be fair, we should have had the tarp area tented.'

'To be fair, again, your people did tent it after they were done laying out the bones. They had no way of knowing a news helicopter would be overhead. And that they would disseminate a photo. Ghoulish.'

'If it hadn't been a news helicopter, it could have been somebody's drone. Welcome to the wonderful world of social media.'

'That's what Eric said, too.'

'He's right. At least the station took responsibility and took the photo down.'

'What's the next step, now that you have the entire skeleton?' I asked Pavlik.

'We'll send the bones to a forensic anthropologist at the state laboratory for analysis. The skull and the teeth should help immensely.'

Teeth? 'He's not going to have dental records. And if he's as young as you think, he'll barely have any teeth at all.'

'We're all born with a full set of teeth hidden in our jaws. We just don't see them until they start moving down through the gums.'

Teething. 'So the anthropologist will be able to tell how old the baby was when he died by the number of teeth he's cut?'

'And the position of what he hasn't cut. Also, they'll analyze the bones and bone marrow to better estimate how long ago the baby lived.'

'What about DNA?' I asked. 'Could it be matched to Vana's or Vivian's?'

'Maybe,' Pavlik said. 'Depending on what has survived the years. And, also, whether Vana and Vivian will give us their DNA.'

'Can't you make them?' I asked.

'Probably not. It would be merely for means of identification. Besides,' Pavlik continued, 'it may be months before we get the full analysis on the skeleton.'

'A murdered baby isn't a priority?'

'A baby who was murdered decades ago will be put behind current cases that can be resolved.'

'You can't solve this?' I couldn't quite believe my ears.

'I hope we can, as far as who Baby Doe is and what happened to him or her. But it's possible any suspects are already dead.'

Which brought us back to the Koepplers. 'I asked Philip whether he thought there might have been other people living on the site.'

Pavlik picked up a now even browner apple slice and sniffed it.

'Don't eat that,' I said. 'Frank will. Or Mocha.'

At the sound of their names, the two dogs appeared from around the corner in alphabetical order. Arriving at the couch, Frank stepped aside to let Mocha precede him. 'I don't know why he lets her push him around.'

'Polite?' Pavlik guessed, giving Mocha a thumbnail size piece of apple and Frank the rest of the slice. Mocha took hers away to enjoy, like a mouse to her hole. Frank swallowed his in one gulp and sat down on my foot to wait for more. 'Besides, he knows she doesn't eat much.'

I slid the foot out from under. 'You don't mind my continuing to ask around about the baby, do you? It sounds like it'll be a while before you have much definitive information.'

Pavlik rubbed his chin. 'I'm trying to decide if that was an insult or just a very artful way of justifying the fact you've already grilled your friend Philip.'

'The latter,' I said. 'But he didn't know much, obviously. He did seem delighted to imagine his mother-in-law being brought up in a commune.'

'Mrs Shropshire does seem very proper,' Pavlik said. 'But your commune idea brings up a good point. We have no idea who might have been around at that time.'

'Walter Benson lives at Brookhills Manor now. You know, Way's father?'

Pavlik nodded.

'Walter knew the Koepplers and they had business dealings around that time. If you're still thinking the 1960s?'

'The remains still support it,' Pavlik said, choosing a slice of cheese this time. Thankfully, it wasn't brown. Or white or green, which has been known to happen in my refrigerator.

'As well as the trash. The rest of the skeleton was found a couple of inches below that magazine I mentioned to you.'

'So Frank did dig up the femur from the same area.'

'Most likely. We lucked out and the inner pages of the magazine were still legible. Apparently if paper is buried where oxygen can't get to it, it takes longer—'

'Longer than it's going to take you to tell me the magazine and publication date?'

Pavlik grinned. 'A teen fashion magazine dated September 1967. Twiggy was modeling something called a coat dress on the cover.'

'That's pretty specific. I thought the inside was all that remained.'

'Eric researched and came up with the issue. He's enjoying the hunt, I think.'

'I know. He told me the compost heap was like an archeological dig, going back through the decades. Maybe he's going to be an archeologist,' I said, settling back into him.

'Or, better yet, a cop,' the sheriff said in my ear.

We were all sound asleep – Eric in his room, Pavlik and I in ours, Frank on Eric's floor, Mocha on ours – when my mobile phone rang.

I reached for it. 1:49 a.m. Who was calling at such an hour?

'Philip?'

Pavlik had his arm over his head, frowning at me. 'Woodward?' he mouthed.

I nodded.

'Maggy,' the man on the other end of the line said, 'I'm so sorry to disturb you at this time. I didn't know who else to call.'

'What's wrong?'

'Vivian didn't come home last night.'

I turned over and sat up, a little irritated. It was still last 'night', so far as I was concerned. 'She's probably still out. Or at the hotel with her mom. Maybe they had wine with dinner and she didn't want to drive home.'

'I thought of that, of course, and Vana is the first person I called,' Philip said, as Pavlik's own phone rang.

He groaned and rolled over to retrieve it from the table on his side of the bed. 'Pavlik.'

Philip was still talking. '. . . She might not have wanted to call and wake me, but Vana was sound asleep, and I ended up waking her. She says that Vivian dropped her off at the hotel about twelve thirty and was coming straight home. It's less than half a mile.'

'Vivian never got there?'

'That's what's so odd,' Philip said as Pavlik listened to whoever was calling him. 'I woke up and thought I heard her – you know, the gravel crunching as she pulled in? But I just rolled over and went back to sleep.'

'What time was that?'

'I don't know,' he said. 'Like I said, I fell right back asleep.'

'And the car isn't there now?' I asked, watching as Pavlik got up and pulled on a pair of jeans. 'Maybe she changed her mind and parked on the street because of the county trucks.'

'The trucks are gone,' he said. 'And the Lexus isn't on the street.'

'Have you called the sheriff's department?' Pavlik was sitting on the edge of the bed, putting on his socks and shoes.

'I . . . no, I didn't know if I should. You know how they say somebody has to be missing twenty-four hours. I thought maybe you would know—'

Pavlik reached over and took the phone. 'Philip? It's Jake Pavlik. We'll be right there.'

I blinked as he clicked end. 'We will?'

'At least I will.' He held up his own phone. 'Nine-one-one took a call from Brookhills Manor. Someone is reporting headlights.'

Seemed a silly reason for calling 9-1-1. Though I'm sure the residents of the Manor had called for less. 'You think they may be Vivian's?'

'I sincerely hope not.' He handed me my jeans. 'They're submerged in Poplar Creek.'

SEVEN

'It's like that movie you were talking about,' Amy said, arms wrapped around herself against the early-morning cold.

'*The Big Sleep*?' I shivered under the blanket Philip had brought me from the house to augment my jacket. 'Yes, it is.'

Vivian Woodward's dark green Lexus was being lifted from Poplar Creek, water pouring out of it. One door hung, pried open by the dive team who had removed Vivian's body shortly after we'd arrived at two a.m. Recovering the car had waited until sunrise so the crane could be brought in and the chains attached safely.

I was not working today, and Amy had seen the commotion and stopped on her way to join Sarah at Uncommon Grounds for her shift. 'You should go help Sarah,' I told her now. 'Thanks for stopping.'

'My . . .' she put her arm around my shoulders, '. . . well, not my pleasure. But you know.'

I did.

I watched Amy get into her car parked behind the Land Rover on the street and drive to the coffee shop/train depot's parking lot just around the corner. Philip was inside the house talking to Deputy Kelly Anthony. Pavlik had sent a car to the Hotel Morrison to pick up Vana and she was now sedated in the cottage.

'Mom!'

I turned to see Eric, who'd been asleep when we'd left. The only one who'd taken notice of our leaving was Mocha who, disturbed by our movements in our bedroom, had huffed her way over to Eric's. 'What's going on?'

'Vivian Woodward's car went into Poplar Creek last night.' I nodded toward the nearly identical spot on the gravel where Eric had parked yesterday. No concrete barrier to mark the edge and keep the tires of any vehicle from rolling right—

'Oh my God,' Eric said, getting closer to peer at the land-slide of gravel that marked the Lexus' path over the edge and down the bank to the water. 'She didn't set her brake?'

'We don't know,' I said. 'She came home late and in the dark. Maybe she just misjudged where the edge was.'

'You're not saying she's still inside?' His face had gone white, as the crane positioned on the far side of the shed swiveled to bring the car over dry land.

'They pulled Vivian out of the car earlier,' I told him, putting my hand on his arm. 'But it was too late.'

He closed his eyes for a second, then pulled me into a hug. 'Thank you.'

'For caring enough to nag you about setting your brake, you mean?' There was a time when I could have kissed him on the top of his little head. Now I just had to settle for a cheek. And stand on tiptoes to do that. 'You're welcome.'

'Why . . . why didn't she get out?'

'I don't know,' I said. 'The headlights were still on when we got here.'

'What does that mean?'

'That at least part of the electrical system was still operating, but that doesn't necessarily mean the windows worked.' The days when you actually 'rolled' down the windows with a crank were far past, unfortunately.

'If she couldn't open the windows, she probably couldn't open the door because of the pressure difference, right?' Eric was moving toward where the crane had set the Lexus.

Pavlik was talking to one of the technicians and looked up, hearing Eric's question. 'Exactly right, Eric. It might be possible to open the door or window before the car sinks, but it takes a lot of presence of mind. Even taking off your seatbelt is a struggle.'

Eric raised his eyebrows.

'I know,' Pavlik said, holding up his hand. 'Seems elementary but people panic, even look for their cell phones, thinking they should call for help first. But your fine motor skills deteriorate, and the simplest things become difficult. If you can't get out before the car sinks, you can try breaking a window – side windows, not windshield – or, if you wait calmly until the car fills with water and the pressure equalizes, you should be able to open the door.'

The difference between a man and a woman. Or at least this man and this woman. I tell Eric how not to roll his car into the water, Pavlik tells him how to survive when he does.

'You have to remember to think your way out,' Pavlik summed up. 'Don't panic.'

'Is that what happened to Mrs Woodward?' Eric asked. 'She panicked?'

'I . . . yes,' Pavlik said, glancing at me. 'Probably so.'

I'd seen Vivian's body when it was placed on the gurney. Her fingers were bloodied, nails broken from trying to claw her way out. The woman's last minutes would have been a nightmare, something I wouldn't stop thinking about for a long time. I didn't want to put that image in Eric's mind.

'Do you think she just didn't stop soon enough?' Eric was moving around the car. 'That Lexus is like brand new – she told me she just got it in December. It shouldn't be brake failure or something.'

My son, the policeman.

'Electronics in new cars are pretty complicated,' Pavlik told him. 'Luxury models have as many as a hundred computers or processing units. And if something is going to go wrong, it's likely to do so early on so—'

As he spoke, I heard a double-knock and saw Kelly Anthony on the back doorstep of the cottage. Inside, the sound of running water stopped and a shadow passed by the frosted window before Philip stuck his head out the door.

'Oh my God,' a voice behind me echoed Eric's exclamation a few minutes earlier.

I turned to see Oliver coming up the driveway toward us.

'Mrs Woodward's car went into the creek,' Eric told him.

'Is she OK?' The boy's face had gone pale.

'I'm afraid not,' I told him, putting my hand on his arm. Oliver had suffered too much violent death already in his young life. This wasn't somebody close, but it had to bring up echoes of his parents' deaths.

'She's dead?' He was staring at the workers detaching the

slings that had lifted the Lexus from the water. 'Did she drive into the water? Like on purpose?'

'Oh, no,' I said, and then exchanged looks with Pavlik. 'At least we don't think so.'

Pavlik took over. 'We think it was an accident. She drove home late after dinner and maybe became disoriented as she parked, not realizing how close to the edge she was.'

'There's no divider or anything,' Oliver said, glancing around a little frantically. 'There should be something.'

Eric slung an arm around his buddy. 'We should talk to Mr Woodward. Maybe we can help him do that.'

'Too late for Vivian,' Oliver said still staring, and then shook himself. 'I just met her a couple of days ago.'

'Even so,' I said, 'it's a shock.'

'But why didn't she just get out of the car?'

'Pavlik and I were talking about that,' Eric told him. 'It's really important to make a move to get out right away. I was thinking, though. Once you're submerged, how can you tell which side is up?'

'You watch the air bubbles,' Pavlik said. 'They'll always rise to the surface.'

'And wouldn't the air pocket inside the car always be up, too?' Oliver contributed. 'Then . . .'

The three of them having moved onto survival tips, I turned toward the cottage. As Kelly Anthony tucked away her notepad to leave, Philip saw me and waved.

Leaving Pavlik and the boys to talk shop, I crossed the grass, gravel and weeds to the back door.

'OK if I go in, Kelly?' I asked the deputy as I passed her.

'Of course.' She nodded to Philip. 'You two are friends?'

'Yes,' I said. When she went to take out her notebook again, I added, 'Only since Philip and Vivian moved here from Boston, though. A month, give or take.'

'That's what I understand.' She finished a quick scribble and stashed the notebook again, nodding to me as she continued toward the crime scene van.

'The deputy was very kind,' Philip said, stepping aside to let me in.

I almost said, *Don't let her fool you.*

The truth was that Kelly Anthony was a good cop who had been burned recently by taking an apparent accident at face value. She'd paid the price for that mistake and learned from it.

Now she was unnervingly thorough, especially when confronted with another accident. I could tell Kelly, though, that Vivian hadn't seemed the most confident of drivers as she backed down the driveway to leave yesterday afternoon. And that it hadn't been dark then and, maybe, she hadn't had a glass of wine in her. And a creek in front of her.

Though the accident's resemblance to Philip's imagined tea strainer was a little unnerving.

'I'm so sorry,' I said as I stepped into the back hallway and he closed the door behind me. 'How are you bearing up?' Then I held up my hand. 'Sorry, stupid question.'

'What else is there to say really?' He led the way down the hall to the main room.

A snore came from behind the closed bedroom door as we passed.

'Vana?' I asked, nodding toward it.

'I gave her one of Vivian's sleeping pills,' Philip said, pulling out chairs for us at their dining table. 'Knocked her right out.'

'How is she holding up?' I asked, compounding my error.

'Terrible. She's been up since I called her around one-thirty and she has a hangover to boot.' He waved for me to sit and took the other chair. 'Apparently, she and Vivian had a couple of bottles of wine with dinner.'

Two bottles, two people. I liked wine, but that was beyond my limits. 'And Vivian drove?'

'Unfortunately she did,' Philip said. 'They ate at that new Italian place in Wauwatosa.'

That would be Luc's, the restaurant Tien's father had opened with a partner just before Christmas. 'That's about a five-mile drive on city streets. A little more via the highway.' Not terribly far unless you had a bottle of wine in you.

'Five miles.' He shook his head. 'I guess she thought she could make it. Dropped Vana off at the hotel and drove home.'

And into the creek. 'Do you think that's what happened, then? She had too much wine and just—'

'Made a mistake?' Philip asked. 'More than likely. I guess it's a good thing nobody else was killed.'

'You mean her mother?'

'No, somebody they could have hit. Vana is as responsible as Vivian. She never should have let her drive, but given the dynamics in that relationship—'

The snoring in the next room abruptly stopped.

We held our breaths and got a shaky inhale before the next snore.

'Both of them were impaired and responsible,' I said, keeping my voice low. I was hoping, quite honestly, that Luc wouldn't get in trouble for serving them. 'They should have called a cab or rideshare.'

'I know,' he said, rubbing the stubble on his chin. His eyes were bleary from grief and lack of sleep.

'I warned Eric yesterday to set his brake when he parked on the apron. In the dark, it would have been easy for Vivian to get a little too close.' Or, given her condition, just plain overshoot and drive right in.

Philip was shaking his head. 'I meant to put up parking barriers. Vivian . . .'

His voice caught and he dropped his head into his hands, sobbing.

'I'm so sorry,' I said, standing up to put my arms around him from behind. He was trembling. 'It wasn't your fault. It was—'

'It *was* his fault.'

We hadn't heard the snoring stop or the door open.

Now Vana Shropshire stood a few feet away in a wrinkled pants suit she must have pulled on, but still all lady. She was eyeing us, and I instinctively took a step away from Philip, dropping my arms.

'My daughter didn't want to come here,' she said, advancing on us. 'I certainly didn't want her to come. But *he* couldn't be talked out of it.' Her unsteady finger poked at me. 'Are you why?'

'Me?' I think my voice squeaked. 'I didn't know Philip or Vivian until they moved here. I had nothing to do with this.'

And yet, here I was. No wonder Pavlik said trouble found me and Sarah called me the corpse-stumbler.

'I was just being . . . nice,' I said, weakly moving away. The smell of wine-past-drunk was wafting off Vana, making me a little sick.

'Don't pay any attention.' Philip lifted his head. 'Vana is a bitter old alcoholic who let her daughter drink and drive.'

Wow. The gloves were off apparently. On both sides.

'I am not,' Vana snapped back.

'Not bitter or not an alcoholic?' Philip asked. 'You made my wife the way she is. Afraid of—'

A knock on the door. 'Come in!' they yelled in chorus.

Eric stuck his head in. 'Sorry,' he said, eyes darting between the three of us. 'The sheriff was looking for my mom?'

I gratefully followed him out as the other two stood-off against each other.

'Pavlik has good timing,' I said, closing the door behind us.

'Not Pavlik, me,' Eric said, with a sheepish grin. 'I could hear the raised voices and thought you might need extracting.'

'Good word, and I certainly did need it,' I said, punching him lightly in the shoulder. 'Thank you.'

I checked the time. Just seven-thirty a.m. Maybe still early enough to catch Tien at the shop. 'I'm going over to Uncommon Grounds. Want to come?'

'Nah,' Eric said, hooking his thumbs over his jeans' pockets. 'I'll stay here in case Pavlik needs me.'

And here I was worried the sheriff and my son might not get on full time. Before I knew it, I'd be the odd man out. 'You do that,' I said. 'Want me to bring you anything back? Coffee? Hot chocolate?'

'No thanks.' He was already halfway to the cluster of crime scene investigators and sheriff's deputies. 'We've got ours here already.'

Ours. Maybe Pavlik was right, and Eric would go into law enforcement or investigative work of some kind. OK by me.

As long as he stayed safe.

Crossing Poplar Creek Road to Junction, I caught sight of Tien Romano leaving the shop's side door to the train platform. 'Tien, wait.'

'Maggy,' she said, coming down to meet me. 'I was just going to call you.'

'About what happened?' I chin-gestured across the way.

'Yes,' she said, lowering her voice. 'My father feels awful. This Vivian and her mother had dinner at Luc's last night.'

'They had wine, I understand.'

'Oh, no. Was Vivian drunk? Is that why she went into the creek?' She opened her mouth and then stopped, seeming to collect her thoughts before saying, 'I was thinking of going over to the restaurant. Do you want to come?'

I did indeed.

EIGHT

Luc and Tien Romano had been fellow tenants in Benson Plaza, along with Goddard's Pharmacy. An's Foods was named after Tien's mother, who died when Tien was still quite young. The father and daughter kept things going, but when the mall collapsed, Luc decided to retire. That had lasted about a year.

'I was surprised when your dad decided to open a restaurant,' I told Tien, as we drove east on Brookhill Road in her little Audi crossover.

'I think he only retired—'

Her hands were on the steering wheel, but I could see she was itching to do the air quotes the last word demanded.

'—to free me up to do something on my own after An's closed.'

'Which you did by opening Romano Catering and baking us the best sticky buns in the state,' I said.

'Thanks to you and Sarah.' She stopped at a stoplight and turned to me. 'I don't know what I would have done without a commercially licensed kitchen.'

'And I don't know what we'd have done without you.' My eyes narrowed. 'Why? Are you thinking about leaving us to partner in the restaurant?'

'Heavens, no,' Tien said, stepping on the gas to leap forward and veer to the right onto the freeway. 'Though I am doing some cooking and baking for Dad. Italian bread and rolls, lasagna, stuff like that. And I've filled in for the wait staff a couple of times.'

Hmm, seemed like she was more involved than she was letting on. But Luc was her dad, after all. 'You didn't happen to be there last night, did you?'

She glanced sideways at me. 'Sadly no, but my dad was, so you can grill him.'

'Great.'

Another sidelong look. 'Why? Is this more than an accident?'

'No, I'm sure not,' I said. 'It is horrific, though. I just warned Eric yesterday to set his parking brake in that lot. Vivian coming home in the dark, after a few glasses of wine—'

'Brr,' Tien said. 'That's what scares me. My dad isn't responsible, is he?'

I hoped not. 'Only if they were over-served, I think.'

'But what exactly does that mean? Do you know?'

'I honestly don't,' I said as she pulled off the 68th Street exit into the Village of Wauwatosa.

'Me neither,' she said, taking another turn. 'An's didn't have a liquor license obviously. Angela will know. She's owned other restaurants.'

'Angela is your dad's partner? In the restaurant, I mean.'

She passed a parking lot and did a U-turn to park on the opposite side of the street in front of a brown, brick building. *Luc's* was stenciled on a curved transom window above the door. 'Partner in life, too, the way things are going.'

'Oh,' I said as she switched off the ignition. 'Do you like her?'

'I do, actually,' Tien said, getting out. 'Even though she's the polar opposite of what I remember of my mother.' She held out her hands, palms up, juggling them as she spoke. 'Italian, Vietnamese, Italian, Vietnamese.'

'Very different cultures.'

'They certainly are,' she said with a grin, 'but since I've been around my dad's Italian side for a long time now, it's not quite culture shock. Angela is kind of like my nona. Except younger. And amplified.'

I was looking forward to meeting this woman.

As we approached the door it was flung open by a man about five foot eight inches tall with salt-and-pepper hair. 'Tien! Maggy! I couldn't believe my luck when I saw you two lovelies pull up.'

'It's so good to see you, Luc,' I said, doing double cheek air-kisses. 'You look younger than ever.'

'That's because I touch up his hair.' A buxom woman with salt-and-pepper hair to match Luc's came up behind him wiping her hands on a dish towel.

'You must be Angela,' I said.

She grabbed and hugged me. 'And you're Maggy. I've heard so much about you and that crazy partner of yours, Sarah.' She let me go and turned to Tien. 'Where've you been? You never call, you never write.'

Tien just got out a laugh and, 'But I just saw you yesterday—' before she, too, was pinned to Angela's bosom.

'It's never enough,' the older woman said, stepping back. 'Come in, come in.'

We did, and I stood for a second, taking in the wood-paneled walls and white linen-topped tables. 'I love it. It feels like a supper club.'

'Exactly what we were going for,' Luc said, pulling out a chair for me. 'Can I get you an espresso or is it a busman's holiday for a coffeehouse owner to drink coffee?'

'Actually, I would love an espresso, especially one I didn't make,' I said. 'I was on my way into the shop when I ran into Tien and we came directly here.'

'Espressos all around?' Angela asked.

'Perfect,' Tien said, taking the chair next to me and then half getting up again. 'Can I help you?'

'Now don't you move,' Angela said. 'Just talk to this father of yours and I'll be back in a jiff.' She bustled off into the kitchen.

Luc sat down across from me. 'I heard about the accident. That was right down the road from you.'

'It was,' I said. 'I understand Vivian and her mother had dinner here.'

'That they did,' he said. 'Veal for the mother and eggplant for the daughter, though like I told them, who could tell the difference?'

I played stupid. 'Between eggplant and veal?'

A cackle sounded from the kitchen. Luc's partner was as good an eavesdropper as my partner was.

Luc grinned in appreciation. 'No, no. Between mother and daughter. They always like when you say that.'

'My father the charmer,' Tien said. 'And getting more Italian with every moment.'

'Whadda ya mean?' he asked, gesturing extravagantly with his fingertips bunched and pointing at the ceiling.

'I mean,' Tien said, 'that you were born in Milwaukee, Wisconsin, not the old country. And so were your parents.'

'Lower east side of Milwaukee,' Angela pointed out from the kitchen.

'Home of the best Italian bakeries and restaurants around,' I said, and then corrected myself. 'Until now.'

Luc smiled. 'I like this front of the house stuff. People expect a little theater.'

'You're not cooking?' I asked.

'We take turns,' came from the kitchen.

I saw what Tien meant about Angela being 'amplified'. 'So last night Angela was in the kitchen and you, Luc, were out in front?'

'I was,' Luc affirmed. 'Seated the two ladies and got them started with a basket of Tien's fresh-baked bread. They asked for butter.' The expression on his face showed what he thought of that choice over olive oil.

'And wine?' I asked.

'Sangiovese,' he said, making a circle of thumb and forefinger and fanning out the other fingers to draw across his body, a beatific expression on his face.

'That means "perfect,"' Tien translated.

'Get all the gestures down, you won't even have to speak,' I said.

'I talk enough for the both of us,' Angela called.

'It's true,' Luc admitted with a grin. 'But as to the wine, it was an excellent choice.'

'And they had two bottles?'

'They did,' Luc confirmed. 'When they ordered the second bottle, my waiter asked – you know, lighthearted, so they wouldn't take offense – how they were getting home.'

'What did they say?'

'That they'd have to take an Uber if they drank the whole thing. As it turned out, Richard said the one laid off the wine because she was driving.'

'The younger one?' I asked.

Luc closed one eye, thinking. 'Must have been. I remember she gave the car to the valet when they pulled up.'

That added up, both that Vivian was driving and that Vana

should be so hungover. 'Vana, the mother, drank the whole second bottle?'

'Oh, no, no,' Luc said. 'They took more than half the bottle with them.'

'They did?' I asked, surprised. 'I thought it was illegal to take an open bottle in a car.'

'Oh, there are all sorts of rules, believe you me.' Angela swept in with a tray containing a plate of cookies and two tiny cups and their saucers. She set the plate in the middle of the table, then one cup in front of me and the other in front of Tien, before reciting, '"The cork must be re-inserted by the restaurant to the point where the cork is even with the bottle and a dated receipt for the wine *and* food must accompany it." We staple it on the bag just to be sure.'

'And don't forget, none of this can happen after midnight,' Luc added. 'Like Cinderella. I remember they just made it.'

'Thank God.' Tien let out the breath she apparently was holding. 'I was so worried.'

'You mean that we'd be responsible?' her father asked. 'I admit the restaurant business is new to me, but if I thought the woman was incapable of driving, I'd have put them in a cab.'

'Rideshare,' Angela said, bustling back to the kitchen. 'Cheaper.'

Luc hooked a finger toward her back. 'Isn't she a card?'

I smiled. Luc didn't look much different, but Tien was right. He'd morphed into an old Italian guy. It was kind of nice.

Tien was watching me, and I gave her the thumbs up.

'I think so, too,' she said.

'Think what?' Angela said, coming back with two more cups.

'That you're a card,' Luc said.

'And that you're good for my dad.' Tien gave her a peck on the cheek as she leaned down with a cup.

Angela flushed with pleasure. 'Well, I surely hope so. Now have a *tadal*.' She pointed at the cookies.

Never one to disobey orders, at least when it comes to eating, I took a small, round, iced biscuit. 'Delicious.'

'You know, Maggy,' Luc said as I washed the cookie down

with a sip of espresso, 'I wanted to ask you about this baby they were talking about on the news.'

'Such a mystery,' Angela said, pulling up another chair and taking a tadal. 'My uncle Donny used to come spend weekends out your way. From Chicago, you know.' She gave us a wink.

I raised my eyebrows. 'Your uncle Donny was mafia?'

She shrugged. 'All I know is my older cousins used to go with Donny on "errands" when they were boys.'

'Collecting protection money?' Tien's eyes were big. 'Where was this? When?'

'Chicago, mostly, but Milwaukee, too. Long time ago.' She picked up her cup and sipped, knowing full well that she had hooked us.

'I've heard that mobsters . . .' I glanced apologetically at her. 'Sorry.'

'Now don't worry about it,' she said. 'Uncle Donny was on my mother's side. They were always a little sketchy, to hear my father tell it.'

'Anyway,' I said, 'I've heard they had lake homes in the Brookhills area. Vacationed there.' I turned to Tien. 'That room under the train platform. That's—'

'—where they stayed out of sight until the train pulled in,' Angela said. 'Then they'd come out, brazen as you like and board the train, smoking their cigars and all.'

Angela sure knew her stuff, mob-wise.

Tien seemed equally awed. 'Your uncle Donny – was he a made man?'

Angela waggled her head. 'Now, I don't know that. Truth is I'm not even sure we were related familywise. Uncle . . . well, it was a pretty flexible term in my family.'

Mine, too, though not for those same reasons. Which brought me back to the Koepplers and the possibility of multiple 'uncles and aunts' living on that property. 'Not to change the subject, Angela, but it sounds like you know Brookhills pretty well.'

'Raised my boys there with my first husband,' she said. 'Then, when he died, I moved to a little place here in Wauwatosa, which is where Luc and I met.' The lovebirds exchanged smiles.

'Do you know the Koeppler place? It's across from Brookhills Manor—'

'Where that poor lady went in the drink last night?' She glanced over at Luc. 'Damn shame. I think we'd have had repeat business there.'

I saw Tien repress a grin.

'That's it,' I said. 'I mean, you're right that the Koeppler place is where Vivian's car went into Poplar Creek. It's also where the baby's skeleton was found.'

'I saw those tiny bones.' Angela's eyes teared up. 'I thought that's not much more than a newborn, that child.'

The picture had gotten wider distribution than I'd have expected before it was taken down. I'd feel sorry for Kate if I liked her. Which I didn't. 'The sheriff thinks that the bones—'

'Oh, that's right,' Angela said, delightedly, giving Luc's shoulder a little shove. 'This is the one who dates the handsome sheriff, isn't it?'

'It is,' I said with a smile.

'They're getting married,' Tien added.

'Now that you said that, I'm going to expect an invitation,' Angela said, and then an idea seemed to hit her. 'They should get married here,' she said to Luc. 'Don't you think so?'

She turned back to me, as my mouth opened. Nothing came out.

'Now don't you worry,' she said. 'Such a deal we'll give you.'

'Well, thank you. That's very kind of you.' I was honestly tempted. If we did it there, the woman wouldn't let me lift a finger. In fact, I wasn't sure Pavlik and I would get our vows in. 'Anyway—'

'Yes, dear, you were saying about the baby.'

'You're right that he was just months old. Pavlik says—'

'She calls him by his last name,' Angela said, sitting back and slapping her hand on the table. 'That is so cute.'

'We met when the sheriff accused me of murder,' I explained. 'Once we got past that, I couldn't think of him any other way.'

'Absolutely understandable.' Angela wagged a finger at me. 'Bet you two have a damned good sex life. Your sheriff probably has his own handcuffs.'

Luc's face had gone bright red.

'Maybe Maggy can get you some,' Tien offered, watching her father as she said it.

Luc choked and started to cough, Angela slapping him on the back. It took me a second to realize he was laughing.

'Now, dear,' Angela said, when she brought Luc a glass of water and things had settled down a bit. 'You were saying about your sheriff and what he had to say. Does he know how long ago the baby died?'

At least one of us could keep track of the conversation. 'Mid to late sixties, most likely. I'm wondering who was living on the Koeppler property back then.' I meant besides the Koepplers, but I wasn't going to bring up communes and free love to this crowd.

'Well now, I was a mere glimmer in my father's eye then. Born in 1968.'

'Hooked myself a younger woman, I did,' Luc said, sliding his arm around the back of her chair.

'I could ask Nona though,' Angela offered.

'Your grandmother is alive?' I must have sounded aghast because Angela, Luc and Tien broke up laughing.

'I meant—' Truth was I actually meant exactly what I'd said.

'I know, I know,' Angela said, waving down my explanation. 'My boys' nona, meaning my own mother.'

'Your mother lived in Brookhills, too?' I asked.

'She went to school at Brookhills College,' she said. 'A very respected school back then. And then she married my father and moved to Chicago, which is where I was born and where she's stayed until now. It's time she moved up here, though, to be closer. She's visiting, and I'm trying to convince her to look at the new units they're building at that Brookhills Manor.'

'I have some good friends living there,' I said. 'Sophie Daystrom and Henry Wested.'

'Oh, yes,' Tien said. 'Carmen would love Sophie. Henry, too.'

'Carmen is Nona?' I asked.

'She really hates it when I call her Nona,' Angela said, waving her hand. 'Only the boys are allowed.'

'Carmen is nearly eighty, but very independent,' Tien said. 'She drives a Ferrari.'

'She's a pistol,' Luc said.

'"Pistol", Dad?' Tien repeated. 'Now you're taking the old Italian guy thing a little too far.'

'Fine, I'll ratchet it back,' Luc said. 'Carmen's pretty hot, though.'

Angela turned and surveyed him. 'You are talking about my mother.'

'Absolutely,' Luc said. He feigned licking a finger and brought it close to her shoulder. 'Ssst, hot stuff!'

Angela swatted him a good one.

NINE

'Angela is great,' I told Tien as she drove us back. 'If her mom is the same, she'll fit right in at Brookhills Manor.'

Tien shifted her eyes toward me and back, even as attending to her driving. 'Which must be why you suggested Angela collect Carmen and meet us at the Manor, I suppose.'

'Well, of course,' I said, looking straight out the front windshield myself. 'We'll introduce her around and—'

'Pump her for information?' Tien turned the little car off the freeway and onto Brookhill Road.

'She's old,' I said. 'She'll love talking about old times.'

'Carmen gives "old" new meaning,' Tien said. 'But if you're right that the baby's skeleton dates back to the sixties, it sounds like she might have been here.'

'That's what I'm thinking,' I said. 'Angela said she was born in 1968, after Carmen got married and they moved to Chicago. Maybe we'll get lucky.'

'I'm glad you didn't say "get lucky" in front of my dad and Angela. They can be . . .' She was searching for a word.

'Frisky?' I supplied.

'Better word than horny, I guess,' Tien muttered as she turned right onto Poplar Creek Road and then took an immediate left into the Manor parking lot. Across Brookhill Road, the investigators were still at work. No sign of the news helicopter, though I thought I caught sight of Eric near the county crime scene van.

'Well, it will be a good opportunity for Carmen to see the Manor. Hopefully, Walter Benson will be around. He drives a flashy car, too. And she can meet Sophie and Henry.' I frowned. 'He served in the early years of Vietnam.'

'My dad was late years, before you ask.' Tien turned the Audi neatly into a parking spot next to a pink crab apple tree just starting to blossom. 'Way beyond the decade in question, unless you think I'm sixty.'

The Vietnam War – or conflict, as it was called, given that Congress had never actually 'declared' war on North Vietnam – had run from 1955 to 1975. 'The war lasted two decades – that's an entire generation.'

'Dad got out in '75 and brought my mom here,' Tien said. 'But I wasn't born until 1989. Just in case you're doing the math in your head.'

'I was, but it made it hurt, so I stopped,' I told her, swinging open the door and climbing out of the crossover. 'The engine is still running.'

'Oops, sorry,' Tien said. 'This new Audi has a push button for the ignition, and I keep forgetting.'

'I saw you push a button,' I said.

She sighed. 'Yes, that was to put it into park.'

Damn newfangled cars. I glanced across the river. 'Best be careful about that.'

Her gaze followed mine. 'I know. One mistake and—'

'Well, look who the heck the cat dragged in,' a voice said.

We turned to see Sophie scurrying down the sidewalk from the main entrance. She wore an elaborate red hat with a purple feather that matched her purple suit.

'Are you heading out to a meeting?' I asked her.

'Would I be wearing this goldarn outfit if I wasn't?'

Sophie belonged to the Red Hat Society, a group of women over fifty who got together regularly.

'I'm sorry you're leaving,' I told her. 'Tien's father's new partner's mother is coming over and I thought I'd introduce the two of you.'

'Father's partner's mother?' Sophie was trying to work it out and who could blame her? Then she brightened. 'Luc has met somebody?'

'Angela is his business partner,' Tien told her, 'but they're also dating.'

'Dating?' Sophie sputtered. 'Your father is a good deal younger than Henry and me, but there's still not time to waste dating. Move in with the woman! Throw it against the wall! See if it sticks!'

Tien looked both confused and horrified.

'Never mind,' I told her. 'Sophie talks big, but she didn't move in with Henry for a long time.'

'What can I say?' Sophie said, patting her feather. 'I like my independence. Luckily, Henry doesn't try to change me.'

An impossibility. 'Speaking of Henry, is he here?'

'Yes, yes,' Sophie said, 'you'll find him in the lounge drinking coffee most likely. It's free here, you know.' That last was meant for me.

'Yes,' I said, as she climbed into her little Hyundai. 'Yet we still count ourselves blessed to have you as customers at Uncommon Grounds.'

'You sure the heck should,' she said, slamming the door. The window rolled down so I could hear: 'Your sheriff was here somewhere.'

'Across the way, you mean?' I gestured toward the Koeppler cottage.

'If I'd meant that, it's what I'd have said now, wouldn't I?'

Fine. 'So what was Pavlik doing here then?'

'I think Walter Benson got him out here. Vandalization on Phase Three, as he calls it. I call it Phase "Give us all your earthly possessions and we'll let you live here until you kick off."'

'Hmm,' Tien observed as Sophie peeled away. 'She's in a good mood today.'

'She is,' I agreed with a grin, just as a horn blared.

Sophie's Hyundai had turned left out of the parking lot, almost cutting off a silver Porsche 911.

'Uh-oh, did they nearly collide?' Tien asked, squinting.

'Not sure. The Porsche just turned in here.' I shaded my eyes. 'I think it's Walter Benson.'

'Nice car.'

'It is,' I said as the little sportscar vroom-vroomed into the spot next to us. 'Hello, Walter, good to see you again.'

'Yes, well,' he said, cracking open his door carefully. 'Just see that you don't ding my baby here.'

Tien was frowning, probably at the affront to her own new 'baby'. She waved her hand at the largely empty lot. 'There are plenty of spots. Why didn't you just park away from us if you're worried?'

'Where one of these blind geezers can slam into it?' he asked, unfolding his lanky form from the seat. 'At least *you* have a decent car and are young enough to be able to see to drive it.'

'Well, thank you,' Tien said, not bothering to hide the sarcasm. 'I think.'

'Tien, this is Walter Benson. Way's father,' I said. Way had been An's landlord, as well as Uncommon Grounds'. And canceled their lease, too.

'That explains it,' Tien said.

'Explains what?'

'Why I took an instant dislike to you,' she said with a friendly smile on her face. Tien was the nicest of persons. Unless you did something to hurt her father, then all bets were off.

Walter Benson's eyes narrowed. 'You're insulting me?'

'More your son,' she said. 'And the way he did business.'

'He's dead, you know.' Seemed to be his go-to line.

'Still an as—' She broke off as another sports car, this one a shimmery light blue convertible, roared into the lot. 'Here we go.'

'A Ferrari,' I said, shading my eyes again. 'Is that Angela?'

'In the passenger seat,' Tien said. 'Nona's driving.'

The car came barreling toward us, hitting the brakes at the last moment and making a neat turn into the spot on the other side of Walter.

'Wow,' he said. 'What a beauty.'

'Why thank you,' the woman in the driver's seat said. 'You're not bad yourself.' She looked him up and down. 'Your car, I mean.'

'That's what I meant, too,' he said, delightedly, opening her door for her. 'New resident?'

'Play your cards right and maybe so,' she said, climbing out and offering her hand. 'Carmen Petra. And you are?'

'Walter Benson,' he said, taking the hand. For a second I thought he was going to kiss it, but he just stared at her.

'Nona, must you hypnotize every man you meet?' Angela had gotten out of the passenger side all on her own and joined us.

'Yes,' the woman said, not taking her eyes off Walter. 'And do not call me Nona. I'm your mother, not your grandmother.'

'I call her that to get her goat,' Angela said to Tien and me.

'She's very . . . vibrant,' I said, taking in all that was Carmen Petra. And it was a lot. Her car the unusual metallic blue. Her dress just a shade off emerald with a scarf in other jewel tones.

She was glancing around, her nose wrinkled. 'I am not certain of this place. I do not see a garage for my car. And whatever can that commotion be?' She gestured across the road.

'A car rolled into the canal,' Walter said. 'Not much of a loss.'

Appalled at even his callousness, I said, 'You met Vivian Woodward, you know.'

'Who?' Walter seemed to have forgotten I – or anyone other than Carmen – was there.

'The woman who died,' I said. 'You just said she wasn't much of a loss.'

'I meant the car,' he said irritably. 'A Lexus, wasn't it? I have no idea who the woman was.'

'Yes, you do,' I insisted. 'Vivian Woodward. You talked to her mother Vana just yesterday. Said you remembered her.'

His head twisted toward me. 'That was Nirvana's girl? The one who died?'

'It was,' I said.

I fully expected him to treat her loss as lightly as her car's, but the man seemed genuinely troubled. 'Well, now. What an awful loss for poor Nirvy.'

'Nirvy?' I repeated.

'Yes, yes.' Walter seemed lost in whatever memory her name had conjured up. 'Paz called her that, because she was such a worrier, poor little thing. Though living that existence, how could she be any other way?'

'Were her parents not good to her?' Tien asked now.

Walter started at the sound of her voice, like he'd forgotten she was there or could speak. 'Oh, I don't know about that, but it was the era. Drugs and all.'

I decided to take a stab. 'I heard there was a commune over there. Must have been quite the happenin' place in the sixties.'

'"Happenin'",' Tien whispered. 'Really, Maggy?'

But Walter had frowned. 'Now where did you hear that?'

'Walter Benson.' This from Carmen, who was peering at him intently. 'Wally Fally?'

Walter's face went crimson.

'All legs and arms, this man,' she said, turning to Angela. 'So clumsy, you wouldn't believe.'

'You knew Walter in the sixties?' Jackpot!

'Oh, yes,' she said. 'My parents, they were from outside Rome, but I came here for school. My uncle Donny, he knew the area.'

Carmen was becoming more and more Italian as she spoke. I glanced at Angela. 'Uncle Donny again.'

Angela just shrugged.

'This place,' Carmen said, waving her hand toward the Koeppler's cottage. 'It was where we hung.'

'See?' I hissed to Tien. 'If she can say hung, I can say happenin'.'

'No. You can't.' End of subject apparently.

'. . . very near to the train station,' Carmen was saying, 'so we travel to town for fun. Still, we have the woods and Poplar River.'

'Creek,' Angela corrected.

'Looked like a river to us back then,' Walter said, still studying Angela's mother. 'Carmen . . . it is you, isn't it? You were Carmen Gianni back then.'

'Petra was my husband's name.' Before he could ask, she added, 'He died.'

'You haven't changed.'

'No,' Carmen said, waving her hand. 'But life, it has. The things we did?'

Angela exchanged looks with me. 'Like what?'

'Oh, now,' her mother said, 'you have no need to know.'

'Oh, but I do, *Nona*.'

A reproachful stare and then the older woman laughed. 'You do it to tease, but—'

'You know who else is here?' Walter interrupted. 'Henry Wested. Now there was a real stick in the mud.'

'Oh, but I loved Henry,' Carmen said. 'So polite and soldierly. Even before he became one.'

'Henry did serve in Vietnam,' I said. 'If you were all in this commune, did that—'

'Oh, no, no. The cottage by the river was not a commune,' Carmen said. 'We played at being flower children, what you call hippies. We were just college students, most of us.'

'Except for Ray and Matilda,' Walter said, nodding.

'They wanted to be called Paz and was it . . . Joy?' Carmen asked, remembering.

'Harmony,' I told her.

'Yes, that is it.' She fluttered her eyelashes. 'Paz was so handsome. But they could be tedious with the . . . how you say back-to-nature thing?'

Back-to-nature thing.

'So tedious,' Walter said, apparently liking the word, 'that we couldn't shoehorn them off the property when it was time to leave.'

'Oh, that's correct,' Carmen said. 'It was your father who owned the land, was it not?'

'This over here' – he swept his arm toward the Manor – 'and that lot across the way. Paz and Harmony said it was theirs by squatters' rights.'

'Adverse possession,' I offered, cocking my head. 'How did that turn out? Were they able to prove it belonged to them?'

The flush 'Wally Fally' brought on had faded, but now it tinged back. 'It was a very long time ago, but as I recall, I spoke to my father and we eventually settled it amicably.'

'1979,' I said, remembering what Sarah had dug up. 'Quit claim deed for a dollar.'

'A dollar?' Carmen repeated. 'Your father must have been a far more generous man than I recall, Wally. I remember his anger when you eloped with that girl you impregnated in our second year. What was her name?'

Now this was getting interesting.

'Paula,' Walter supplied, his jaw clenched. 'The marriage didn't last, but of course, I felt like I had to do right by her.'

Let's all applaud. Sheesh. 'Paula was Way's mother?'

'Yes, she was.' Walter crooked his arm for Carmen to take. 'Won't you let me show you around, my dear? We're just starting Phase Three, which are luxury condos for those of us who demand the finest in life.' He couldn't help but sneak a glance at the car. 'Away from the riff-raff.'

But Carmen hesitated, frowning. 'And a garage? I will not park my baby outside.'

'Maybe it's time you sold the Ferrari,' Angela said. 'You really wouldn't need it here. They probably have transportation to grocery stores and the like.'

'Buses? I think not,' Carmen said.

'Don't you worry.' Walter was leading her away. 'Each new unit will have its own heated garage. The condos are being built on the far side of the skilled nursing facility—'

Carmen stopped, her nose wrinkled. 'A nursing home? I prefer not to be reminded of my own mortality. The smells, the sights.' She shivered.

'Oh, no, no,' Walter said. 'There is not a connection between the buildings. I only meant the condos are to the north. The show model won't be ready until Saturday, but we can walk to the site. Or, if you prefer, we can take your car or mine. It's a fair distance.'

Two scant city blocks, by my reckoning, which Carmen chose to walk. Walter was laying it on thick, making sure he put plenty of figurative distance between the luxury condo living and the imminent possibility of nursing home living. I also noticed he didn't mention that there was a funeral home and crematorium conveniently located a scant block past the luxury condo site.

'Each home will have its own entrance and garage, as I said. No need to . . .' His voice faded as they walked out of earshot.

'If he has garage space,' Tien said, looking back at her Audi, 'why did he park next to me?'

'Maybe luxury cars need to be socialized like dogs,' I said. 'You know, so they don't growl at the riff-raff.'

'Think I should follow them?' Angela was watching the two disappear.

'Only if you want to be further nauseated,' Tien said. 'Or we could go to Uncommon Grounds for coffee.'

Brilliant idea.

TEN

Sarah welcomed us warmly when we stepped into Uncommon Grounds.

Which made me immediately suspicious.

'Tien,' Amy said, coming to the service window. 'Didn't I see you leave?'

'I ran into Maggy, we left to go to my dad's restaurant, stopped by Brookhills Manor and now we're back here again.'

'All that accomplished in' – the barista craned her neck to see the clock above the original ticket window – 'a little over ninety minutes. Well done.'

'Thank you,' Tien said, with a grin. 'By the way, Amy Caprese, meet Angela Fiorentine.'

'Caprese, another Italian,' Angela said, delightedly, only the counter between them probably preventing her from hugging the barista. 'It's wonderful to meet you.'

'Actually, I'm not Italian,' Amy said. 'My father just liked tomatoes.'

Angela's jaw dropped. 'You're kidding.'

'I am,' Amy said, a smile busting out. 'But my father's family *is* from the island of Capri.'

'In the Bay of Naples,' Angela said. 'Beautiful place. Have you been?'

'Not yet,' she said. 'But my boyfriend, Jacque, says we'll—'

Not caring to hear about Jacque Oui's promises, I gestured for Tien to follow me to my favorite table by the window. 'I'll go back and get our drinks when Amy and Angela are done chatting.'

'So what do you think?' Tien asked as she sat down.

'Of Carmen? Angela? Walter?'

'Carmen and Walter, mostly. Did you realize they knew each other before Carmen arrived?'

'No,' I said. 'But they're of the same generation and Angela mentioned Carmen had gone to Brookhills College, so I thought there was a chance.'

'On the other hand, the Koepplers didn't go to BC, Walter said.'

'No, but they were a young couple living off-campus. The cottage would have been the perfect place for kids to hang out, smoking weed and drinking cheap wine.'

'"And making love, not war",' Tien quoted from an era well before her time. 'The peace movement of the sixties really got its start on college campuses.'

'Speaking of making love,' I said, leaning forward, 'what about that bombshell about Walter getting this Paula pregnant? For a second there, I thought maybe we'd found our Baby Doe.'

'Unwanted love child disposed of by wealthy family,' Tien said. 'It would have fit.'

'Except Way lived.' Until May two years ago. 'I'm going to investigate, though. Make sure Way's date of birth checks out.'

'Do you know what it was?'

'No, but I can Google it.' I got out my phone and punched in 'Way Benson date of birth'. 'May the tenth, 1963.'

'Is mine in there?' she asked, peering at my phone.

'I doubt it,' I said. 'You're not famous. Or, at minimum, rich. And murdered.'

'None of the above,' Tien said, sitting back. 'Thank God.'

'Carmen said Paula got pregnant in "our" sophomore year, so they must have been in the same class. Angela said her mom is touching eighty, so . . .'

'Can you just Google Walter Benson's date of birth? He's even richer than Way.' She frowned. 'Though he hasn't been murdered.'

'Still, he probably has a Wikipedia entry,' I said, punching in Walter's name. '1943, so he would have been around nineteen when he started his sophomore year, if he went right from high school to college—'

'1962. With Way born the following May, in 1963.'

'Yes,' I said. 'Damn.'

'Maybe Way was a twin?' Tien offered.

'We couldn't be that lucky,' I said. 'Besides, why would

even the most stick-up-their-collective-butt family recognize one twin and kill the other?'

'Good point,' Tien said. 'Which brings us back to the Koepplers. But they, too, raised one child to adulthood. Why kill another?'

'Walter said Vana was a nervous little thing and that he wasn't surprised given her upbringing.'

'But when I pressed him on why . . .' Tien said.

'He blamed it on the times, drugs and all. But no specifics.'

'Maybe he doesn't know any more.'

'Maybe,' I said. 'Or he doesn't want to talk about it. And it's obviously not a good time to ask Vana herself.'

'With her daughter having died in such a horrible accident, you mean,' Tien said. 'It's just so odd, isn't it? Nothing happens in that location for years—'

'Decades,' I said. 'And then in the space of twenty-four hours, two deaths are discovered. One a cold-case mystery and the other one, like you say, a horrible accident.'

'You're thinking,' Tien accused me.

'I do it occasionally.'

She smiled. 'What about, though?'

'I was thinking about your car and the "Park" being a button, instead of a spot on the shift lever. That would confuse me.'

'Once you get used to it, it's fine,' Tien said. 'It's just that in addition to that there's the button for the keyless ignition and yet another for the parking brake.'

All at the touch of a button, but maybe easy to confuse if you're not used to it. 'My Escape still has a hand brake you pull up. And a shift lever. And a key you turn.'

'I'm sorry,' she said with a little grin, 'but welcome to the modern era of computers in automobiles.'

'My Escape is not even five years old,' I protested. 'But you're right about the computers or processing units in cars. I had no idea, but Pavlik says a typical car these days has maybe fifty. Luxury models as many as a hundred.'

'And that's a bad thing?' Tien asked. 'I can use voice control to tell my car where to go.'

'I tell my car where to go sometimes, too,' I said, with a smile. 'But I'm assuming you're talking directions?'

'Exactly,' she said. 'What's wrong with cars being smart?'

'Nothing really. Except as smart as that Lexus was, Vivian still ended up in the water. And couldn't get out.' I was thinking of her bloodied fingers.

Tien put her own hand on mine. 'I know.'

'You two all right?' Angela asked, arriving at the table with two espressos. 'I didn't know what you wanted, Maggy, so I got two of these for me and whomever.'

'I'd love one,' Tien said. 'Thank you.'

'Amy said she knows what you want, Maggy,' Angela said, sitting down. 'That girl's a pistol.'

Well now we knew where Luc got the expression. I saw Tien suppress a smile.

'Am I ever,' Amy said, setting a latte in front of me. 'Anything else I can get you all?'

'No, this is great, thank you. Why don't you join us?' I was looking around for Sarah. It wasn't like her not to be kibbitzing. Or at least eavesdropping. 'Where's Sarah?'

'Oh, she left,' she said. 'Said you were taking the rest of her shift.'

Of course she did.

'I thought you didn't have to work today,' Eric said, when I dropped my car keys on the end table and flopped down on the couch about seven.

'I didn't,' I said. 'But Sarah decided she should take off instead.'

'I wondered what she was doing hanging around the Woodwards' place this afternoon,' Eric said as he disappeared around the corner into the kitchen. 'I ordered Chinese. Is that OK?'

'More than OK. Did you order enough for me and Pavlik?' A harrumph from the other side of the room reminded me to add, 'And Frank and Mocha?'

'Of course,' Eric said, bringing out two glasses and an open bottle of Pinot Noir.

'Thank you,' I said. 'What a good boy you are.'

'I did bring a glass for you.' He poured his and sank into the chair set at a right angle to the couch with a self-satisfied sigh. 'But I opened it for me, in the first place. I have had a couple of grueling days of observing police work.'

'I'm sure you have,' I said, sitting up to help myself to the Pinot. 'And you're twenty-one now so I can't give you grief.'

'Except for my socks.' He propped up his feet on the edge of the cocktail table, revealing the dirty bottoms of his white socks.

Not sure whether I should nag him about feet on the coffee table or the state of those socks, I settled for neither.

'Then you like wine?' I asked curiously. 'I'm not sure I did at your age. Except maybe a sweet white.'

'Which I absolutely don't like,' he said. 'But, yeah, I enjoy the ceremony of it. Opening the bottle, checking the cork, maybe decanting wine, letting it breathe.'

'All of which you did with this one?'

'Of course,' he said, swirling. 'Except for the decanting. There's mixed advice on whether Pinot Noir should be decanted. And as for the breathing, this is all it's going to get.' He took a sip.

I did the same. 'Nice.'

'It's kind of like what you taught me about making a good espresso drink,' my son continued. 'Tamping the espresso into the portafilter and pulling the shots at the correct pace. Frothing the milk to the right consistency and temperature. The fully automatic machines just aren't the same.'

Probably not the time to tell him we'd considered carrying the automatic machines in the store. 'Are you and Oliver still going to do work for Philip?'

Eric shrugged. 'If he wants us to. But for now the yard is a crime scene.'

Which seemed to suit Eric just fine. 'Is Oliver all right? He seemed pretty shook by Vivian's accident.'

'I was kind of surprised,' Eric said. 'Like he said, he barely knew Mrs Woodward.'

'It's probably not so much the person as sudden death, in general, for him.'

'Like his mom and dad,' Eric said, nodding. 'I suppose that's natural.'

He'd stopped, but I didn't think he was finished. 'But?'

He pulled his feet off the coffee table and leaned forward in the chair. 'Oliver liked Mrs Woodward. But I think it was just the opposite for Mr.'

'Why don't you call both of them by their first names?' I said. 'It'll be easier.'

'Pavlik doesn't,' Eric said. 'At least when he talks to them.'

'That's a police thing,' I said. 'To maintain professional distance.'

'Oh, gotcha,' he said. 'That makes sense.'

'Anyway, why don't you think Oliver likes Philip?'

'I'm not sure,' Eric said. 'But he waited to go up to the house on Tuesday morning until he knew Philip wouldn't answer the door.'

'Had Philip left?'

'No, he was in the shower.' The feet were back on the coffee table.

'How would you know that?' I asked, frowning.

'Have you ever looked at that house from the backyard? There are only two rooms facing that direction and one has a frosted window.'

'The bathroom.' I remembered from my tour and from seeing Philip's shadow cross the window as he went to greet Kelly Anthony at the back door. 'You can hear the water running, too.'

'Yup. And the toilet flushing. Must not be any insulation in those walls.'

'But how did he know it was Philip not Vivian showering?'

'Not that hard, Mom. Light goes on, door closes. Half an hour later, the toilet flushes and the shower goes on. Gotta be a guy.'

He had a point. 'But why avoid Philip?'

Eric lifted his shoulders and dropped them. 'Got me. I'd say maybe he figured Vivian was a softer touch, but all he wanted was permission to work for free.'

Philip was the softer touch between the two Woodwards, in my opinion. 'It might be that Oliver just feels more comfortable with women. His father wasn't exactly warm and fuzzy.'

'True,' Eric said. 'And Mrs G is the one he's close to, not his grandfather.'

Good call. 'I hate to think how Oliver will take it when she dies.'

'Mom,' my son protested, 'Mrs G is not going to die. Not soon, at least.'

What can I say? I'm a planner. 'Did you say Sarah was at the Woodwards' this afternoon?' I said, changing the subject.

'Yes, talking to Philip,' Eric said. 'I think she's trying to get him to sell the property.'

'Ms Sensitivity,' I said, exasperated yet unsurprised.

'She was actually pretty sensitive. For Sarah, I mean. She said she could understand if Philip wanted to just leave, given all that had happened. First the baby's bones and now his wife's accident.'

'And she offered her help.'

'Yeah,' Eric said. 'But I did, too. You know, if he needed anything more done while I'm here.'

'That was kind of you, and self-serving of Sarah,' I said.

'That's not fair,' Eric said. 'Sarah has a good heart. Look at how she took in Courtney and Sam after their mom died.'

Their mom being Patricia Harper, who had been my partner – along with Caron – during Uncommon Grounds' first iteration in Benson Plaza.

'You're right about that,' I admitted. 'But—'

'I think Sarah just wanted Philip to know she'd be interested.'

It was true that if Sarah didn't speak up and Philip sold or listed with somebody else, she'd never forgive herself. Or me.

'. . . was really, really mad.'

'Wait,' I said, coming back to the conversation. 'Who was angry?'

'Vivian's mother,' Eric said. 'She came by as Philip and Sarah were talking. Said the property belongs to her, and as far as she was concerned it should be left as it is.'

'Vana owns it?' That was new.

'Guess so.' He leaned forward. 'I think she's scared of the place. Like it's cursed or something.'

'I guess you can't blame her, given all that's happened,' I said. 'She also blames Philip for bringing Vivian there.'

'And for her dying? That's not right,' Eric said. 'Vivian was an adult and could make her own decisions.'

'Absolutely. But being her mother, your—'

'"Your kids are always your kids," I know,' Eric said in a sing-song voice.

'And you want to protect them,' I finished for him with a smile.

'But from a house? A piece of land?'

'I know it seems crazy,' I said. 'But Vana left when she finished high school and seemingly has had nothing to do with her parents since. I don't even know if she came back for their funerals.'

'Seems extreme.'

'It does. But now that we know that the baby's skeleton you and Frank found had signs of abuse before he was killed—'

'Wait,' Eric said, holding up his hand. 'How do we know that?'

Because me and my big mouth had just told him. 'I'm sorry. I thought you knew. Please don't share it with anybody.'

'Who am I going to share it with? You and Pavlik are the only people I'd tell, and I assume he's the one who told you.'

'I'm sure he's going to tell you, too,' I said quickly. 'But the inquiry into the skeleton was pretty much sidelined with Vivian's accident and all.'

'That's OK, Mom,' Eric said, reading my face. 'My feelings aren't hurt.'

'I just want you two to like each other,' I confessed.

'We like each other. Sure better than I liked Rachel.' His father's dental hygienist/wife, who happily wouldn't be an issue for twenty to life.

'That's good.' I twirled my glass, wondering how much I should reveal. 'Thing is, the baby had a broken leg and arm, the clavicle—'

'Collarbone, right?' Eric rubbed his chin, which he kept a little stubbly in the style that was popular these days. 'I thought I saw something on the femur. A line going down, but not like it was broken into pieces.'

'It was mended or mending, Pavlik said.'

'The baby was abused before he died then.'

'We don't know for how long. Children heal quickly and, well, Pavlik says the baby was only a few months old.'

'Still. It was his entire life.'

'I know.' I reached over and touched his shoulder. 'But maybe it explains why Vana hates the place so much.'

He turned to face me. 'You think she was abused too?'

'Maybe,' I said, sitting back. 'Though she hasn't said that. Or that she knows who the baby is.'

Eric cocked his head. 'Maybe he was born before her.'

'Maybe,' I said. 'Or she was so young—'

I was interrupted by the thundering paws of both sheepdog and chihuahua as the door opened and Pavlik stepped in.

'Off!' he ordered Frank, who was nearly at eye level with him when the sheepdog jumped up in joy. Which he did, whenever he saw Pavlik. Mocha was more an ankle biter.

'Just in time,' I said, going to the kitchen and bringing out a wine glass. 'We have Chinese coming.'

'Good deal,' Pavlik said, taking the glass to pour himself some Pinot. 'What did you order?'

'Eric ordered it,' I told him, smiling at my son. 'So probably lots of everything.'

'Even better,' he said, as I took his hand and pulled him to sit next to me on the couch.

'I'm glad that you're home,' I said.

'Me too.' He took a slug of wine and set down his glass. 'What do you two want to know?'

'He's assuming the apple doesn't fall far from the tree,' I told Eric.

'I have no idea what that means,' my son said, giving Frank a scratch as the sheepdog walked by his chair to curl up in the corner.

'It means that your mom pumps me for information every night.'

'And that you expect the same from me,' Eric said, pushing a lock of hair out of his face. 'Gotcha.'

'What did you learn today, Maggy?'

Pavlik's question startled me. 'Me?'

'Yes, you. I saw you go off with Tien, presumably to her father's restaurant, and then I saw you again at Brookhills

Manor where you seemed to be pumping the elderly for information. Am I wrong?'

'Absolutely not,' I said. 'By the way, what's going on at the Manor? Sophie said there's been some vandalism.'

'Graffiti mostly,' Pavlik said. 'But tell me about your trip to Luc's. I assume you went in search of information about Vana and Vivian's dinner last night.'

'Specifically, how much they'd had to drink. Tien was worried her dad might be in trouble for serving them alcohol, so I went with her to check it out.'

'Considerate of you,' Pavlik said. 'And what did you find out?'

'Presumably what your officers did. Vana and Vivian finished one bottle of Sangiovese and had the waiter open a second. They drank about half of that.'

'But even one bottle would have put them over the limit, wouldn't it?' Eric asked. 'A seven-hundred-and-fifty-milliliter bottle would be, what? Two-and-a-half five-ounce glasses each. And they're women, remember.'

'I'd resent that, if I didn't know what you mean,' I said.

'Assuming weights of one hundred and twenty or one hundred and thirty pounds, two drinks would put their blood alcohol level at the legal limit of point zero eight,' Pavlik confirmed.

'And they could have been impaired before that,' Eric said.

'Impaired enough,' I said, 'for Vivian to pull in too fast or not pay attention to how close she was to the creek bank when she went to park. What can you tell from the car?'

'Yeah, what about that?' Eric asked. 'The electronics must have been messed up by the water. Is it possible to know if the car was running or the brake on?'

'Or what gear it was in,' I added. 'Tien was showing me her new car. You push a button to start it and another to put it in park and yet another to put on the parking brake.'

'I've heard about those kinds of technological advances,' Eric said. 'Not that I'd know from the vehicle I drive.'

My son was being facetious. 'Tell your dad to buy you a new car.'

'Or save your money,' was Pavlik's contribution.

'Whoa,' Eric said, grinning between us, 'tough crowd.'

'Only because we care,' I said sweetly. 'Now back to Vivian's Lexus?'

'It's been towed to the impound garage,' Pavlik said. 'We'll know more tomorrow, but as you say, if she was impaired, she could have easily overshot the gravel parking area in the dark. There are no parking barriers or lights back there.'

And her headlights would have shown straight out, of course, not down. 'Do you have her blood alcohol level yet?'

'That will be at the autopsy, which will also be tomorrow,' Pavlik said. 'Intoxication levels are more difficult to get post-mortem.'

'Really? Why is that?' Eric asked, genuinely interested. 'I mean, I know you can't use a breathalyzer, but what about a blood or urine sample?'

'It's difficult to interpret the results because there are changes that occur in the body after death that can produce ethanol, which is what you're measuring. Or, conversely, the ethanol in the drinks themselves can be dispersed or diluted depending on the time of death and condition of the body.'

'Cool.'

'So maybe the easiest way to know was to ask at the restaurant,' I said, a little self-satisfied.

'Which you did, and we did, as well.'

I didn't ask if it was before or after me. 'Vana is understandably upset, but she's being really nasty to Philip. Blaming him for bringing Vivian here. Blaming Brookhills in general. Blaming everybody, in fact, but herself. If both Vivian and Vana wanted to drink, they could have gotten a cab or rideshare.'

'People always think they're OK,' Pavlik said. 'Right up until they're not.'

'Philip called Vana an alcoholic,' I said. 'I'm not sure if that's technically true or he only said it in anger.'

'Or both,' Pavlik said. 'But if she does have her own drinking problem, it explains why she doesn't want her daughter's death to be branded drunk-driving.'

'Because it would make her feel responsible,' I said.

'Apple and tree,' Eric said.

'Exactly,' Pavlik said, with a grin. 'Like it or not, though, we'll have to wait for the autopsy to know more.'

'Speaking of the autopsy.' I'd been thinking. 'Will they take DNA samples from Vivian?'

'Samples will be taken, like blood, urine, saliva and mucus, et cetera. But a DNA analysis wouldn't be run unless there was a reason. Why?'

'Baby Doe,' I said. 'You said you couldn't require DNA samples from Vana or Vivian to see if they're related to Baby Doe. But since Vivian's will be right there—'

'At autopsy,' Eric said, leaning forward. 'That's genius, Mom.'

'And likely illegal without either permission or a warrant.'

'Don't you want to know who he was?' I asked Pavlik as Frank got up and stretched, dislodging Mocha who had been using his paw as a pillow.

'Of course I do, but we have current cases to work on. People who we can help now.'

'He's waited more than half a century,' I said.

'I know,' Pavlik said. 'And you know I do care. But old cases like these are complicated and sometimes' – he raised his hands in apology – 'they end up at the back of the line behind the active cases. The state lab has Baby Doe's remains and a forensic anthropologist will be assigned. As I understand these things, though, it's likely the only DNA at this point will come from the bone marrow. I don't know if that could be used for paternity tracing.'

'If it's mitochondrial DNA,' Eric said, 'I think it only gives you the maternal side.'

'How do you know that?' I asked. 'School?'

'Ancestry testing,' Eric said. 'Remember I gave you a kit?'

Oh, yeah. Should have read about it. Which gave me an idea. 'Is there a way the baby's DNA could be compared with what's on record through those online places? They'd have tons of data, I would think.'

'All of it private,' Pavlik said. 'Or at least private to us.'

Meaning the police, I assumed. Not me.

Or my son. 'I could nose around,' Eric offered. 'See if anybody in their family has a public family tree or DNA profile. Oliver can help. He did his DNA and posted it – that's where I got the idea of doing mine and sending you and dad kits.'

Good to know he didn't think he was adopted. Or that one of his parents was fooling around. Besides his dad. Later.

But Pavlik was shaking his head. 'You guys should be careful about all the private information you put up online. It's—'

The dogs going into a frenzy interrupted him, just before the doorbell rang.

'Saved by the bell,' Eric said with a smile.

ELEVEN

'Don't you want to know what information I was able to coerce from the elderly?' I asked Pavlik as he pulled the trash bag out of the basket under the sink to dispose of in the bins outside.

'Of course I do,' he said, straightening. 'But shouldn't the takeout containers go in recycling?'

'I'm not sure,' I said, wrinkling my nose at the collection of mangled and sauce-stained boxes in the bag. 'If they do, they probably have to be rinsed.'

'They might be plastic coated,' Pavlik said, poking at them. 'Maybe ask Eric. He probably knows.'

'I will next time,' I said. 'I think he went to bed.'

'You just don't want to dig the containers back out,' Pavlik accused me.

'Absolutely,' I said, grimacing. 'Especially since the dogs chewed on them. But you're welcome to do so.'

'No thanks,' he said, pulling the drawstring closed. 'Next time. Like you say.'

He took the bag out and, when he returned, must have seen something on my face. 'What?'

I drew my breath in between my teeth. 'I was thinking how easy it is, just to dispose of something you don't want and forget it.'

He wrapped his arms around me. 'You mean the baby.'

'Yes.' I shivered. 'And just . . . death, in general. Look at Vivian. She died a horrible death in that car, clawing and pounding at the windows, trying to get out. But from above, you'd never know all that. All you'd see would be the headlights.'

'Until they went out, too,' Pavlik said. 'I get it. And I'm not going to forget that baby either. I promise.'

'I know you won't,' I said into his shoulder.

We stood that way for a count of ten, then I lifted my

head. 'There were more people around back then than you might think. In the sixties, I mean. People other than the Koepplers.'

'That's what your senior snitches told you?' Pavlik asked, loosening his embrace so he could see my face.

I nodded. 'For example, Walter Benson and Carmen Petra went to school at Brookhills College.'

'I don't know Brookhills College,' Pavlik said, having only lived in Brookhills about five years. 'Where is it?'

'Gone now,' I told him. 'But back then it was very well respected, apparently, and drew students from all over the country, even the world. Carmen, for example, was from Rome. She and Walter remember hanging out at Paz and Harmony Koeppler's house.'

'Who is Carmen?' Pavlik asked.

Long story. 'She's the mother of Angela Fiorentine, who is Luc Romano's partner in the restaurant. Carmen is thinking of moving to Brookhills Manor, so Angela and I took her over and introduced her to Walter. Turns out they knew each other from way back.'

'Your connections never cease to amaze me,' Pavlik said. 'Who else was around back then?'

'Henry Wested went to BC, too,' I told him. 'This was before he enlisted and was sent overseas. I'm not sure he was one of the inner circle, given the anti-war sentiment back then.'

'I'd talk to him especially then,' Pavlik said, going to the sink to wash his hands. 'He's an outside observer.'

'Who probably wasn't high as a kite,' I agreed. 'You know you hugged me with those garbage hands you just washed.'

'You don't know the worst of it,' he said, waving them at me. 'Picked up dog poop on the way.'

'With a bag, I hope.'

'What kind of cretin do you think I am?' he asked, pulling me close again, now with wet hands.

'Get a room.' Eric stuck his head into the kitchen. 'And speaking of rooms, I'm going to mine. Night.'

'Night,' we called after him. And then followed orders.

* * *

Cognizant of what Pavlik had said about an outside observer, I kept an eye out for Henry as I latte'd and cappucino'd my way through the next morning.

Pavlik tolerated my nosing around, but it wasn't often that he actively encouraged it. He understood that I needed to know more about Baby Doe and the Koepplers in the sixties. Besides, what damage could I do some sixty years later? There were very few non-arthritic toes left to step on.

I, in turn, understood that Baby Doe couldn't be the sheriff's department's top priority. Pavlik had been called out at five this morning on an armed robbery that had turned into a murder. People were dying in real time, and I got that.

The autopsy results and forensics tests would come in and be followed up on. But for right now, Baby Doe was my baby.

The sleighbells jangled on the door, and I glanced up hopefully from the counter I was scrubbing.

Not Henry, but almost better.

'Vana,' I said. 'How are you doing?'

'I could use some coffee,' she said, standing in the center of the room. 'And is your partner – that real estate agent – here?'

'Sarah will be in' – I glanced at the clock – 'in about half an hour.'

'I'll wait.' She sat down at the closest table. 'Latte, please.'

I considered how to approach her as I pulled and brewed the shot and frothed the milk. Coming up with nothing, I took her drink to the table and sat down across from her.

She looked surprised. 'Don't you have things to do?'

'Not just this second,' I said. 'I wanted to say again how sorry I am about Vivian. You must be devastated.'

'I am,' she said. 'And anxious to get away from here.'

I didn't say anything, and she continued, 'Oh, I know that sounds awful. But I have hated this place, this town, for years and years. Now my daughter has died here and all I want to do' – her lip trembled – 'is run away again.'

'I don't blame you,' I said, pulling a clean napkin from my pocket and handing it to her as a tear rolled down one cheek, leaving a watermark through her otherwise flawless makeup. 'I . . . Can I ask you something?'

'What's that?' She'd dabbed her face.

'Your childhood here obviously wasn't happy. Was that because you were abused?'

She just stared at me.

'You were so young when you left. Barely eighteen. You said just now that you wanted to run away again. Meaning that back then you were—'

'Running away from something? Absolutely. My parents couldn't be bothered with me because they were so much in love. But once my father was gone, my mother was almost helpless without him. Childlike. I knew if I didn't get out the moment I was old enough, I'd be stuck there forever.'

There was a lot to unpack there, but I started with: 'Your parents never hit you?'

She crumped up the napkin and carefully set it in the middle of the table before saying, 'Why do you keep asking that?'

'The baby.' I watched her face as I said it.

'I told the sheriff's deputy,' she said tautly, her voice getting measurably louder with each staccato word. 'And I told you. And Philip. And Vivian. I don't know anything about a baby.'

'You did say that,' I confirmed.

'And it certainly wasn't mine.' These words came out in a rush.

'I know that,' I said. 'He would have been near your age. When were you born?'

'Is that any of your business?'

I just waited. Pavlik had already told me the year of the woman's birth, but I wanted to get her talking.

Her shoulders dropped. '1962.'

'And the sheriff's department thinks the baby was born sometime in the sixties as well. Think back. You don't remember another child somewhere in the neighborhood? Maybe one that didn't live long?'

She cocked her head, studying me. 'This child they've found. It was abused? Is that why you're asking if I was, too?'

'*This child*—' My tone came out icier than I had intended given Vana could be a victim as well, so I stopped myself, then continued softly, 'The baby boy or girl had broken bones. His leg, his arm, his collarbone. A rib. Some of the injuries were inflicted days or weeks before he was finally murdered or simply left to die in a trash heap. So, yes, I'm asking you if you remember anything that would help and, specifically, if your parents ever hit you.'

'I . . . I . . .' Her hand played at her neck, like she was wearing a necklace. 'I try not to think of those things.'

'Then they did.'

'No . . . just . . . maybe a slap, a spanking. Or my dad yanked my arm, mostly . . .' She seemed to be casting about in her memories back then. 'Mostly it was like I wasn't even there.'

'Were there other people staying at the house? Besides your mother and father?'

She sat up straight. 'This commune idea? Was that yours? I told Philip it was ridiculous. *I did not live in a commune.*'

I didn't know if she was trying to convince me or convince herself. But before the vein pulsing in her forehead blew out, I gave her a reprieve. 'No, not a commune. But I know that kids from the college – friends of your mom and dad like Walter Benson, Carmen Petra, Henry Wested – hung out at your house. Do you remember them?'

'I try,' she said succinctly, 'not to remember anything about that time. Not their friends, not them.' She stood up and scrabbled through her purse. 'Tell your partner to call me if she's interested in the property.'

'But isn't selling the property Philip's decision?' I asked, wanting to clarify what Eric heard her tell Sarah. 'I assume it passed to him after Vivian died?'

'The deed has never been transferred from my parents' names.' She paused with her hand on the doorknob. 'I have no inten—'

The door was pulled open abruptly and Vana stepped back, a sour expression on her face.

'Sorry,' my son said, panting. 'But—'

'Hang on a second, Eric.' I held up a finger. 'You were saying, Vana, that—'

'Pavlik just took Philip Woodward in.'

'Philip?' Vana looked as astonished as I felt.

'Yes.' Eric was still trying to catch his breath. 'The accident – Mrs Woodward – it apparently wasn't an accident at all.'

'What do you mean?' I asked, waving him in. 'How could it be anything else? Vivian was drinking . . . sorry' – I held up a hand in apology to the woman's mother – 'and overshot the parking area.'

'No, that's just it,' Eric said. 'Walter Benson was across the way at the Manor. He says he saw somebody standing next to the Lexus, arguing with the driver.'

'And?' I didn't like where this was going.

'And he's pretty sure it was Philip Woodward.'

Vana Shropshire hit the floor.

TWELVE

Eric helped me get Vana into a chair.

'Oh, my God, oh, my God,' she kept saying over and over, holding her head. 'Oh, my God, oh, my God.'

Sarah, who'd come in just in time not to help, looked unimpressed. 'She didn't strike me as the religious type,' she whispered.

'Give the woman a break,' I said, beckoning my partner away to where Eric now perched on a high stool by the window overlooking the tracks. 'Her daughter died in an accident yesterday and today it turns out to be a murder?'

'You uncharacteristically are framing that as a question. Is it the murder you don't believe or who they think did it?'

That was a good question. 'I . . . just . . . why would Philip want to murder Vivian?'

'Money,' Vana's voice said from the table. 'They'd been having trouble and Vivian hated it here. She told me at dinner that she was going to file for divorce.'

I swiveled to face her. 'Did Philip know that?'

'I don't know,' Vana said. 'But I do know that he had all these big plans.'

'And now Vivian was going to leave and take half of everything,' Sarah said.

Philip did have big plans, but he wasn't stupid. 'What then? He killed her *and* in a way that echoed a scene in *The Big Sleep*?'

Vana cocked her head. 'Echoed what?' The other two were also looking at me with equally blank looks.

Unwilling to give the same dissertation on *The Big Sleep* that Philip and I had subjected Amy to, I left it at: 'It just seems crazy.'

'So is murder,' my son pointed out.

Vana was sniffling. 'I kept telling myself that Vivian must have passed out or fallen asleep. That she didn't even realize what had happened. But this—' She started to sob, her face in her hands.

None of us being great with emotions, we all just stood there, willing somebody else to go over and comfort the woman.

Eric finally cleared his throat. 'Um, the sheriff said that Walter heard raised voices. He thought maybe there was an argument.'

'Vivian telling Philip she wanted a divorce?' Sarah hazarded.

'And Walter heard all this from inside Brookhills Manor?' I was skeptical.

Sarah shook her head. 'You really don't want it to be Woodward, do you?'

'That's not . . . well, no.'

'He's a charmer,' Vana said tearfully. 'Don't let him get in your head like he did my daughter's.'

Eric shot me a look that said, *Who are you letting into your head?*

'She only has eyes for Pavlik,' Sarah assured him.

'Anyway,' I said. 'Where was Walter?'

'In the Manor parking lot,' he said, 'having a cigarette.'

'That's just across Brookhill Road,' Sarah said. 'Maybe thirty feet. It's possible.'

'Was it Walter who reported the headlights submerged in the creek then?' I asked Eric, who seemed to have the direct line to the sheriff these days.

'No, he didn't realize the car even went into the creek. He had just finished his cigarette and was going inside when he heard raised voices and looked over. It was Sophie Daystrom who saw the lights later and called it in.'

Of course it was.

'What in the world was everybody doing up at that time?' I asked Pavlik that night.

He shrugged out of his jacket and draped it over a chair. 'Hello, dear. Yes, it's been a tough day. How was yours?'

'Sorry.' I wrapped my arms around him and laid my head on his chest. 'Mine was better than yours, I'm betting. Though

Eric and I had to pick Vana up off the floor this morning when she heard about Walter's statement.'

'Resilient woman,' Pavlik said, giving me a kiss on the top of the head before moving away. 'This afternoon she was down at the station badgering us.'

'About what?' I asked.

'Wanting to know why we hadn't charged Philip yet. And smearing him, of course. She's not a very pleasant woman.'

'No.' I perked up. 'I don't suppose Vana could have done it?'

'Sorry,' Pavlik said. 'She passed through the hotel lobby a little after twelve-thirty on her way to her room after Vivian dropped her off. Benson says he saw the Lexus and heard the argument about twelve-forty.'

It was maybe a five-minute drive from the hotel. What with pulling in, parking and Philip coming out, the time would fit. I frowned, snagging Pavlik's jacket to hang up in the closet. 'How can he be sure?'

'Checked his phone as he finished his cigarette, weighing whether to have another before he went to bed.'

Let's see: lung cancer or sleep; lung cancer or sleep. I pick sleep. 'But he didn't hear what they were arguing about? Or see the car go over the edge?'

'No. He said he was just irritated they'd interrupted the peaceful night. Checked the time and went in.'

'And Sophie reported seeing the car lights in the creek how long after that?'

'I got the call while you were on the phone with Philip, remember?' Pavlik took the jacket from me and hung it up himself.

'That was one forty-nine a.m., according to my phone. What was Sophie doing up at that time?'

'Going to the bathroom,' Pavlik said, sinking onto the couch. 'She tells me it comes with aging.'

I needed no such excuse. 'And Sophie and Henry's bathroom has a view of the creek?'

'It does,' Pavlik said, and patted the couch. 'You can ask her more when you see her. She's very eager to share information about her "frickin'" bladder.'

'Sophie is very eager to talk about many things, the more

off-color, the better,' I said, then sighed, settling next to him. 'What did Philip have to say?'

'Exactly what he told you on the phone that night. He went to bed and when he woke up in the middle of the night, he realized Vivian hadn't gotten home.'

'And called us.'

'Yes,' Pavlik said. 'That struck me as a little odd at the time. Didn't it you?'

I hesitated. 'I'm not sure. I guess I thought because he was new in town and we've gotten close—'

'Another thing, by the way, that Vana Shropshire brought up.'

'Me?' I turned to face him. 'What a bitch.'

Pavlik chuckled. 'She just said that Philip had a way with women and used you as an example.'

'Not a reason for Philip to get rid of his wife?'

'No.' He held up his hands in defense. 'Not that you're not worth killing for.'

'Thank you.' I settled back down. 'You do realize he and I are just friends, right?'

'Of course. Just like you and your ex-husband's brother-in-law—'

'Stephen Slattery.' I sighed. 'Stephen is a sweetie.'

'As is Bernie Egan.'

'Caron's husband,' I said. 'Cute. Bald.'

'Father Jim?'

'Priest.'

'See? You're just a guy magnet.' He closed one eye to survey me. 'What are you thinking about for dinner?'

'I haven't really,' I admitted, then did have a thought. 'We could go to Luc's.'

A groan. 'I'm done in. Plus, I know you must have an ulterior motive.'

'Not really,' I said. 'I've pretty much exhausted the line of questioning there. I could, though, really go for some pasta.'

'We could have it delivered.'

'Done.' I picked up my phone.

'What did we do without restaurant delivery apps?' I asked, rubbing my full tummy. We'd ordered pesto penne with chicken and angel hair with meatballs and a red sauce from Luc's. Both dishes had been delicious.

'What did we do?' Pavlik asked, wiping a bit of red sauce off my lip. 'Leave the house at night occasionally.'

'You were the one who didn't want to go out, you know.'

'I know.'

Companionable silence commenced as we digested.

'Where's Eric?' Pavlik finally asked.

'His dad's,' I said. 'He's leaving tomorrow, you know. Or Sunday.'

The weekend and, therefore, the end of spring break was on our doorstep.

'Don't worry, he'll be back. Summer is coming.' Pavlik glanced around. 'And the dogs?'

'With Eric,' I told him. 'Mia wanted to play with Frank, and Mocha wouldn't be left behind.'

'That's good.'

I twisted to look at him. 'Why good?'

'Because we just ate Italian with neither of the dogs begging. Either they're not here or dead.'

'Not here is better, I agree.' I was thinking. 'What about the wine?'

'It's gone,' Pavlik said, gesturing toward the empty bottle. 'You don't want me to open another one, do you?'

'Heavens, no,' I said, sitting up. 'But I meant the partial bottle of wine Luc packaged up for Vivian and Vana to take home. Was it in the car?'

'I don't know,' Pavlik said. 'Anthony didn't mention a bottle. I can check with her tomorrow.'

'Either it still should have been in the car with Vivian,' I said, 'or Vana took it with her to her room when Vivian dropped her off.'

'Which might be most likely,' Pavlik said. 'Especially if Vana is an alcoholic, like you said.'

'It was Philip who said she was an alcoholic,' I said, frowning. 'I keep revisiting everything he said to me, wondering if it was a lie. You really think he did this?'

Pavlik shrugged. 'We questioned Philip Woodward but

couldn't hold him. So far it's his word against Walter Benson. But Benson seems pretty credible.'

'He's sure it was Philip.'

'Yes, wearing a dark robe.'

'I suppose you checked to see if Philip has a dark robe?' Stupid question.

'We did,' Pavlik confirmed. 'Navy blue. Monogram.'

'Did he let you in to look or did you need a warrant?' I picked up the empty wine bottle and set it back down again.

'He brought it to us,' Pavlik said. 'Sure you don't want me to open another? It is Friday night.'

'No, we would just have a glass each anyway.' Even cheap wine deserved to be drunk the night it was opened.

And of course, Philip had cooperated with the sheriff. To do anything else would make him appear guilty. 'What's the working theory? Philip heard Vivian pull in and went out and they had a row?'

'It's possible,' Pavlik said, stacking our plates. 'Vivian had been drinking and even her mother admits she could be a nasty drunk.'

I handed him the forks to put on top. 'They argued and she obligingly got back into the car while he pushed it into the creek? That's crazy.'

'Or they had the fight while she was still in the car—'

'That's what Walter saw?' I interrupted. 'Philip outside the car, Vivian inside?'

Pavlik nodded. 'Maybe the car started to roll—'

I interrupted again. 'Was Vivian in the driver's seat when the divers found her?'

To his credit, the love of my life didn't even roll his eyes. 'No, she had managed to undo her seat belt.'

'She had at least some presence of mind then,' I said.

'Or she'd already taken it off.'

'Either when she stopped the car or as she and Philip were arguing,' I said. 'But then what?'

'Then we don't know,' Pavlik admitted. 'Maybe she does get out of the car after Walter Benson goes inside and Philip hits her. According to the autopsy, there's a pre-mortem contusion above her right eye.'

'She was hit before she died?'

'Or she hit her head on the steering wheel or windshield as the car went into the creek. She would have lived for a few minutes, as you know, before running out of air.'

Unfortunately, I did know that. And that Vivian couldn't have been unconscious, as Vana had hoped, since she'd tried frantically to get out.

I put that aside for now, trying to reason it out. 'Philip and Vivian fight, Philip hits her and, thinking he killed her, panics. He puts her back in the car, takes off the brake and pushes it into the creek, where Vana is revived by the cold water.'

'But Philip doesn't know that,' Pavlik says. 'He goes back into the house and waits an hour or so to call you, all innocent and concerned about his wife.'

'Calls me because he knows I'll be sleeping next to you,' I said, crumpling the foil take-out containers a little more aggressively than necessary to fit them into the Luc's bag for disposal.

'Not quite an alibi, more an opportunity to play the concerned husband.' Pavlik yawned. 'Sorry.'

'I'm tired, too.' I held out my hand to help him up. 'Anything further on the baby since we're talking about horrible things just before bedtime?'

'Sorry again, but no. Like I said, cold cases take a back seat to ongoing crimes and the pathology and DNA, especially, is going to take a while.'

He wrapped an arm around me. 'Now let's forget death. OK?'

'OK.' Until morning.

Saturday morning arrived and I had the day off. Unfortunately Pavlik had gotten another call in the night and was still gone when I woke up.

No Eric, Frank or Mocha either, of course, since they'd all stayed overnight at Ted's. I didn't begrudge it, really. Being alone in an empty house was admittedly rare since Pavlik and Mocha had moved in. But it was all too familiar, too.

It had been three . . . no, nearly four years since my dentist ex and I had split. He'd fallen for his hygienist, Rachel Slattery, and had timed leaving me with Eric's leaving us for his first year of college away. It was the first time I'd lived alone or even been alone for more than a few nights at a time. I had Frank, though, and now not even he was in the house.

There was nothing. Nothing but silence.

Whiner.

I checked my phone. Nearly eight. I would luxuriate in the quiet. Have a cup of coffee.

Pulling on a pair of yoga pants to go with the oversized T-shirt I so romantically slept in, I padded barefoot into the kitchen and dragged my old coffee maker out from under the shadow of the overhead cabinets.

I was thinking about Sophie, herself padding barefoot to the bathroom, only to see the eerie glow of headlights submerged in the creek outside her window. Had she awakened Henry before she called 9-1-1? Had they perhaps investigated? Heard something?

And, now that I thought of it, why hadn't they been outside, hovering nosily, when Pavlik and I arrived in the early hours of the morning?

Blowing dust off the top of the drip coffee maker, I swung the basket out. 'Ugh.'

Apparently, whoever used it last – most likely me – hadn't emptied the used grounds and they had sprouted a fine layer of white mold.

'Coffee grounds,' I said to myself. 'Perfect for the compost heap. If we had one.'

Which reminded me, of course, of poor Baby Doe. Discarded as easily as the coffee grounds I was about to dump in the trash.

Instead, I swung the filter basket closed again.

THIRTEEN

I showered, dressed and still no sign of Eric, Frank and Mocha. But none of the three were anything approaching early risers, given their druthers. Pavlik had texted he'd be gone most of the day.

My intention was to grab a cup of coffee at Uncommon Grounds and, making sure I didn't let Sarah slip out the back again, take myself and my to-go cup to Brookhills Manor. As I went to turn left off Poplar Creek Road onto Junction, though, I caught sight of Philip Woodward backing the Land Rover into his driveway.

Now why did my mind immediately go to disposing of a body? None were missing, after all.

Regardless, instead of turning, I continued a block farther and parked on the street. Philip's Land Rover had stopped just short of where Vivian's Lexus had gone in the water, liftgate open.

As I walked up the driveway, Philip disappeared around the back of the Land Rover.

'Morning,' I called, coming around the SUV to look in the back.

Inside were five six-foot black-and-yellow parking blocks. If your vehicle sits high, like my Escape or Philip's Land Rover, your tires stop at the block. If the car is low-slung, like Walter's Porsche or Carmen's Ferrari, you scrape the hell out of the under body on them.

Either way, though, the automobile doesn't go up, over and – in this case – into the creek.

Philip was inside the Land Rover, having managed to wrestle one of the parking blocks down to the edge of the vehicle, where it hung cantilevered in space. 'Sorry, they loaded these for me at the building yard. They're rubber, so not so much heavy as unwieldy. They don't slide.'

'Can I help?' I said, grasping the end sticking out. 'If you can push it just a little farther, I can tip it down to the ground and then we can lift it.'

Instead, he hopped out and stripped off his work gloves. 'I know what you're thinking. I'm closing the barn door.'

'After the horse is gone' was the rest of the expression, but it wasn't what I was thinking.

I'd noticed the eighteen-inch steel rebar spikes already on the ground and was wondering how long ago he'd bought them. But that was just me.

Philip had tears in his eyes. 'Vivian told me to do this a month ago. Get the parking blocks and spike them in place. How long would that have taken me? But I was too busy coming up with marketing concepts and stupid ideas for tea infusers. If only . . . if only . . .'

'I'm so sorry, Philip.' I went to him and he pulled me close, sobbing into my hair.

'I really did love her,' he said finally, pulling back. 'We had our problems, but this was to be our project.' He waved his hand toward the little shop.

'The police questioned you.'

His nose was red and running and now he swiped at it with the back of his hand. 'Yes. I just don't understand it. I called you, Maggy, the minute I realized Vivian hadn't come home.'

'You didn't come out here first to check? Maybe pulled on your robe and . . .' I interrupted myself. 'The crime scene tape is gone. And the van.'

'You mean, if they now think the accident is murder, why aren't they still scurrying around here like ants?' He held up a hand. 'Sorry, I know your Pavlik is one of them. The main one really . . . so . . .' He seemed to realize he was babbling and left off.

'No offence taken,' I said. 'But you're absolutely right that I assumed the area would still be cordoned off.' I was trying not to glance toward the furrows the Lexus' back tires had made as the front slipped off over the bank and into the water.

'Apparently they'd already done everything they would have for a murder, even when they were calling it an accident,' Philip said a little dryly. 'Very efficient, your sheriff.'

Not much to say to that, except, 'He is.'

The fact was nothing was assumed when a violent/sudden death was investigated. Sure, it could be accident or suicide or murder. You didn't know if you didn't investigate. Fully.

Philip cleared his throat, nudging one of the steel spikes on the ground nearer the rest of them with his toe.

'Can I help?' I asked again.

'I was thinking maybe I'd ask Eric or maybe that Oliver to give me a hand.' He shrugged. 'But what's the difference? I won't be opening the place now.'

'But wouldn't Vivian want you to?' I knew what Vana had told me about her daughter's marriage and the ownership of the property. Now I wanted to hear Philip's side.

'Honestly?' He lifted his shoulders and dropped them. 'I don't know. Maybe she only moved here because I insisted and' – his voice got low – 'we didn't have any other place to go.'

'What do you mean?' I asked. 'What about Boston?'

'Boston,' he said, lifting his head, 'is a very expensive place to live. And I lost my teaching job.'

'I thought Vivian was the teacher,' I said, confused. 'And you were in marketing.'

'I taught marketing,' he corrected. 'You know what they say: "Those who can't do, teach."'

'You came here to put what you know into practice. There's no shame in that.'

'There is shame, though,' he said, 'in giving up a tenured position.'

Tenured, meaning 'for life' unless you were fired for cause. 'Not if you wanted something different.'

Philip ran his hand over his face. 'Who am I kidding? That's just what I told Vivian.'

'I don't understand,' I said. 'If you told Vivian you didn't want to teach, that's not a crime.'

'No, but it was a lie. I was going to lose my position. They gave me a chance to leave before that happened.'

'Oh.'

He was nodding. 'Aren't you going to ask me what I did? What "cause" they had?'

I wanted to ask, but I didn't think that I needed to. 'It's none of my business.'

'You're right that I'm a brilliant marketer,' he said, 'but of myself. I'm the devoted husband for Vivian. The charismatic college professor for my students. The serious academic for my colleagues. The brilliant, slightly nerdy marketer for you. It's gotten so I don't really know who I am at the core.' He was staring at the ground.

I stayed silent. Though the 'nerdy' thing kind of hurt.

'Anyway,' he continued after a few seconds, 'I guess I started to believe my own advertising. I stepped over the line with a student.'

As I had suspected. 'And it rightly bit you in the backside.'

He raised his eyes to mine. 'It was one time, one student. I swear.'

'Did Vivian know?'

'I didn't think so.' He was gazing across Brookhill Road toward the Manor.

'Didn't? Is that what you fought about in the parking lot?'

'No, no.' He was shaking his head. 'I don't know what that old man saw, but it wasn't me doing . . . that. Vivian's death had to be an accident. Or maybe she . . .'

'Did it on purpose?' Oliver had wondered the same thing. But it would be a horrible way to commit suicide. And if Vivian had tried to kill herself, she'd changed her mind. Panicked as the car slid under the water . . . I shook my head, trying to get the image out of my mind.

'I didn't think so either,' Philip said, misinterpreting my gesture. 'But then Vana told me that Vivian knew about what had happened and I started to wonder.'

'What about this girl? The one you had the affair with—'

'One night stand,' Philip said.

'No such thing for a college age girl,' I said. 'Especially with an older man, one she admires.'

'You honestly believe my student followed us here and killed my wife?'

'Honestly? No. But if somebody did . . .' I shrugged.

'Better a poor college student than me?'

Not necessarily. 'You should tell the police.'

'Absolutely not. I'm not going to compound what I did in Boston by bringing an innocent person into this nightmare.'

'Unless you have to.' I knew I was being cynical, but I wasn't sure if it was so much the girl that Philip wanted to protect or what was left of his professional reputation.

'I . . . I don't want to talk about this anymore,' he said. 'I have work to do.' He went back to tugging at the barrier and I left him to it.

'Oh, and Maggy,' he called, as I walked to my car. 'I'd appreciate if we kept this to ourselves. Not say anything to the sheriff, you know.'

Sure, I knew.

I didn't answer him.

I don't know why I got into the car and drove the half-block to Brookhills Manor. Probably because I had already stalked away from Philip and getting in the car and roaring away was a better exit than circling the car on foot and crossing back to the senior center.

Driving did, however, give me the opportunity to park just a little too close to Walter Benson's Porsche. I noticed he'd been careful to stop a few inches before the parking block in the Manor's lot.

I was surprised, though, that he hadn't moved it into the garage he'd told Carmen about. Or maybe he had and moved it back out again. Either way, it was accumulating a sweet layer of crab apple blossoms from the tree overhanging the spot.

Not that I had any legitimate reason to dislike Walter. His son Way was a dick, but I shouldn't just assume it ran in the family.

'Hey! Watch your door!'

Or maybe it did.

'I'm being very careful of my door,' I told him. 'But you should watch where you park. The tree is dropping petals and sap all over your poor 911.' I shivered. 'I'd move it before the paint is permanently damaged.'

Any irritation he'd felt over my daring to park my five-year-old Escape next to him was now redirected at the tree. 'Damn weed. You're absolutely right.'

'I know,' I said smugly. 'Why don't you put the Porsche in the garage?'

'The garage?' He glanced around as if somebody might be listening. 'You mean the parking structure. As far as I'm concerned, the car is safer out here than it is in there.'

'Even with the vandalism?'

'What vandalism?' Walter demanded. 'Oh, you mean the graffiti. That's been confined to the construction site, but I'd sooner take my chances with the graffiti artists than the blind old bats that park in that structure.'

'But you were using the indoor parking as a selling point when Carmen was here.'

'And it is,' he said. 'The condos will each have their own attached garage.'

No bats, presumably, blind or otherwise. 'When will these new units be done?'

'Not for another six months, minimum,' he said. 'Until then, I feel better with the 911 parked out here. The lot is lighted and there are people passing on Brookhill Road.'

Directly across Brookhill Road, of course, was The Big Steep. 'Is this where you were when you saw the argument between Vivian and Philip? Catching a smoke in your car?'

I'd appalled him. 'Please. I do not smoke in my cars, not any of them.'

If I were interested, I'd ask how many he had. 'So where were you then?'

'By the door there,' he said, pointing toward an unmarked side entrance. 'There's an ashtray there. It's where the staff congregates for a smoke during the day. I find it soothing at night.'

'After midnight?'

'Anytime there aren't people around.' He peered at me. 'Please. You're not one of those Midwesterners who eat at six thirty and are in bed by ten, are you?'

Damn right and proud of it. 'You weren't out here long enough to see the car go in the water though?'

'I find other people's unpleasantness . . . unpleasant.' He gave a half-shrug. 'My tranquility having been disturbed, I opted to go in and read before going to sleep.'

I cocked my head. 'Your room is on this side of the building?'

'Street side, no,' he said, with a little shiver of disdain. 'The larger two-bedroom apartments face the back – the Water's Edge units.'

Water's Edge sounded ever so much better – and more expensive – than 'Creek Side'.

I frowned. 'Henry and Sophie have a two-bedroom. Aren't they on this side?' With a bathroom view of the creek.

'Wested and Daystrom? They're on the corner up there,' Walter said, pointing at the back corner unit on the fourth floor.

I glanced up at their apartment windows and across the street to where the Lexus had gone in. 'They have a view of both Brookhills and the creek.'

'Yes,' he said. 'From what I understand, though, they didn't notice the car until it was too late for the poor woman.' He seemed genuinely sad about that.

Fact was, though, he hadn't exactly done anything to help. 'What about you? Did you think she might be in danger? I mean, you said they were having a fight.'

'I didn't say that exactly,' Walter said, cocking his head. 'They didn't scream at each other. It was more of an intense discussion.'

'But you couldn't hear what they said?'

'No, I couldn't make out any words at all. Not that I was trying. I heard the car pull in on the gravel and then a door open.'

'A house door or car door?' I asked.

'House, definitely,' Walter said, rubbing his chin. 'I glanced away, but then back when I heard an undercurrent of conversation. A man in a robe was standing by the car and things seemed a bit tense, as I said. I thought she must have been out, and he didn't like it.' He shrugged. 'I didn't want them to think I was eavesdropping, so I went inside.'

Damn. Where was somebody like Sarah when you needed her? My partner was eavesdropper extraordinaire, and she didn't care who knew it. 'Too bad.'

He glanced at me, startled. 'Well, yes, I suppose it is.'

This time I broke the silence. 'Are you heading out?'

'Out?' he said, seeming to have forgotten he had his car key in his hand. 'Oh, yes, I'm just pulling around the other side to our sales office for the new phase of the development. We're hosting a reception in the model unit this afternoon at two. Come, if you like. Carmen will be there.'

'She's really interested then?' I asked, a little surprised. Angela's mother had struck me as someone who wasn't ready to give up her independence.

'It's not just senior living at its best,' Walter intoned, as if he'd read my mind. 'It's *living* at its best.'

'It's the new slogan,' Sophie Daystrom said, sliding a one-sheet flyer over to me. 'I voted for "God's waiting room". It never wins.'

I laughed. 'I can't imagine Walter going for that.'

We were sitting in the light-filled living room of their corner unit. The room's floor-to-ceiling windows on the south faced Brookhill Road and to the west, Poplar Creek.

'Walter Benson?' Henry said, coming in with a cardboard tray of to-go cups from the coffee urn in the lobby. 'The man has no sense of humor. But he does have divine talent.'

'As in God-given?' I asked, as Henry set the tray on the counter that divided their front room and their kitchen.

Henry just smiled at me.

'He's having one on you,' Sophie said. 'Playing those word games. He means divine as in dowsing.'

'Dowsing.' The more they said, the less I understood.

Henry chuckled, wiggling the Styrofoam cups free of the holder, one by one, before he answered. 'Divining or dowsing as in finding water or oil or the like.'

Ah, like a divining rod. Or dowsing rod, apparently.

'Another good one would be "metal detector,"' Sophie told him.

'Metal? As in steel?' Henry asked, puzzled.

'No, m . . . e . . . t . . . t . . . l . . . e,' Sophie said.

'Oh, yes, yes,' Henry said, 'that's wonderful, my dear.' He set a cup in front of her.

She took a sip from her reward. 'I thought so.'

'So, detecting somebody's resilience?' I tried.

'What they're made of,' Henry confirmed, sliding me a cup. 'Or divining, as in finding or zeroing in on something.'

Hmm. OK. 'And why do you say this is Walter's talent?'

'Because the Bensons have always had a talent for finding a niche,' Henry said. 'And profiting from it.'

'Or a weakness and exploiting it,' Sophie contributed.

'Like baby-boomers aging, you mean?' I asked.

'Exactly like that,' Sophie said. 'Or building strip malls, when people abandoned cities for the suburbs.'

'That was Way,' Henry said, digging in one cardigan pocket, then the other. 'Oliver has the gene, not that he's inclined to use it.'

'Nurture over nature,' Sophie said. 'Thank God that Way and Aurora never had time for him.'

And Mrs G did. 'He and Eric will be heading back to Minneapolis tomorrow.' I had to stop myself from sighing.

'He was just here,' Henry said. 'Wanted to ask Sophie about what she saw the other night.'

'Eric was here?' I asked, inordinately proud that my son had inherited my nosy gene.

'No, Oliver,' Henry said, dashing my hopes. He was checking his trouser pockets now.

'What are you looking for?' Sophie demanded.

Henry came up with a handful of cellophane-wrapped fortune cookies. 'Cookie?'

'Oh, sure,' I said, taking one. It squished like soggy cardboard. I set the thing down, ostensibly to remove the lid from my cup. I took a sip. 'This is pretty good.'

'Not five dollars and not Uncommon Grounds, but they do keep it brewing so it's fresh,' Sophie picked up a cookie and made a face. 'A lot fresher than these darn things.'

'I like them soft,' Henry said. 'You should try them, Soph. Be easier on your digestion.'

A glimmer in his eyes said he was kidding.

'There's nothing wrong with my digestion,' Sophie said, elbowing him. 'He's always on me about my trips to the bathroom.'

'Which, I presume,' Henry said, sitting down across from me, 'is the reason you've graced us with your presence?'

'You know me too well,' I said, ruefully. 'But it's not that I haven't wanted to see what you've done with your new place. It's just that I . . .' since I didn't have an excuse, I settled for, '. . . haven't.'

'Do you want to see the window?' Sophie said, getting up eagerly. 'You'll see why I couldn't miss it.'

Following her through a short hallway and into the next room, I stopped short. 'There's a floor-to-ceiling window next to the toilet?'

'Disturbing, isn't it?' Henry said, from behind me.

'Oh, pish-posh,' Sophie said, sitting down on the lidded commode. 'I find it freeing. Let them look.' She swept her hand toward the window. Going closer, I could see down to the gravel apron where the Lexus had gone into the creek.

'When I come in here at night,' Sophie said, 'I don't bother turning on the light. Normally there's a glow from the two streetlights, which is enough to see what I'm doing.'

'Should you actually wish to see,' Henry said.

'Besides,' Sophie said, ignoring him. 'It's more restful. If I turn on the light, I have trouble getting back to sleep.'

I could see that.

'. . . thought I was seeing double.'

'Double?' I asked, thinking I'd missed something.

'Or maybe just a reflection in the creek that I hadn't seen before. Of the other two lights,' Sophie finished.

'Reflection of which other two lights?' I asked.

'The two streetlights, of course.'

Of course. 'You saw the two reflected streetlights, plus the two headlights in the creek. What time was this?'

'A little after one-thirty,' Henry said. 'Sophie called for me to come see right away.'

'Once I got up off the john,' she said, standing up from the toilet. 'Had to be presentable.'

Apparently at two-plus years, the relationship was new enough Sophie and Henry didn't converse with each other while on the pot. Pavlik and I were the same at this point. Frank and I, on the other hand . . .

'We conferred,' Henry said, taking up the story. 'And decided it was not a reflection, but a vehicle in the water. I called nine-one-one. I believe the sheriff's office called Sheriff Pavlik after that.'

'Yes,' I said, loving Henry's precise way of doing things. 'Could you actually make out the car?'

'Yes,' Sophie said. 'We got out the binoculars and there it was.'

'Now, Sophie,' Henry said, 'I'm not so sure that's true. In the interest of time, we called it in immediately.'

'Oh, right,' Sophie recalled. 'For all we knew, there still was somebody alive in that car. So we called it in first and then got out my night-vision binoculars.'

Sophie had night-vision binoculars. And these big ol' windows. Which probably explained why they weren't outside freezing with the rest of us that night as Vivian's body was recovered. They could see more clearly from up here.

'With the infrared,' Henry took up again, 'we could make out the car and even what looked like tire tracks leading off the bank into the creek. Before that, we saw just the lights and a vague shape, and our minds came up with "car."'

'And our minds were right,' Sophie said, as a figure came out of the house across the street.

'Should we step back?' I said uneasily, as Philip glanced around. 'He'll know we're looking.'

'Well, let him, goldarned it,' Sophie said, emphatically.

Thatta girl. But I still felt exposed.

Henry, bless him, was more sensitive to other people's feelings. In this case, mine. 'Sophie was just having a little fun with you, Maggy. People can't see in. The windows are mirrored.'

'One way, like in interview rooms,' Sophie said, leading us back into the living room. 'You being related to law enforcement probably know all about that. Now I want to hear exactly what you and your sheriff think about all this.'

FOURTEEN

'How much did you tell her?' Eric asked later that morning, as I handed him a T-shirt to stuff into his duffel.

'As little as I could get away with,' I said. 'Which is a good thing, since it got me back here before you took off on me.'

'I would have called you before I left,' my son said to the note of recrimination in my voice.

'Or, better yet, stayed until tomorrow,' I suggested. 'It's only a five-hour drive to Minneapolis, so if you left at ten or even eleven tomorrow morning, you'd be home by late afternoon.'

'I'm dropping Erin off for her flight to Boston, then hitting the road. Things to do, people to see before classes start up again on Monday.' He straightened up from his bag, grinning.

'More important things and people than—' I broke off. 'Oh, my God. Who have I become?' My mother, that was who. 'Sophie and Henry said Oliver stopped by this morning.'

'Oh, yeah?'

'Presumably saying goodbye to Mrs G since you guys are heading back, but he was also asking about their reporting Vivian's Lexus in the creek.'

'Just like you were.'

'Yup. They didn't have much to add. Other than reminding me that there are streetlights on Brookhill Road.'

'Meaning it wouldn't have been quite as dark in the Woodwards' backyard?'

'Exactly,' I said. 'It explains why Walter was able to make Philip out from across the street. Oh, other thing, Sophie has night-vision binoculars.'

'Cool,' Eric said. 'They probably can see all sorts of stuff from up there.'

'Unfortunately, they weren't looking at the pertinent time.' I sat down on the side of the bed. 'I wonder why Oliver is so interested.'

'Me, too.' He turned. 'Maybe it's like that movie, *Mrs Robinson*.'

'The song is "Mrs Robinson." The movie is *The Graduate*.' What were they teaching kids in school these days? 'You think Oliver was interested in Vivian?'

'Who knows? She's nice-looking for an older woman, I guess.' He cocked his head, thinking. 'You know that saying, "not getting any younger"? It's really true, isn't it?'

'Which is why it's a truism,' I told the young whippersnapper.

'No,' Eric said seriously. 'I mean, like the people at Brookhills Manor. Even they shouldn't waste time feeling old, because today – this very day' – he was pointing his finger for emphasis – 'is the youngest any of us will ever be again.'

He was right.

And it was freeing and depressing, all at the same time. Thanks, son.

'Epic, huh?' Eric had turned to the dresser to pull out socks. 'Oliver isn't driving back with me today.'

'He's not? Why?'

'I think it has to do with his grandfather,' Eric said. 'Family stuff.'

'See?' I said, rising. 'Another reason you should stay. The two of you can get an early start and drive back tomorrow.'

'And I'll have to wait for him, so we'll get off to a late start and never get back. You know how he is. Anyway,' Eric continued, 'Oliver's going to fly back. His grandfather has the money.'

He certainly does. 'I bet Oliver is staying for the open house Walter is having to show off the new condos at Brookhills Manor.'

'Condos?' Eric said. 'Is that what they're building? I thought it was rentals.'

'It kind of is,' I said. 'From what I understand, you practically sign everything over to them to live there.'

'What do you mean?'

'Sophie was explaining how it works to me.' With appropriate expletives. 'You buy the place for a set price, but also agree that when you die, the Manor gets another big chunk called an endowment. Plus, they get the condo back. In return, they promise you can live there the rest of your life.'

'Sounds like a racket.'

'It does, doesn't it? I'm going to go to the open house this afternoon and see what it is people are willing to sell their souls for.'

'Why buy a condo at the Manor?' Eric asked, nose wrinkled. 'Why not just buy a house? You can live there until you die, too.'

When I was Eric's age, I figured you just lived until you died, too.

It's that mushy part in between that scares the bejesus out of you. 'But if you had a stroke like Mrs G, they'd have to accept you into the nursing home or assisted living, even if you didn't have enough money at the time.'

'That's because you've already given them everything you have. Or promised to give it to them.'

'I know,' I said. 'I guess it's the feeling of security.'

'Sounds more like giving up,' Eric said. 'Or prison. What happens if Brookhills Manor goes out of business? Or you don't like it there?'

'Well, then . . . I don't know.'

'I wouldn't do it,' Eric said, zipping up his bag. 'And you don't either. I'll take care of you when you're old.'

Aww. Every mom should have a gay son who doesn't have a partner yet. 'I will not move in with you. And I won't sign anything at the Manor.'

He hefted his duffel. 'But you're going anyway?'

'*Not* for me,' I said, emphatically. 'Luc's partner's mother Carmen is looking.'

'And you know her so well that you're helping?' He waved for me to precede him out to his van.

'I just met her,' I admitted, as he opened the back and tossed in his duffel.

'Then you're being nosy,' he said, slamming it harder than I would have. 'Or do you have a suspect over at the Manor?'

'Suspect for what?' I asked, innocently trailing him from the back to the driver's side.

He climbed in and then rolled down the window. 'There

are old people there,' he said, holding up one hand, 'and you have an old crime to solve.'

'Baby Doe.' I leaned through the window to give him a hug. 'You have a point.'

'And you have an appointment,' he said. 'Love you.'

'Love you, too,' I said to the receding minivan.

I arrived back at Brookhills Manor at two p.m., just as the reception was slated to start. Opting to leave my Escape in the nursing home lot, I walked toward the entrance of the building site. The lot had been cleared and foundation poured, but there wasn't much more progress than that. A large excavator was perched near the street, a smiley-face spray-painted on the cab. Pretty cheery vandals.

Cones and concrete barriers had been used to funnel visitors' cars away from the unsightly construction area toward a parking lot where Walter had left his 911, front and center. I didn't see Carmen's Ferrari yet, though.

A path led from the lot to a modular building that reminded me of the portable classrooms brought in to relieve the overcrowding at Eric's elementary school. Open house banners were draped from the roofline. A senior-friendly ramp covered in green indoor-outdoor carpeting ran up from each side to the center door, a safety railing in place to keep people from plummeting the two feet from the landing onto the asphalt below.

As I mounted the ramp, I saw Walter talking to somebody on the side of the building. It took me a second to realize it was Oliver. I couldn't hear what they were saying, but it seemed heated. Oliver trying to convince Walter of something or vice versa.

Maybe the plane fare home wasn't a done deal. Or, horror of horrors, Oliver didn't want to go back to school at all, which would explain why he hadn't driven back with Eric.

It not being my business, I continued around the bend of the ramp to the center door. Opening it, I felt a little like Dorothy. Except instead of stepping into the Land of Oz, I was stepping into the Land of Benson. And the condo was spectacular.

There already was a crowd and I could see Sophie and Henry chatting with a few other residents of the Manor next to a faux window with a faux view of Poplar Creek.

'What do you think?' Walter Benson's voice asked in my ear and I jumped. The man must have come up the ramp right behind me without my realizing.

'Spectacular,' I told him. 'You're very light on your feet.'

'Do you think so?' he asked, straightening the lapel of his navy chalk-stripe suit. 'How old do you think I am?'

Tien and I had looked the man up, so I knew exactly how old he was. But I also know a trap when I hear one. 'I'm terrible at guessing ages.'

'Just try,' he pressed.

'No.'

'Please.'

'I'd rather not.'

He glared at me, as the sound of footsteps tip-tapped up the ramp.

When the door opened behind me, though, his face lit up. 'Carmen, please. Come in.'

Angela's mother was wearing camel pants and turtleneck with a large colorful scarf knotted casually about her shoulders.

'Hermes,' a voice at my elbow said. 'Hand embroidered.'

I turned to see Vana Shropshire. 'What are you doing here?'

She cocked her head. 'You do ask the impertinent question, don't you?'

'Sorry,' I said, holding up a hand. 'But you're the one assessing people's clothes.'

'Not assessing, admiring,' she said, her chin gesturing toward Carmen. 'That scarf goes for at least five thousand dollars, something that hasn't escaped Walter, I'll venture.'

'Is it Walter or Carmen's style you admire?' I asked curiously.

She shrugged. 'I do appreciate business acumen. For example, did you see what they're serving?'

A server with a tray passed conveniently by. 'Caviar and champagne, you mean?'

She held up her glass. 'Prosecco. There's one fish Benson is trying to hook today, and she's Italian.'

'I'm not sure who is hooking whom,' I said, as Carmen's light laugh wafted over the crowd from where she stood speaking to Walter.

'They're playing each other,' Vana said, claiming a glass of Prosecco for me as another waiter passed by. She handed it to me. 'We'll see if anybody is landed.'

Enough with the fishing metaphors. 'I'm still surprised to see you here.'

'Because my daughter is dead and my son-in-law probably killed her?' She took a sip. 'But that's exactly why I'm here. This is so much classier than sitting at a bar alone or drinking up the minibar in my room, don't you think?'

She nodded toward the gigantic marble island that separated the living area from the kitchen. It was set with all manner of alcoholic beverages in addition to the Prosecco, plus a healthy array of hors d'oeuvres.

If Vana really was an alcoholic, she wouldn't have trouble drinking pretty much anywhere.

'I saw Philip this morning. He swears he didn't hear Vivian come home.'

'So? He swore to Vivian that he didn't have an affair with a student when he left the school,' Vana said, setting down one glass on the marble island and claiming another. 'He had, and it ruined Vivian's life.'

I almost said 'and his', but the truth was that Philip had made the choice to have the affair, or one-night stand, as he put it. Vivian didn't. 'You really think Philip killed her?'

'I think that Vivian had enough to drink that night to tell Philip exactly what she thought of him. She punctured his overblown ego.'

I had to admit it tallied with what Philip had admitted about his own personality. 'They argued and he killed her?'

'Ask the eyewitness,' Vana said, nodding toward Walter and Carmen. 'Personally, I wouldn't have thought Philip had the balls. All talk and no action.' She laughed a little too loudly. 'Well, except the once, of course.'

Two twenty in the afternoon and I was tempted to tell Vana to go home and sleep it off.

'Is that boy Oliver around?' Her head was swiveling. 'He

left a message at the hotel, saying he was sorry about Vivian.' She grasped my hand. 'Such pretty manners.'

Ugh. Hopefully, Oliver was safely out of range.

'You should go back to the hotel and lie down,' I suggested, disengaging myself.

'Why? You think I'm drunk?' she demanded, as Walter glanced our way, frowning.

'I didn't say that,' I said, as Walter excused himself and started toward us. 'It's just a little early—'

'Walter Benson,' Vana interrupted, giving the man her hand. 'Nice of you to pry yourself away to greet your other guests. Prosecco?' She waved at a lineup of fresh glasses on the counter.

'Not for me,' he said, a disapproving tone to his voice. 'I prefer to remain in control of myself.'

'You know, it's difficult looking at you now, all upright,' Vana said, 'to believe you were the same man who used to smoke joints with my parents. But I do remember.'

Walter smiled a little painfully. 'Upright, meaning uptight? I suppose you're right. But it was the excesses of youth that showed me the pitfalls to avoid if I wanted to make myself a success.'

'Well put,' Vana said, raising her glass in *salute*.

Vana now being Walter's problem, I took the opportunity to move toward Carmen who was examining the floorplans arrayed on one wall.

'Walter seems smitten with you,' I told her.

She glanced past me toward the man and smiled. 'Walter Benson was perpetually smitten as a young man. He is no different as an old one, I'm afraid.'

I grinned. 'You dated?'

'Oh, Maggy,' she said, shaking her head. 'Of course we didn't date. We had sex. Many times. It was the sixties.'

'You and Walter?' I think my eyes got wide, but that was better than grimacing in revulsion, I suppose.

'Everyone with everyone.' She shrugged at my expression. 'You have to remember, it was women's liberation. We had the pill – the original pill, before that little blue one that makes old men rut like randy deer.'

That one, presumably, being Viagra. 'Oral contraceptives were available.'

'Yes,' she said with a smile. 'Another reason I was quite happy to come from Italy for school. My parents would have been scandalized.'

'Birth control wasn't available in Italy?'

'Not until later,' she said. 'And my family was very, very Catholic.'

I frowned. 'You've been here since . . .'

'1961,' she told me, seeming to know where I was going.

'And yet your accent . . .?'

'Is charming, no?' Now she outright laughed. 'It makes me memorable. Besides, it is my right. My birthright.'

I couldn't fault her. I hadn't even been to Norway but managed to adopt my mother's native 'yah'. Didn't pick up many men with it, though.

'Did Walter offer to show you the rest of the condo?' I asked. 'The bedrooms, perhaps?'

A smile. 'He did not, yet. Shall we explore?'

A doorway to the left did indeed lead to a spacious bedroom, with a walk-through closet that went on to a bathroom. 'Master suite?'

'One of two, I think,' she said, poking her head into the bathroom. 'This washroom also can be accessed from the hallway.'

'And has a walk-in tub,' I pointed out, 'for when you're old.'

'I'm already old,' she said, opening the mirrored cabinet, 'but when I can no longer step into a bathtub, I think I will just settle for a shower. Or stay dirty.'

'Are you and Walter the same age?'

She closed the cabinet door and glanced sideways at me in the mirror. 'And that age would be?'

'I don't know,' I fibbed. 'You interrupted our game. He wanted me to guess.'

'Oh, ta,' she said, waving her hand. 'You are right that it's a game. A game for those who believe they look younger than their age. I am seventy-nine and proud of it.' She raised her chin as she said it.

'You do look younger than that. By a decade,' I said, quite truthfully.

'I am youthful. Which is why I don't play the games.' She waved me over to a sitting area that had been staged under a window with two reading chairs and a small round table. 'But you are being disingenuous, no?'

'No.' I glanced out the window, which of course, wasn't actually a window.

'Nice light, no?'

I laughed. 'No. But you're right that knowing when you were in school and assuming Angela is in her mid-fifties, like Luc, I guessed you were somewhere in your late seventies.'

She thought for a moment and then undid the flap of her clutch. 'I brought something you may like. I thought perhaps to show it to Walter.'

She pulled out a black-and-white photo. 'It is of all of us, from my senior year.'

I took the photo. 'Where was this taken?'

'Paz and Harmony's backyard. There were more trees then, but you can just make out the creek behind us.'

'Oh, yes,' I said, peering at a partial wall of two-by-fours to one side. 'Is that the cottage then, being built?'

She took it. 'The shed, I think. The cottage was behind the photographer. We would all bed down on their living-room floor or outside, if the night was mild.'

'Who was the photographer? I think I see you. And is that' – I looked up, surprised – 'Vickie LaTour?'

'The redhead?' Carmen asked, peering at the grainy photo. 'Yes, Vickie. Though I do not believe LaTour was her last name then.'

'And the couple is Paz and Harmony?' The man had long hair pulled back in a ponytail. He had his arm around a woman with curly hair nearly down to her waist.

'Yes. And this is Walter.' She pointed to a mustachioed man on the other side of Harmony, his head tilted toward her.

'They seem close,' I said, studying it. 'Walter and Harmony. Were they—'

Carmen shrugged. 'Who knows, but I think not. For one

thing, Paz would have killed him. And Walter, he is not very brave. For another, Walter was married then and has the boy.'

'Paula got pregnant in Walter's sophomore year, you said.'

'Correct,' she said. 'No, I think it was that Walter – and Henry, too – were protective of Harmony, not so much in love. She was very much the . . . how do you say, hippy-dippy?'

Hippy-dippy. 'Protective – was Paz violent?'

She did a head wobble. 'Maybe yes, maybe so. He did have a hot temper, much like an Italian. But I never saw the man hurt anyone.'

Even a baby? 'No Henry in the photo?'

'He took the photo. I think because he already had the short hair for the service. Henry was very handsome.'

'Still is,' I said, nodding out the door toward the living room where I could see Henry holding his fedora as he greeted the aforementioned Vickie LaTour.

'His hat, always with the red feather in the brim,' Carmen said with a sigh. 'It is dashing, even all these years later.'

'Don't tell me he wore the fedora back then?'

'He did, yes, before he traded it for his army cap. Like my accent, his fedora marks Henry as unforgettable.'

I tried to imagine Henry coming home after the war with his dapper fedora balanced just so over his army buzz cut. 'I love Henry. Do you mind if I snap a photo of this?'

'Of course not,' Carmen said, as I took my phone out.

'Everyone does love Henry and always has,' Carmen said fondly as I snapped the pic and slid my phone back into my pocket. 'Which is the answer to the question you asked the other day.'

I frowned as I handed her back the photograph. I ask a lot of questions. 'Which question?'

She chuckled. 'Perhaps you didn't quite ask it. But you wondered how it was that a soldier going to fight in an unpopular war was embraced by . . . I think you called us flower children?'

It was Carmen who used that expression, but I let it slide. 'What else do you remember about that time? Were there actual children about?'

'Children?'

'Yes.' I felt myself flush. 'For example, did Paz and Harmony have Nirvana yet? Or Nirvy, I think Walter said they called her.'

'Paz called her that.' Her tone was disapproving. 'Nirvana was born in perhaps my first year of college. A pretty little thing. I would sit with her sometimes when her parents couldn't be bothered.'

I couldn't quite picture Carmen as a babysitter, but OK. 'You didn't like Paz and Harmony?'

'Paz, specifically. He was a fine friend to get high with,' she said, shrugging. 'Less so, I imagine, as a father.'

'Did you ever see him hit her?'

'Maybe a slap on the arm,' she said. 'Or how do you say? Backside? Why do you ask?'

I don't know. Why did she pretend she didn't know the American word for butt after living here for fifty years? It's what we do.

'Vana doesn't have anything good to say about this place or her parents.'

'Her father sometimes was not kind to her mother. Bossed her around, we used to say.'

'It was Vana I was talking to earlier,' I told her, not sure if she'd met the adult Nirvana.

'I did see,' Carmen said. 'I was going to offer my condolences on the loss of her daughter, but it did not seem the right moment.'

I'll say. 'She's been drinking too much, as you probably saw.'

Carmen shrugged a very Italian shrug. 'Alcohol lets her forget for a moment.'

'She's been "forgetting" in that way for years, from what I understand. I wondered whether there was a reason.'

'The reason being that her father hit her sixty years ago? Or her mother?' Carmen was dubious. 'I do not know.'

'But can you tell me if Nirvana was their only child?'

It was Carmen's turn to glance out the non-existent window. 'This is not Nirvana you care about. It's the skeleton I saw on the news. The baby.'

'Yes,' I said, quietly.

I thought I saw a trace of moisture come to her eyes. She blinked. 'I saw no other children. Not of Paz and Harmony's and not of anyone else, before you ask.'

'You did say there was a lot of sex.'

'And a lot of birth control,' she reminded me, standing up. 'I also told you that.'

'When was the last time you saw them?' I followed her into the outer room.

'Harmony and Paz?' She stopped and gave that some thought as she rearranged her scarf. 'That would be the summer following my senior year. So, 1965.'

She settled her scarf and gave me a small finger wave before starting toward the door.

1965. I glanced around the room.

Vana had gone thankfully – hopefully on foot, not driving. Sophie and Henry were sipping Prosecco with Vickie and a few others from the Manor. I could hear Walter's voice from the other end of the unit in what must be the second master suite.

'Maggy?'

I turned to see that Carmen was standing in the doorway. Her hand was on the knob, a frown on her face as she stared off into the distance.

'Did you forget something?' I asked.

She seemed to bring herself back and met my eyes. 'It was that summer I left.'

'Summer of '65.' Just four summers short of the Bryan Adams' song.

'We were all wearing the baby doll dresses.'

I cocked my head. 'Cute?'

She shook her head, a little impatiently. 'The tented mini-dresses – high waisted or no waist at all. And the shorter, we thought, the better.'

'Like Twiggy wore,' I said, catching on.

'Exactly.' She glanced around as if to see if anyone was listening. 'Well, Harmony had one that she wore many, many times. Blue floral.'

'So? You just said you all had them.'

'Yes.' She stepped out onto the ramp and turned. 'I just

remember thinking, as I said my goodbyes, that Harmony was filling hers out just a bit more.'

I made a grab for the edge of the door before Carmen could let it go. 'Are you saying Harmony might have been pregnant?'

I got an elaborate Italian shrug for my answer.

'Did you ask her?'

'Don't be silly,' she said, tossing the end of her scarf over her shoulder as she turned to leave. 'Only an American would ask such an impertinent question.'

FIFTEEN

'You *are* an American,' I wanted to scream after her. At least for the last sixty years or so.

But since I had asked a friend at a high school reunion when the baby was due a month after she had given birth to it, I had to agree with the rest of Carmen's logic.

Still . . .

Summer of 1965, Harmony Koeppler might have been pregnant. Or, perhaps, just put on a few pounds. Munchies, from all that pot.

I turned back and surveyed the room as the tip-tap of Carmen's shoes on the asphalt outside faded.

Who was here that might know? Henry was still chatting with Vickie by the window and, as luck would have it, Sophie had moved off to become part of a group of oldsters gathered at the end of the kitchen island that contained the food.

I started toward the window.

'Maggy,' Vickie called, a little too loudly considering I was now within two feet of her. 'Thinking about buying a place or are you here detecting?'

'Now, Vickie,' Henry said, 'is that a fair question? She might be here freeloading liquor and food like the rest of us.'

Vickie chortled at that, drawing a dark look from Sophie across the room.

'I don't blame you a bit,' I told them. 'After all, you have to put up with the inconvenience of the building site. The noise and dirt. The developers should be wining and dining you.'

'We're also props,' Vickie said, patting her burgundy hair. 'From my count, your friend was the only real prospect here and how would it have looked if it was nothing but crickets when she walked in?'

'You do know that was Carmen,' I said.

'Carmen? Carmen—' Her eyes widened. 'Don't tell me that was Carmen Gianni?'

'It was,' I said, pulling out my phone. 'She was just showing me a picture of all of you—'

'Did Carmen leave?' Walter had zeroed in on us. He was glancing around the room in a bit of a panic, so maybe Vickie was right about the turnout being mostly current residents of the Manor.

'She did,' I told him. 'But she said she'd be in touch. She's extremely interested.' Of course, I knew none of that.

'She is? That's wonderful. Maybe I should just catch—' Walter's cell phone buzzed.

'I wouldn't go after her,' I said, as he punched up a message. 'Carmen strikes me as a woman who doesn't like to be pressured. That Italian temperament.'

Besides, I wanted to pressure Walter for a few answers.

But he was still glancing around the room as he slipped the phone back into his pocket.

'Gerald,' he called, catching sight of a man passing by with a tray. 'Take over here. I have to meet with' – he glanced at me – 'a client.'

'Right, yes. I guess so,' the man said, seemingly at a loss.

'If it's Carmen,' I said to Walter, 'I really think—' But Walter was already out the door.

Damn. Talking to him would have to wait.

I turned to Gerald, feeling like we were being rude. 'Hi, I'm Maggy Thorsen. Are you one of Walter's associates?'

'No, I'm a rent-a-waiter,' he said and then shrugged. 'But I guess I've been promoted.'

'I guess you have,' I said, smiling. 'Want me to take that tray?'

'Would you?' he asked, handing it over. 'I really appreciate it, though I'm not sure exactly what I'm supposed to be doing if I'm not pouring or passing drinks.'

'Do what Walter does: stand and look important,' I suggested. 'Answer the occasional question, maybe.'

'Except I don't know anything.'

'Sure, you do,' I told him. 'Brochures are on the counter. And remember, "Brookhills Manor Luxury Condos aren't just senior living at its best, they're—"'

'"*Living* at its best,"' Henry and Vickie chorused.

'Right,' Gerald said with a grin, going off to retrieve a brochure.

As he thumbed through it, I turned to Henry and Vickie with my tray. 'Another Prosecco?'

'Don't mind if we do,' Vickie said, handing one to Henry before taking one herself.

I claimed the last glass and set down the silver tray.

I was taking a sip as Vickie said abruptly, 'Now what's this about a skeleton?'

Choking, I held up a hand, struggling to clear my throat.

'I was going to ask you, actually,' I said, as the burning in my windpipe subsided.

'You were going to ask questions? Now there's a surprise,' she said. 'Have they identified the poor little thing?'

'Not yet,' I told them. 'They believe that he may have died in the sixties. You were all here then, right?'

'Sixties and prior to that,' Vickie said, nodding. 'Henry and I met in grade school.'

'Townies,' Henry said. 'Walter, too. Carmen came here for school, so she was the exotic import.'

Like her car.

'But then you went off to war and became more interesting,' Vickie reminded him.

'I wasn't already interesting to you?' Henry protested.

Vickie giggled.

I was glad Sophie wasn't in earshot of the conversation, which I now made a yeoman's effort to steer back in the direction I wanted. 'What about the Koepplers?'

'Paz and Harmony,' Sophie's voice said flatly from behind me.

'How would you know about them?' Vickie asked her. 'You're not even from here.'

'Yes, I'm a newcomer.' Sophie's jaw was tighter than Vickie's unlined forehead. 'Just thirty-two years and counting now.'

'And I'm even newer,' I said, trying to defuse the tension. 'So, elucidate. Henry, Vickie and Walter were all locals. Carmen, not. What about Paz and Harmony?'

Vickie tried to wrinkle her brow. 'I think they just showed up, didn't they?'

Henry's head was cocked, thinking. 'I was cutting through the woods along the creek one day and just ran into Paz. He was building a bedroom set for Harmony who had just given birth to Nirvana. That was probably freshman year of college.'

'I remember being surprised there was even a cottage there,' Vickie said. 'The whole area here though was wooded, so we wouldn't have seen the cottage from the street. Which came in handy as it turned out.'

'For what?' Sophie demanded.

'Smoking dope,' Henry said. 'Not me, of course.'

'Straight arrow, even back then,' Vickie concurred.

'Or stick-in-the-mud, depending on who you listened to,' Henry said. 'But I wanted to go into military intelligence and needed to keep my nose clean.'

Sophie gasped. 'They were doing cocaine?'

I frowned. 'I don't think the expression has anything to do with snorting cocaine. It's too old.'

'What does it mean then?'

'I honestly don't know,' I admitted.

'What I meant was I needed to stay out of trouble,' Henry explained. 'And steer clear of other people's.'

'Well, hopefully you've gotten past that,' Vickie told him. 'Because Maggy wants to ask us some questions.'

'I do,' I said. 'Carmen told me she thought that Harmony might be pregnant the last time she saw her.'

'Which was when?' Vickie asked, tilting her head.

'August of 1965,' Henry stated, earning him a glance from both women. He shrugged. 'It was the summer after we graduated.'

'"We"' – Sophie made finger quotes – 'being you and Carmen and Vickie.'

'So we were in the same class,' Vickie said. 'I don't know what you're getting all upset about. You're younger than any of us.'

'I'm not getting upset,' Sophie said. 'You're the one who told me you think Carmen had work done.' Sophie turned to me. 'Though she's a fine one to talk, if you know what I mean.'

I wasn't touching that one. 'What do you think? Was Harmony pregnant?'

Henry rubbed his chin. 'I have to say I didn't notice if she was. Everybody wore this loose stuff and all. And I had other things to think about.'

Like going to war.

'By the time I returned to Brookhills four years later,' he continued, setting down his glass, 'it was just Harmony and the little girl there.'

'How old was Nirvana?' I asked.

'Seven or eight, maybe?'

'Whatever did happen to Paz?' Vickie asked, then turned to me by way of explanation. 'I got a place in Milwaukee after graduation.' She did jazz hands. 'Single girl in the city.'

Sophie rolled her eyes.

'Paz just took off on them, was what I heard,' Henry said. 'Gone, split.'

'He left?' Vana had said her father was 'gone,' but I'd assumed the man died. Which he probably had by now. 'This would have been 1969–70?'

'Probably before,' Henry said. 'He wasn't here when I got out of the service in '69. Ready to go, Soph?' He held out his arm.

She took it possessively and flashed Vickie a smile before saying, 'Yes, dear. Let's go home.'

I waved goodbye before turning to Vickie. 'So do you remember?'

'Remember what?' She was still watching the two of them leave. 'I don't know why Sophie has a problem with me. She's not only younger but got the guy.'

'Because she wants to keep the guy and you flirt outrageously.'

'Yeah, well, there is that,' she said, twisting her toe into the floor like a little girl. 'But I've got to get my money's worth out of all this.' She used the palms of her hands to frame her carefully maintained face. 'The day I stop flirting, I'll be dead. Sophie knows that.'

The two had been friends all of Sophie's years in Brookhills. 'If she gave you permission to flirt with her husband, would it still be fun?'

She pursed her volumized lips, thinking. 'No. No, it would not.'

'Then you should thank her for making your life worth living.'

Vickie let out a cackle. 'I should, you know that? Thank you, Maggy.'

'You're very welcome.' I set down my glass. 'A pleasure seeing you, Vickie. As always.'

'Same here,' she said as I went to the door.

'Maggy?' Her voice stopped me.

'Yes?' I turned, holding the door ajar.

'You didn't finish your question.'

Some detective I was, allowing myself to be diverted to the point I forgot the question. 'Um. Do you remember—'

'Carmen was right.'

I let the door close again. 'Right about?'

'Harmony was pregnant.'

I retraced my steps to where she stood. 'Did she have the baby?'

'Yes.' She was obviously uncomfortable. 'Well, at least I think so.'

'You didn't see him?'

'No. Of course not. Why would you think that I did?' She seemed startled, though her eyebrows couldn't lift much higher than they already were hoisted.

The reaction seemed odd. 'Because if she had a baby, you might have seen him.'

'Oh, you mean the baby.'

'Of course I meant the baby. Who else would . . .' I'd said 'him,' referring to Baby Doe. 'Did you think I was asking if you saw Paz?'

'Well, maybe for a second I thought that,' she admitted. 'But I never did see the baby.'

I was thinking furiously. It had been the sixties, after all. 'See how? As in socially?'

She frowned. 'The baby?'

Now she was just playing dumb. 'No, not the baby. Were you seeing Paz Koeppler? Did you two have an affair while Harmony was pregnant?'

She held up a hand. 'No, no, not an affair. It was just once or twice, but not when Harmony . . . well, at least I didn't know she was pregnant.'

Oh, my God. And these people have the nerve to complain about the younger generation?

I counted to ten and, keeping my voice low, said, 'Getting back to the baby. Did you ever see him? Or her?'

'No,' she said. 'Never. The only child I ever saw was Nirvana.'

'Harmony was pregnant, but you never asked what happened to the baby?'

'Like I said,' she protested, 'we graduated the spring of '65. I hung out here through that summer, but then I got a place in the city.'

'Your parents were still in Brookhills.' This was a stab in the dark.

It landed. 'Well, yes. I'd come back occasionally, bring my wash.'

More than half a century later, kids were still kids, parents still parents.

'What about Paz?'

'If my roommates were gone, sometimes he'd stay with me in the city.'

'How long did this go on?' I asked.

'Just a couple of months really. Paz was . . . well, he was kind of a jerk,' Vickie said. 'Thank God I didn't get pregnant. My parents would have killed me.'

Odd to hear those words from a near octogenarian. 'When was this?'

'That fall after Henry left for the service. 1965.'

'And when did Paz split, as Henry put it?'

She shrugged.

'Come on, Vickie,' I said. 'Henry went off to war, but you were still around. Your parents lived here. You'd had a thing with a married man. You're telling me you don't know when he left?'

Another shrug. 'People came and went back then. Paz would take off for a few days when being married with a kid became a drag.'

'Sometimes visit you?'

She shook her head definitively. 'Not after that fall. I was done with him.'

'But it was after that fall that he took off for good?'

'I guess so,' she said vaguely.

She was a tough interview. Maybe she'd been stoned the entire time. 'OK, fine,' I said, turning back to the door. 'Have it your way.'

'You don't have to get huffy, missy.' Old Vickie was back.

'I'm not being huffy,' I said. 'But if you're not going to tell me anything, I might as well leave.'

'It's not that I don't want to, I don't know. He just . . . left.'

The almost sob at the end indicated the past wasn't quite in the past for her. That maybe she felt like he'd left her, as surely as he'd left Harmony and the child or children.

Which opened another possibility.

If Paz Koeppler thought kids were a drag, maybe he hadn't wanted another child. And he'd done something about it.

SIXTEEN

'You think Vivian's grandfather killed the baby and then took off?' Philip unfolded an aluminum-framed lawn chair for me to sit on.

I'd intended to go to Uncommon Grounds to talk through my possible epiphany at Brookhills Manor with Sarah. But it was Saturday and Uncommon Grounds closed at four. I'd gotten there five minutes after, and my industrious partner was already out the door. Which meant I'd be lucky if the place had been vacuumed, and the till counted.

Talking to Pavlik was my next thought. But when I called, he'd been tied up in a meeting. Eric was halfway to Minneapolis and I preferred he didn't talk on the phone – even hands-free – when driving.

Philip, a possible murderer, hadn't been my first, second or third choice, but as I went to retrieve the Escape from the nursing home parking lot, I saw Philip across the way getting groceries from his car and offered to help. First I'd unburden him, then myself.

Shopping safely put away, I settled into the green-and-white woven webbing as Philip opened another chair for himself. Just in case he was a murderer, I'd suggested we sit outside rather than in, putting our chairs on the concrete slab behind the cottage to catch the last of the afternoon sun.

More secluded than sitting in front, certainly, but then there was the safety net of the corner units at Brookhills Manor. Who knew how many pairs of eyes were trained on us as we spoke? And, when night fell, Henry and Sophie had their night-vision binoculars.

'You sure you're OK sitting out here where it happened?' I asked a little belatedly.

'You mean here where a baby's bones were found?' he asked, nodding to our left. 'Or' – his head swiveled right – 'there where my wife drowned in her car?'

The rubber parking blocks were out of the Land Rover but still not staked in place, instead laying haphazardly like six-foot black-and-yellow pick-up sticks.

'There's nowhere here I can go to escape,' he continued woefully. 'Vivian or her family are everywhere.'

'But you're here, too,' I reminded him. 'The sheriff's office hasn't arrested you.'

'Yet,' he said. 'Apparently your sheriff would like some physical evidence to go with the eyewitness report from the eagle-eyed coot from across the way.'

That was my sheriff for you. Always wanting evidence. 'I'm sure they're going over Vivian's car, for one thing.'

'They'll certainly find evidence of me in it,' he said, sounding a little desperate. Or maybe that's just what he wanted me to think. 'We both drove the Lexus occasionally. And they took my robe.'

'Have you ever been in the Lexus with your robe on?'

'Of course not. I told—' He broke off and looked sideways at me. 'Oh, I see. Benson says I had the robe on, so if they find particles inside the car it means I got in that night.'

'Maybe.' I wasn't sure what else to say.

'Maybe hit Vivian in the head. Maybe released the brake. Maybe pushed the car in the creek.'

'We don't know any of that happened,' I pointed out. 'Her death still could have been an accident.'

'And what Benson saw?'

That, admittedly, was more of a stumbling block than any of the parking curbs.

He sighed, lifting and sliding the arms on his chair so the back reclined a bit. 'So, let's talk about the baby. Which, I'm sad to say, is the less depressing of the two subjects.'

'Because it's history not current events. And it's not your wife who is dead. And you couldn't have done it.' I offered him a meager smile.

He reached across the plastic arm of the chair and took my hand. 'Have you forgiven me?'

'Me? What for?' I pulled my hand back a little too fast, maybe, but then he might be a murderer.

'For cheating with a student.'

'That's none of my business,' I said.

'But I saw your opinion of me drop like a rock.' Dry laugh. 'Not as much as if I killed my wife, of course.'

'Of course.' I studied his face. 'Did you?'

'No, I did not,' he said.

He seemed sincere, but I'd known a lot of sincere killers. Which probably said something about me.

'Back to the Koepplers,' I said. 'When we were talking about them at the shop with Sarah, I guess I assumed that Paz had died before Harmony.'

'He didn't?' Philip thought about that, a vertical line appearing between his eyes. 'I think it was Sarah who said he'd died.'

Oh, yeah. '"The old man wasn't living, period, full-stop," I think were her words. Though she also said his name was still on the deed.'

'That's right,' Philip said. 'Does it matter?'

'Only that we don't know when he actually died. According to Henry and Vickie, he abandoned Vana and her mother sometime between 1965 and 1969.'

'I had no idea,' Philip said. 'I have to tell you, though, that when the lawyers asked for Paz – or Ray's – death certificate to transfer the deed, Vana didn't have it.'

'Because maybe he's not dead,' I said. Then asked, 'Why did they need the death certificate?'

'The property deed,' Philip said. 'It was in the names of Ray Koeppler and Matilda Koeppler. We had Matilda's death certificate because that just happened in the last year. But Ray's . . .' He shrugged.

Vana had told me the deed hadn't been transferred from the Koepplers, but she hadn't said why. 'Did Vana say why she or her mom didn't have Ray's death certificate?'

'You've talked to her,' he said, exasperated. 'She wants nothing to do with that period in her life or this place in general. She just wants to leave.'

'She was at the reception across the street,' I told him. 'For the new condominiums.'

'Just now? Was there booze?'

'A little after two,' I said. 'And yes, there was booze.'

'Which explains why she was so blitzed when I saw her,' he said. 'I'd left her a message saying I was leaving for the grocery store and asking if she needed anything.' He shook his head. 'I guess I was thinking booze.'

'Enabler,' I said.

'I know.' He was running his hands up and down the arms of the chair. 'But she just lost her daughter. I didn't think it was a good time for her to go cold turkey.'

'No need to worry about that,' I said. 'She already had a head start when she got to the reception and then added Prosecco. I was hoping she'd gone back to the hotel to sleep it off.'

'Unfortunately, no,' he said. 'When I came into the front room to get my phone and keys there she was sitting at my table. Just drunk as hell and screaming her head off.'

'When was this?' I asked.

'Maybe two-thirty, quarter to three? I got rid of her as quick as I could and left.'

Vana must have staggered right over to Philip's from the reception. 'Was she always a drinker?'

'I don't know,' Philip said. 'We didn't really see that much of her. But every time we did . . .' He shrugged.

'Did Vivian ever talk to her mother about it?'

'And set Vana off? Heaven forbid.' Philip went to roll his eyes and then caught himself. 'What the hell am I thinking? My wife is dead and here I'm bad-mouthing her.'

Yes, he was. 'Did you love her?'

'I loved her achingly once.' He was gazing past the creek toward the windows of Brookhills Manor across the street. 'But the more I tried to be what she wanted, the less she seemed to want it.'

'Maybe she just wanted you as you are,' I suggested quietly.

'That would have been too easy, I guess.' He resettled himself in the chair. 'Now let's get back to the other crappy husband in the family: Paz-slash-Ray Koeppler.'

'You do have something in common,' I told him. 'He was fooling around, too.'

Philip did a double take, but thankfully didn't remind me it was just a one-night stand. 'With whom?'

'I'd rather not say,' I told him. 'But she probably wasn't the only one anyway.'

'At least they had the sixties to blame.'

'Free love apparently wasn't so free,' I said, thinking about the baby. 'Even back then. Birth control was available, but probably not foolproof.'

'What about Baby Doe?' Philip asked. 'You think he was the result of this relationship? It would explain why his body was hidden.'

I shifted uncomfortably. 'The woman says no. She didn't get pregnant.'

He raised his chin. 'And you believe her?'

As much as I believed Philip these days. 'I think I do. Besides, both Vickie and Carmen believe Harmony was pregnant the summer of 1965.'

'Maybe she wanted another baby but Paz didn't.'

'Then he shouldn't have gotten her pregnant,' I said pointedly. 'But he did "split", as Henry put it, sometime after the more observant women in the group believed Harmony might be pregnant. And before Henry got back in 1969.'

'That's a big window,' Philip said.

'I know. Maybe Vana can tell us more.'

'Us?' Philip held his hands up. 'You'll do better without me.'

Yes, I would. 'The royal "us,"' I clarified. 'I'll probably wait until morning when she's sobered up.'

'If she's sobered up.'

'It would help if we knew when the baby was born and when it died. I'm just not sure how much the autopsy will be able to narrow it down after all this time.'

'And no birth or death records, I assume?'

Wouldn't that make life easy. 'No.'

'Could the child have died of natural causes?' Philip asked.

'And buried himself in the compost pile?'

Philip dipped his head. 'Point taken. But if this baby was born at home, there would be no official record, right?'

'Right, assuming the birth was unattended by a doctor or licensed midwife,' I said. 'From what we can tell, Harmony and Paz were doing the mid-century version of living off the grid.'

'If there was no birth registered, would they have reported the death of a child who didn't exist on the books? Or just buried it?'

I had to agree with Pavlik that referring to Baby Doe as 'it' was dehumanizing.

'Back into the earth, from whence he came,' I said, rubbing my forearms like I'd had a sudden chill. 'I suppose it depends how he died and whether they felt they needed to hide the fact. Do you know if Vana has a birth certificate?'

'No idea,' Philip said, as a crow swept by, landing on the shed. A forgotten scrap of police tape was still knotted on the door handle.

'You asked if the baby could have died of natural causes. The autopsy is still pending, but I think you should know that there were broken bones.'

'Oh, God.' Philip's head went down, practically to his knees.

'I asked Vana whether she was abused by her parents and she danced around the question. Did she or Vivian ever say anything that might have made you wonder?'

'No.' His head jerked up. 'Are you saying she knew about the baby?'

'Being abused?' I shook my head. 'She says she doesn't even remember a baby.'

He squinted into the sun, as another bird swooped by, landing on the gravel lot. 'That's right, of course. We don't even know that the baby was a Koeppler. Or even half a Koeppler, if the other woman is lying. But surely they can do DNA.'

'They might be able to get some from the bones, I understand,' I said, having a thought. 'How would you feel about giving permission for Vivian's DNA to be compared to the—'

'Hello?' a male voice called from the front of the house.

'We're back here,' I called back, forgetting I was the guest. I grimaced. 'Sorry.'

'No, that's fine,' Philip said. 'As long as it's not a reporter. And it's obviously not Vana.'

'Oliver?' I said, as the young man stuck his curly head around the corner. 'Eric has already left if you're looking for him.'

'No,' he said, seeming a little embarrassed. 'I stayed so I

could go to my grandfather's open house for the new condos.'
He gestured across the street. 'It's a big deal for him.'

I did know that because I had been there. Oliver, on the
other hand, had not actually gone in.

'I was there,' I told him now. 'The model looks great and
there was a nice turnout.'

He had the grace to flush. 'I got delayed.'

'Walter left early anyway for an appointment, so even if
you hadn't been late' – a seemingly perpetual problem for the
boy – 'you might have missed him anyway.'

'Good to know,' he said, biting his lip. 'I can tell him I
stopped in, but he wasn't there.'

Since I'd provided the alibi, I suppressed a smile.

'Were you looking for me then?' Philip asked Oliver, starting
to get up. 'I probably owe you for your—'

'Oh, no, no,' Oliver said, waving him to sit back down.
'You don't owe me anything. I was just wondering if Mrs
Woodward's mother was here. I needed to talk to her . . . um,
to tell her how sorry I was. And you, too, sir, if I haven't
already said it.'

'Thank you, Oliver. That's very ki— Watch it!' A third crow
had swooped by, this one low enough to brush Oliver's head.

'Wow,' Oliver said, rubbing his hair. 'He didn't poop on
me or anything, did he?'

'No,' I assured him, peering off toward the shed roof where
the culprit was watching us. The other two had disappeared.
'Maybe there's a nest nearby.'

'They get very protective of their young. And we're
disturbing them,' Philip said, standing up. 'Anyway, Maggy,
I'm happy to authorize the DNA, if you tell me how.'

'DNA?' Oliver asked.

'To see if Vivian was related to the baby,' I told him.

'Oh, yeah,' Oliver said. 'That's really smart.'

'I'll ask Pavlik,' I told Philip, standing myself. He was already
folding up his chair, so I did likewise, handing him mine.

'Well, I guess I best go,' Oliver said, still rubbing his head.

'Thanks for coming, Oliver,' Philip said. 'I'll tell Vana you
dropped by. Or try her at the Morrison. That's where she's
staying.'

'Still?' The boy looked surprised Vana hadn't moved to the cottage.

Philip leaned the chairs against the house and paused, his hand on the back door. 'Want to come through the house? Avoid playing Tippi Hedren and whoever was the male lead?'

'Rod Taylor,' I told him.

'I was sure you would know,' Philip said.

Philanderer, murderer or not, I did appreciate Philip's mind. Oliver was baffled. 'The lead in what?'

'Alfred Hitchcock's film, *The Birds*,' I told him. 'The female lead character is attacked by crows. It's a very memorable scene.'

'Uh-huh,' was all Oliver had to say. He was probably wishing he'd gone with Eric.

'I think I'll take my chances and cut across Brookhill Road here by the creek,' I said. 'I have to get my car in the Manor parking lot anyway.'

'I'll go with you,' Oliver said.

'But—'

Another bird swooped in, this one much bigger than a crow. The rest of the birds scattered.

'Was that a turkey vulture?' I said curiously, stepping over a parking barrier to get a closer look.

'Careful,' Philip said, joining us. 'I meant to get to those.'

'Turkey what?' Oliver was looking doubtful.

'Turkey vulture,' I told him. 'Haven't you ever seen one before? I read that they migrate to South America but come back here every spring.'

'Which is now,' Oliver said.

'Exactly,' I said, glancing around for the bird. The thing had a six-foot wingspan, so it should be hard to miss.

Philip touched my arm as I stepped closer to the creek bank. 'Careful.'

'I will.' Nothing wrong with being solicitous, I guess, but the man was getting annoying. I wasn't twelve. I didn't need walking home. Besides, I wanted to see the vulture.

'What's that smell?' Oliver asked, wrinkling his nose.

'The vulture must be around here somewhere,' I said, glancing up into the trees. 'They eat carrion and vomit a lot.'

'Not surprising,' Philip said, curling his lip.

Oliver, on the other hand, was beaming now. 'Are these the ones that projectile vomit at you, if you get too close to them or their babies? That is so cool.'

'It is, and I bet he went in there,' I said, nodding at the half-open shed door. 'They lay their eggs in caves, hollow logs and even abandoned buildings.'

'Is this the time of year they breed?' Philip asked, hanging back.

'I think so.' I went to shove the door open, but it seemed to catch on the shed floor.

'Careful,' Philip warned yet again.

'I will,' I said, putting my shoulder into it. 'Help me.'

Philip hung back. 'I'm not sure we should—'

'Here,' Oliver said, waving me to get back, too.

I got out of the way as Oliver leaned into the door and gave it a mighty shove.

No movement of the door, but we all jumped back at the sudden sound of wings flapping. Big wings.

'I bet it is a nest,' Oliver said. 'But no vomit so far. I'm going to stick my head in and see.'

'Careful!' This was me, this time.

Like my own son, Oliver ignored me. 'Whoa, big bird,' he said, peering in. 'I see why they call them turkey vultures. The head is red and kind of naked like a turkey, and—'

He pulled back; his face was ashen.

'Did it vomit on you?' Philip asked.

At the word 'vomit' Oliver turned to one side and did so, just missing my shoe.

I slid past him and stuck my own head inside. The big bird was on the concrete floor, but facing away from me, its wings spread wide.

I froze as it turned toward me, folding its wings. But it was what I could now see clearly on the floor beyond the bird that made me stumble back. 'Call nine-one-one.'

'Why? What is it?' Philip had his hand on Oliver's back as the boy purged.

'Not what, but who,' I said. Then lowered my voice to whisper, 'Walter Benson, and I think he's dead.'

Or I hoped he was.

SEVENTEEN

'And when you saw the deceased, what did you do?' Deputy Kelly Anthony asked me.

Pavlik was talking to Oliver since he preferred not to interrogate his own wife-to-be. I was glad of that because I knew Pavlik would be gentle with the boy who'd just caught a vulture scavenging his grandfather's body.

'I told Philip to call nine-one-one.'

'You didn't touch anything?'

'There was a bird the size of my sheepdog standing over Walter's body, acting pretty territorial. I wasn't about to go in.'

'The size of Frank?' Kelly asked doubtfully.

'Not fluffy Frank,' I explained. 'Soaking wet Frank. But it was big.' The vulture had taken flight when the first responders arrived.

'You didn't touch anything?' she repeated.

'Just the door, trying to shove it open.' I pointed toward the shed where the coroner was leaning over Walter Benson's body. The door had been taken off its sole hinge and removed.

'I thought about pulling it fully closed to preserve the crime scene,' I continued. 'But with the turkey vulture inside, it seemed . . .'

'Good call,' Kelly said, making a note. 'What made you go to the shed at all? Were you looking for Mr Benson?'

'No, we had no idea he was there,' I said. 'It was the birds that caught my attention. First just crows, but then the vulture.'

'Birds.' Anthony swiveled her head toward the roof of the cottage where a pair of crows stood watch and gave a little shiver. 'I hate them.'

I didn't know if that was all birds or just the ones that ate dead people. I gave a matching shiver. 'The crows practically dive-bombed us—'

'Us?'

'Philip Woodward, Oliver Benson and me,' I said, nodding toward the back door, where Pavlik now stood with the other two. 'We were chatting and . . .'

Deputy Anthony was looking at me like I'd lost my mind. It wasn't for the first time. 'You do know Woodward is a person of interest in his wife's death, right?'

'Yes, I—'

She waved her hand. 'Never mind. That's exactly why you were talking to him, wasn't it?'

Partially. 'Not really,' I said. Then added, 'I mean, not this time. I wanted to talk to him about his wife's family and the baby.'

'Ahh,' Anthony said. 'The other case we have centered here.'

'But it's a cold case,' I said, cringing at her tone. 'I figured it wasn't off-limits.'

'Up to the sheriff,' she said, as in *let him deal with you.*

Then she asked, 'You say you went to the shed to investigate the birds?'

'Yes, the crows were congregating there and then the turkey vulture arrived and chased them away. I thought the vulture might have a nest in the shed.'

'That's when you looked in and saw—'

'No, the door was stuck.'

Anthony glanced up from her pad. 'It was open and practically falling off earlier this week.'

I had noticed the same thing. 'Somebody must have pulled the door closed a bit. Not enough to keep the birds out, of course.'

'Of course,' Anthony muttered.

'With only the one hinge, it got hung up on the uneven concrete. Oliver thought he could muscle it, so he waved me out of the way.'

'And pushed it open.'

'No,' I said again. 'It didn't give at all. But we could hear the vulture inside, so Oliver stuck his head in.'

'That was stupid,' Anthony said without thinking, then added, 'or reckless.'

'Both. He's young.'

She nodded for me to continue.

'Anyway, Oliver looked in and then jumped back, visibly shaken. That's when I stuck my own head in.' I raised my hand. 'Yes, stupid, as well. And I'm not young.'

I got a smile. 'And you saw . . .'

'Walter Benson.' I couldn't help glancing over at the body, face-down, the back of the navy chalk-stripe suit jacket ripped by the birds. A bloody rebar was on the ground next to him.

'How did you know it was Walter Benson? Did Oliver tell you it was his grandfather?'

'No.' Oliver had been busy getting sick. 'It was the suit.'

'You recognized Benson's suit?'

'Yes, I'd just seen him at—'

'Where?'

'I'm trying to tell you,' I said, irritably. 'If you give me a chance.'

Anthony opened her mouth and then closed it. 'Sorry. I'm just trying to be thorough.' A glance over her shoulder. 'You know.'

I knew. I gave her a sympathetic grin. 'Ask away. I'm all yours.'

'Thanks.' She said it under her breath and added more audibly, 'Now you say you saw Mr Benson earlier today?'

'Yes,' I said, raising my own voice and drawing a curious glance from Pavlik. 'He was hosting an open house for the new condos at Brookhills Manor.'

'The ones they're just starting?' Kelly asked more conversationally. 'My parents were talking about those.'

'The model is beautiful,' I told her truthfully. 'I have no idea if they're a good investment.'

'Or whether they'll even go ahead, now that Walter is . . .' She gestured toward the man in question.

'True,' I said. 'Though it can't hurt to ask. According to my partner Sarah, sometimes you get a deal by being the first few investors in a complex. Especially if . . .'

We both cast our eyes toward the corpse and then back again, equally shamefaced. And I'd bad-mouthed the vulture for picking over the body.

'Anyway,' Kelly said, raising her voice again. 'You say Mr Benson was wearing this same suit?'

'He was,' I told her. 'He left the reception—'

'When was the last time you saw him there?'

I resigned myself to interruption and thought about the question. 'About two forty-five maybe? The reception started at two and—'

'And you left at two forty-five?'

'No,' I said, patiently. 'Walter did. A woman who had shown interest in the condos had just left and he—'

This time I interrupted myself. Walter had been asking after Carmen, but . . . 'He got a message on his phone and said he had to meet a client. Told a waiter to take over.'

'A waiter.'

'Yes, I thought it was curious, too.'

'What was Oliver doing here?'

'He was looking for Vana Shropshire to tell her how sorry he was about Vivian. Oliver worked for Vivian and Philip, you know.' I said it matter-of-factly, but I found Oliver's interest in Vivian, and now Vana, a little odd.

Anthony wrote it down and then tapped her pen on the pad. 'This meeting Walter Benson mentioned. Did he say where it was? Or who it was with?'

'No,' I said. 'But the text message should be on his phone.'

Kelly Anthony excused herself to consult with the coroner. The two women spoke and then the deputy returned. 'Benson didn't have a phone on him.'

Now that was odd. Though so were vultures and death by rebar. At the home of a man the victim had accused of possibly killing his wife. 'The murderer must have taken it.'

'Or tossed it in the creek,' she said.

'Right here, though?' I said a little doubtfully. 'Wouldn't it have been smarter for the attacker to take it with them and dispose—'

'I've got a phone,' a deputy called from the nearby bank of the creek.

But then what did I know.

'It just seems too obvious,' I was saying to Pavlik as he unlocked the back door of the house for us. We'd driven home simultaneously, if not together, from the scene of the now three crimes.

'You should probably stand back.' The rumble of thunder followed by the pitter-patter of little feet sounded across the wood floor inside. Pavlik pulled open the door and stood out of the way himself, as Frank and Mocha plunged out the door and into the backyard.

'Sorry, guys,' I told the pups as they settled on the closest pee-spots. Frank's, unfortunately, were his feet. 'I thought I'd be home earlier.'

It had been approaching two in the afternoon when I'd waved goodbye to Eric and gone back to the Manor for the reception. Now it was nine. It seemed longer because so much had happened.

Walter being murdered, for one.

Philip being arrested, for another.

Oliver losing immediate family for the third time in just two years.

'We should have made Oliver come home with us,' I said, for maybe the third time.

'He's staying with Gloria Goddard,' Pavlik said. 'Which is probably the best place for him.'

'Unless he's badgered by Sophie and company,' I said, turning on the water to hose off Frank's front feet.

'Gloria will protect him,' Pavlik said. 'And he knows he can come over here whenever he wants.'

'I guess,' I said, waving Frank to come over and stand for me. 'I wish Eric hadn't left.'

I set the nozzle on mist and sprayed first Frank's right front paw and then his left. He harrumphed.

'If you don't want me to rinse off your paws,' I told him reasonably, 'lift your leg like a normal boy-dog. You're not built like Mocha. She squats. And has girl parts. If you stand on all fours and let loose, it's naturally going to shoot forward like a firehose. And you know what you get?' I picked up a towel I kept on the porch. 'Wet paws.'

'I'm glad I wasn't around for Eric's potty-training,' Pavlik observed, as I dried Frank's furry feet.

'He got himself, too, sometimes. But mostly the floor.' I

finished with Frank's second paw and draped the towel over the porch railing. 'I should call him.'

'To reminisce?'

I turned the water spigot off. 'To tell him about Oliver's grandfather.'

'Oliver won't call Eric himself?'

Maybe. But my plan had the added bonus of checking to make sure my son made it home all right. 'I think it would be nice if Eric reached out.'

The dogs were still sniffing around the yard. I stepped into the house and tossed my purse on the couch.

'Wine?' I called back to Pavlik as I continued into the kitchen.

'I was thinking bed,' he said, giving up on the dogs finishing up any time soon and closing the door.

I stuck my head back into the living room. 'It's Saturday night. Live a little.'

'I feel like I lived a lot today,' he said, sinking onto the couch the long way.

'Then wine to decompress.' I returned to the kitchen and picked up the corkscrew, considering. There was a nice Pinot on the kitchen counter. Or I could go with the Chardonnay in the refrigerator. It had a screw top.

I set down the corkscrew. White it was. Taking two glasses out of the cupboard, I retrieved the Chardonnay from the fridge and went into the living room.

'Which reminds me,' I said, unscrewing the cap. 'Did you find the wine bottle in the car?'

Pavlik peered at me uncomprehendingly. 'What reminds you?'

'The wine. Or, the red wine I didn't choose,' I said. 'It was Pinot, of course, rather than Sangiovese, but . . .' I shrugged.

'Having seen neither the Pinot, nor the Sangiovese,' he said, sitting up to take a glass from me, 'I'll have to take your word that they reminded you of something. But what?'

'Sorry,' I said, pouring Chardonnay in his glass and then doing the same for myself. 'Different crime, though involving the same people and probably, according to you, the impetus for this most recent one, but . . .' I glanced at Pavlik's face. 'Too much preamble?'

'By far.' He took a sip.

'You were going to check with Kelly Anthony to see if the partial bottle from the restaurant was in Vivian's car.'

'It wasn't,' Pavlik said, setting down his glass. 'Anthony followed up and apparently Mrs Shropshire took it with her when her daughter dropped her off.'

Room booze. Made sense, from what I'd seen. 'Vana was drunk when she arrived at the reception mid-afternoon.'

'Her daughter is dead,' Pavlik reminded me. 'She's probably not herself.'

'She's exactly herself, according to Philip.'

'Philip, who may have murdered an old man.'

'And his own wife.' I sat down next to him and tucked my legs up under me. 'But the only witness to Philip and Vivian arguing is dead.'

'Funny how that worked,' Pavlik said.

'But, as I was saying when you unlocked the door, don't you think Philip is a little obvious as a suspect?'

'Because the victim was killed on Philip's property, struck on the head with a rebar spike that Philip bought?'

I was almost afraid to ask, but: 'Does the rebar match Vivian's head wound, too?'

'No, her wound was more a bruise. Barely broke the skin. Besides, Woodward bought the parking blocks after the car went into the creek, remember? That was supposedly the reason.'

I'd seen the steel spikes on the ground this morning as Philip attempted to unload the unwieldy parking blocks. But had he removed them from the Land Rover before I arrived or did he already have them? 'We're sure he bought the blocks and the rebar spikes at the same time?'

A grin. 'Yes, we're sure. The receipt for both the rebar spikes and parking blocks is dated today.' He shook his head. 'Face it, Maggy. Woodward had the means and also the motive. Or is that too obvious, as well?'

'Well, I—'

'Sometimes it is obvious, Maggy. Most people who commit crimes aren't geniuses.'

'But Philip is smart,' I protested. 'And a crime buff. Noir, like *The Big Sleep*.'

'Liking crime literature doesn't make somebody a master criminal,' Pavlik said, getting up to let the dogs in.

Frank sniffed the coffee table and, finding nothing, laid down on the floor in front of me. Mocha waited for Pavlik to sit back down on the couch and then climbed into his lap, circling three times before settling, head on his thigh.

'But it's just stupid stuff,' I protested. 'Walter's body is in the shed, but Philip sits down to talk with me in the backyard facing that shed?'

'Was it Woodward who wanted to sit there?'

'No,' I admitted. 'I suggested it after I helped carry the groceries into the house, just to be safe.'

'Because he might be a killer.'

'Exactly,' I concurred. 'But Philip didn't object.'

'For all you know, he had bloody clothes stashed in the bathroom.'

Aren't we Mr Sunshine? 'That's another thing.'

'What is?' Pavlik was scratching the little dog behind her ear.

'Walter probably left the reception at about two forty-five. I got to Philip's at about a quarter past four and we discovered Walter's body about a half hour later. From two forty-five to four-fifteen is an hour and a half. That's not a lot of time to kill somebody and get cleaned up. And Philip has an alibi for most of that time. He was grocery shopping.'

'But not exactly a major buy from the sounds of it. At four he checked out after buying a gallon of milk, a carton of cereal, a loaf of bread and a pound of butter. What did you help him carry in?'

'The milk. They put it in a separate bag so it wouldn't crush the bread.' The bags had been from Schultz's Market, maybe a five-minute drive away. 'You're saying he killed Walter before that?'

'The message to meet was sent to Benson at two forty-three.'

'You recovered what was on the phone?' I asked a little surprised. 'I thought that might take a while, given it was wet.'

'We got lucky. It got hung up on some foliage just short of the creek.'

'That was careless,' I said.

'He was in a hurry. Grocery shopping to do.'

We scowled at each other.

I gave in first. 'What did the message say?'

'Shed, three p.m.'

Pavlik was right. There was plenty of time for Philip to hide in the shed, brain Walter at three, tidy up and still get to the store to check out sixty minutes later. 'But why would Walter agree to meet Philip when he had practically accused him of murder?'

'There must have been some earlier communication, something we haven't found yet. It's possible Benson was blackmailing Woodward.'

'Not very successfully. Walter had already reported that he'd seen Philip.'

'Yes, but not immediately, as you'll recall.'

The car had gone into the creek on Wednesday night. It was Friday morning when Eric told me that Benson had come forward about the argument. 'Walter didn't say he'd seen anything beyond the two talking.'

'Maybe there was something else that he was holding back for a price.'

'That he actually did hear the content of the argument? Or saw the car go into the water?'

Pavlik shrugged.

'This is all supposition,' I pointed out.

'Says the woman who supposes all the time.'

True. 'Wasn't Walter taking a chance, though, meeting somebody he knew had already killed?'

'During a domestic dispute. That's different than a cold-blooded, calculated killing.'

'And yet, you think Philip committed a cold-blooded, calculated murder to cover up the domestic dispute killing,' I said. 'I'm not sure I buy that. In fact, I find it hard to believe he'd kill Vivian because she was going to leave him.'

'Heat of the moment,' Pavlik said. 'He might have felt he was losing everything.'

Everything that he already hadn't lost. 'Still. Normal people don't do these things.'

'And yet they do. Every day.'

'Cynic.' We'd been face-to-face during this exchange and now I turned and leaned against him, displacing Mocha.

She hopped down.

'It's my job,' he said, putting an arm around me. 'I have one more piece of information you're not going to like.'

I glanced back at him. 'What's that?'

'The message on Walter's phone suggesting they meet. It was from a Boston phone number.'

'Philip's?'

I felt, rather than saw him nod. 'And just to make things tidy, we've found the corresponding sent message on Woodward's phone.'

EIGHTEEN

'How stupid would he have to be, I ask you. If you were setting up a meeting with your blackmailer, wouldn't you use a burner?'

It was Sunday and I'd opened the shop at six.

Sarah had walked in the door at seven thirty to my question. 'Well, I—'

'Especially if you planned to murder the man.'

She set her purse down on the counter. 'Of course I would. And to answer your first question, very stupid. Now who are we talking about?'

'Philip Woodward.' I was pacing. Good thing there wasn't another soul in the store besides Sarah and me. Bad thing, too, of course. Business-wise. Sundays were kind of a bust except for the seniors coming by.

'We're supposed to believe,' I continued, 'that this intelligent man invited the victim over to his house by text message *from* his own phone, killed the victim with one of the rebar spikes he'd just bought and then left the body in the shed – with the murder weapon – to attract birds.'

'Why did he want to attract birds?' Sarah asked, tying on her Uncommon Grounds apron.

'He didn't want to attract birds, they just came to pick over the body,' I said. 'Crows first, and then one very large turkey vulture.' I shuddered.

'Dramatic touch.' Sarah circled behind the counter to reappear at the espresso machine. 'Maybe he didn't plan to kill the victim.'

'So why invite him over?'

'To play pinochle? How the hell should I know?' Sarah was pulling a shot to brew.

'Pinochle? Who the hell plays pinochle?' I could swear, too.

'How should I know? It was the stupidest-sounding game

I could think of. You said this was a stupid person.' She was frothing milk now.

God forbid I should come between her and her latte. 'But even if it was an accident, wouldn't you cover better?'

'Like seal the body in heavy-duty plastic to keep the birds away? Or dissolve it in lye? Of course, I would.' She dumped the espresso into a mug and topped it with the milk. 'But that's just me.'

I glanced uncomfortably at her. 'Yes, well, accident or not, our victim is dead.'

'Which is why he's a victim.' She took a sip and made a face. 'Why do you keep calling him that?'

'Victim? Because both the perp and the victim are men. Got to keep them straight.'

'Gotcha.' She added a little more foam. 'Smart. Unlike your perp, as you say.'

'Exactly. So, tell me this: the victim is dead, but his phone contains a message from you luring him to the scene. What do you do with it?'

'Take it, wipe it, destroy it.'

'Right, right and right. Except this guy just tossed it in the creek but missed by so much that it landed on the bank undamaged.'

'Idiot.'

'Like I said.'

Sarah was leaning elbows on the counter. 'The victim is Walter Benson, right? I heard it on the news.'

'Oliver found him,' I told her. 'With the vulture, um . . .'

'Aw, jeez,' Sarah said, raising her hands to the top of her head like it might blow off. 'Kid can't catch a break. First his father and the snow-blower and then—'

'I know,' I said. 'Oliver spent the night with Gloria at the Manor, which was probably the best place for him.'

'Is he still planning to drive back to school with Eric?'

'Eric's already up there,' I told her. 'Oliver decided to stay here and fly back today.'

'Now he's probably sorry he did,' Sarah said.

'At least he got to see his grandfather one more time,' I said.

Sarah's jaw dropped. 'Dead and being eaten by vultures? If you think that's a good thing, I have a therapist for you to see.'

It was reassuring that Sarah had a therapist, at least. 'No, a couple hours before that I saw Oliver and Walter speaking.' I left out the part about arguing.

'What else?' Not much got past Sarah.

'It's just that they seemed to be having a disagreement.'

'Aw, jeez.' For the second time. 'You didn't tell Pavlik that, did you?'

'I barely told you,' I pointed out.

'I know. I had to beat it out of you,' Sarah said sarcastically.

'I just don't think it's relevant.' I was trying out the reasoning I'd use with Pavlik should I have to.

'Save it for Pavlik.'

I would. 'Anyway, I texted Eric late last night and told him what happened. He gave me Oliver's phone number, so I left a message for him to call me when he got up.'

'Call you?' Sarah was skeptical.

'Call, as a euphemism for text,' I said. 'Though Oliver has such nice manners, I thought there might be a chance.'

Sarah stuck her head out the service window and looked up at the clock. 'Not quite eight. It'll probably be a while.'

'I know,' I said. 'But I thought I might run over to Gloria's when we get a break here.'

'You did, huh?'

'Please?'

Sarah sniffed. 'You never tell me anything these days, yet you expect me to cover for you.'

'Sorry,' I said sincerely. 'Our shifts haven't been corresponding the last few days. But I'm here now, so what can I tell you?'

'Why Philip Woodward would want to kill Walter, for one thing.'

'Because Walter saw Philip arguing with Vivian before the car rolled into the creek, of course.'

'I know he said that, but the accusation didn't seem to go anywhere. Philip wasn't arrested. At least so far as *I* heard.' She wasn't going to let me off the hook.

'Not for Vivian's death. At the time, there was no physical evidence that it was anything but an accident. And Philip's motive – that he was a failure and a cheat and Vivian was going to leave him – was kind of weak.'

'People would be getting murdered all over the place if that was enough,' Sarah agreed.

'Right. Thing is that all changed when Walter was murdered. They found the message to Walter confirming a three o'clock meeting on Philip's phone.'

'He not only fumbled getting rid of Walter's phone, but didn't delete the message off his own?' Sarah rolled her eyes skyward. 'I assume he's been arrested.'

'Brought in last night,' I said. 'Charged this morning.'

'What's his explanation for the messages?'

'He hasn't given one,' I said. 'In fact, he's not talking at all.'

Sarah seemed to size up my expression. 'You warned him not to, didn't you?'

'Last night, before I knew about the text messages.' I grimaced. 'It seemed only fair. He's such a—'

'Idiot, like we said. Are you also going to get him a lawyer?'

'He's on his own for that,' I said, holding up my hands. 'I'm already in hot water for advising him to clam up.'

'Oooh. Sleeping on the couch?'

'Nah, it's Kelly Anthony who is ticked with me, not Pavlik. I think she was hoping this would be her big break.'

'Cuz her suspect is an idiot.'

'Exactly.' I brightened. 'But he is from Boston, so he probably has some good lawyers on speed dial.'

'He'll need them,' Sarah said, straightening up and glancing around. 'Is that your phone ringing?'

'Yeah, but I'm not sure where I left it.' I started toward the office, but the thing stopped ringing.

'Aside from all the angst over Philip, anything else going on?' Sarah had carried her cup and a sticky bun around and now took a seat at a table. 'I mean, anything besides our little corner of the world blowing up all of a sudden?'

I accepted the unspoken invitation and came to take the chair across from her. 'It is odd, isn't it? Baby Doe is discovered, Vivian dies, Walter is murdered – all in less than a week. And all centered around—'

'Philip.' She was cutting the sticky bun in eighths and now took one. 'Help yourself.'

'Eighths today? What happened to quarters?'

'I'm on a diet.' She took a second and shoved a piece toward me.

I took it. 'You know, you're right.'

'That eighths are better?' She frowned. 'I was thinking just the opposite.'

'No, that the common denominator is, if not Philip, the property he's living on. The Koeppler place sat there for years, but now something has been stirred up.' I set the bun down. 'This whole thing started with the discovery of Baby Doe. Maybe that's what this is all about.'

'We don't even know who Baby Doe is, though.'

'I think he was Paz and Harmony's son,' I said.

'Older or younger than Vana?'

'Younger, by maybe three or four years. Both Vickie and Carmen think Harmony was pregnant the summer of 1965.' My phone was ringing again, but I let it go. 'Vana was born in '62.'

'Don't you want to get that call?' Sarah asked. 'It might be Oliver.'

'I set up a special ring for him,' I said. '"Consider Yourself" from the musical *Oliver*. And "Gloria" – you know, the disco song? – for Mrs G, just in case.'

'You scare me.'

'Thank you,' I said, blushing. 'Mrs G's was easy, with her first name—'

'No,' Sarah said, reaching out to put her hand on mine. 'I really mean you're scaring me. I'll text you that therapist's name.'

I pulled back my hand. 'I don't need a therapist.'

Sarah, happy to have gotten a rise from me, grinned. 'Vickie LaTour thought Harmony was pregnant? What was she doing here back then? And who's Carmen?'

Sarah was right that it had been a while since we talked. I filled her in the best I could.

When I'd finished, she shook her head. 'This baby was maybe months old, but obviously lived long enough to be used as a punching bag. Yet nobody saw him. Not even Vana?'

'If she did, she's not talking,' I said. 'Or maybe she's just shut it out. She didn't even tell me that Paz ran off. I just assumed he'd died.'

'I thought he had, too,' Sarah said. 'Are you thinking he killed the baby? Mothers abuse their children, too.'

Sadly true. 'It's the timing. Paz left – split, as Henry put it—'

Sarah was holding up a hand. 'Wait. Henry was there, too?'

'Before he went into the service.'

'We have Harmony and Paz, Henry, Vickie, this Carmen, Walter – am I missing anybody?'

'Probably, but nobody who's still around, from what I can tell.'

'No Sophie?'

'She's a new transplant, came here thirty years ago. I think she feels left out. She keeps throwing dagger eyes at Henry when we talk about the sixties.'

'Sounds like she should be grateful she wasn't here,' Sarah said. 'You said that Paz and Vickie had something going. Was anybody else doing the dirty?'

'Carmen insinuated that she fooled around with pretty much everybody, but that might just be talk. Hers, I mean.'

Sarah grinned. 'I have to meet this woman.'

'Oh, you will. She might move into the Manor.'

'Which is the other side of the intersection of iniquity, isn't it?'

And they say I get dramatic. 'What do you mean?'

'I mean you have the Koeppler place here.' She took her cup off the saucer and used the saucer to illustrate. 'And across the way, Brookhills Manor.' For this she used the now empty bun plate.

'Which wasn't there then,' I reminded her.

'But a lot of people who were here are now at the Manor. The intersection of the two.' She shoved the two pieces of china together, lifting the edge of the saucer to go over the edge of the bun plate.

'Is a figure eight?'

She threw me a dark look.

'I get it,' I yielded. 'The intersection is the conflict over the land back then.'

'Ooh,' Sarah said, looking surprised. 'I was thinking more of the shed, the gravel lot and the compost heap. It is kind of the epicenter of evil, isn't it?'

'It is,' I said, feeling a little shiver. 'Next thing you know, a demon will emerge from the creek.'

'Somebody killed a child and dumped them in a garbage heap,' Sarah said, as my phone shrilled a message. 'We've already got our demon.'

Good point. 'I think I'll ask Pavlik if he can find anything on Paz,' I said, standing to go get my phone. 'His real name was Ray Koeppler?'

'Raymond on the deed. We could try Google, but since he disappeared before the Internet was around, we may not find anything.'

'Disappeared from here,' I reminded her. I was standing at the door to the office with my phone and punched up a missed voicemail. 'But we might find something in a search.'

I held up a finger while I listened.

'What?' Sarah asked, seeing my face.

'It was Pavlik.' I lowered the phone from my ear. 'The forensic anthropologist's initial results on the baby's skeleton are in sooner than expected. From his teeth, they estimate that he was somewhere around a year old.'

'A year?' Sarah looked as puzzled as I felt. 'Didn't they think he was younger from the size of the bones?'

'Yes, but there's more.'

'Don't tell me.' Her hand was over her mouth. 'He was not only beaten but starved.'

'No.' I waved for her to come into the office and sat down at the computer. 'Baby Doe's bones show clear indications of a disease. *Osgenesis* . . .' As I spoke, I was typing it into the search window.

'*Imperfecta*,' Sarah read over my shoulder, pointing at the results that had already popped up. 'Brittle bone disease. I've heard of it, but . . .'

We were both reading. I sat back first. 'The broken bones weren't the result of abuse. They were part of the disease.'

'Along with stunted growth. It says here,' Sarah was still reading, 'that in type two, the most severe form, the bones can even be broken in utero.'

'Some babies don't survive birth.' I couldn't imagine how they would, given the size of the birth canal and the pushing and . . . it didn't bear thinking about.

'Our Baby Doe must have,' Sarah said, as I reached past her and pushed print. 'Poor thing.'

I turned and met her eyes. 'But then what happened?'

'Raymond Koeppler? Google him.'

'I will, but wait a sec.' I punched a few lines into my phone and pushed send. 'Wanted to get Pavlik going on him, as well.'

'You don't think they already are?'

I cocked my head. 'Yes, but not in an immediate way. Baby Doe is a very old, very cold case.'

'Unless it's connected with what's happening here now.'

'Exactly,' I said, turning back to the computer.

'So search, already.' Sarah was hovering over my shoulder.

I did search for Ray or Raymond Koeppler, but too much information came up, too little of it applicable. 'We need a date of birth or place, even.'

'We don't know if Ray was born here, but maybe he and Harmony were married in the area,' Sarah suggested.

I searched marriage, Ray, Koeppler and Matilda and got a 'Looks like there aren't any good matches, you might want to try' message. 'It would help if we had her maiden name.'

'We could ask Vana,' Sarah suggested. 'Does she know that Philip has been picked up?'

'Probably not,' I said. 'Given everything she's said about him – and him about her – I kind of doubt Vana would be Philip's one phone call.'

'I'm surprised you weren't.'

I ignored that and checked the clock. 'Eight twenty on a Sunday morning. There's a chance Vana is sober.'

'And awake?'

'Probably not,' I admitted and snuck a glance at Sarah. 'But that doesn't mean I can't pound on the door until she is.'

'Caron will love that at her hotel,' Sarah said.

'Maybe I'll stop in at Mrs G's first.'

Sarah raised an eyebrow. 'You honestly think Oliver will be up? He's a teenage boy.'

'He's twenty, though that doesn't change sleeping habits. Regardless, Mrs G will be awake.'

'And she, in turn, will get him up and make him answer your questions,' Sarah said, tapping in more search terms.

'Exactly.' I waited. 'So maybe . . .'

She turned, resting her chin on one hand to regard me. 'You're honestly asking my permission to leave.'

'No, I . . .' I started to rise and then sat down again. 'Well, yes. I am.'

'Go.'

I got halfway up again. 'Are you sure?'

'Get out!'

You didn't have to tell *me* three times. I got the printouts from the computer and stuffed them in my purse. 'You're an angel.'

'Oh, Maggy,' Sarah called as I was about to go out the door, 'if you don't report back to me, I'm going to be less angel and more that demon we were talking about.'

'The one emerging from the epicenter of evil? Got it.'

NINETEEN

'Maggy?' Gloria Goddard peered at me as she tied the sash on her robe. 'It's a little early on a Sunday, is it not?'

'It is,' I admitted.

'Has something happened?' she asked, stepping back so I could come in. 'Something else, I mean, besides Walter's awful death.'

'Just Philip Woodward's arrest.' I followed her into the kitchen past open bedroom and bathroom doors. There was a blanket and pillow on the couch.

'Well now, that can't be much of a surprise, can it?' She was busying herself, putting water in the coffee machine. 'You'll want coffee?'

'If you're having one,' I said, sitting down at the table by the window. Gloria's apartment was on the second floor with a similar view to Sophie's and Henry's.

'You just woke me two hours before I'd be showing up for coffee at your shop,' she said, lifting her chin so I could see her profile. 'I would have expected you to bring it.'

Gloria Goddard of the high cheekbones and leggy . . . well, legs, should have been an old-time movie star or a famous model, instead of a drug store owner. But she'd fallen in love with a pharmacist named Hank with a gambling problem and the next fifty years were history.

'I should have thought of that.' I apologized. 'I like your place.'

'It's not an apartment above a pharmacy,' she said with a wry smile, plugging in the drip pot. 'But it is home. And I don't have to go down to the lunch counter to cook my meals.'

I laughed. 'I can't remember. Is this one or two bedrooms?'

'Just the one.' She cocked her head. 'Why?'

'Oliver,' I said. 'I was hoping to catch him.'

She sat down across from me. 'Catch him doing what?'

I laughed and ran my hand over the gold-and-black-swirled linoleum that topped the table. 'Is this from the pharmacy?'

Gloria nodded. 'It was intact under all that snow and fallen building, if you can believe it. Oliver just repaired a loose leg for me.'

'How is Oliver?' Where is Oliver?

She took a deep breath and let it out in a rush. 'I'm not sure, Maggy.'

I was getting worried. 'He did come here after he . . . after Walter and all, right? Told you what happened? What he saw?' I knew I should have made Oliver come home with us.

'Oh, yes, yes,' Gloria assured me. 'The vulture and all.' She shivered. 'It's awfully hard for the boy, you know. He's not quite sure what he should feel.'

'The Bensons were not exactly warm and fuzzy,' I said. 'In fact, Oliver is the only one—'

'The only one worth his salt,' Gloria finished for me. 'And that was my doing. Not Way, not Aurora, and sure as hell not Walter.' She shrugged. 'But he was his grandfather, and you know what they say.'

'Blood is thicker than water?'

'Nope. You can choose your friends, but you can't choose your family. So, Oliver was stuck with him.'

Until now. 'Is Oliver all right?'

Gloria hesitated, not meeting my eyes. 'I hope so. He left in the middle of the night.'

'But why? And how? Did he go back to school?' How would he get there?

She shook her head. 'He's afraid, Maggy.'

My heart dropped. 'Of what? He didn't do anything, did he? To Walter?'

Gloria's face changed from concern to anger. 'What kind of boy do you think my Oliver is?'

'A good one,' I said. 'It's just that I saw Oliver and Walter talking yesterday afternoon and it seemed like they were arguing.'

She cocked her head. 'He told me he talked to Walter, but nothing about an argument.'

'Then what were they talking about?'

Gloria's jaw had a stubborn jut to it. 'No idea.'

'It could be important. And you know that I would never do anything to hurt Oliver.' I reached over and took her hand. 'You know that I protected him back—'

'Yes, yes.' She yanked her hand away and stood up. 'Back when Way died. I do know that. It's just . . .' She turned to face me. 'He didn't tell me what they talked about. Only that they spoke and a few hours later Walter was dead.'

'People die,' I said, as she fiddled with the coffeemaker. 'More than they should in Oliver's young life.'

'But that's just it,' Gloria said, coming back to the table with the pot. 'Since his mother and father's deaths, I think he has felt like he was cursed or something. Like Jonah in the Bible.'

'A jinx?'

'Yes.' She realized she hadn't brought mugs and went back for them. 'When I had my stroke, I had to convince him that it wasn't because he'd left for college.'

'And now he thinks Walter is his fault?'

'It's worse than that.' She set the mugs on the table and went back again for the pot.

I took it from her and poured coffee into the mugs. 'Worse how?'

She let out a sigh and sank into her chair, wrapping her hands around the mug I slid to her. 'Twice as worse, if that's an expression. This woman, the one who drowned.'

'Vivian?' Where was this going?

'Yes, that's it. Oliver said he was working there and talked to her.'

'And then she died.'

'He's afraid it's going to happen to me.' Gloria was staring into her coffee cup.

'Which is why he left?'

'Yes.' She looked up. 'I tried to make light of it. Tell him I'm an old woman and was going to kick off sometime anyway.' She cleared her throat. 'Sometimes I worry about that, you know? How he's going to cope when I'm gone?'

'I think we'll get him a dog,' I said, without thinking, and then caught her expression. 'Did that sound callous?'

'A little.' But Gloria couldn't quite suppress the smile that was playing at her lips. 'Apparently you've given this some thought.'

'Nothing personal,' I said. 'But the fact is that most situations are made better by the right dog.'

'Unconditional love. Which you got from your Frank.'

'And gave.' I picked up my cup now. 'Ted gone, Eric at school. Nobody died, but I felt like my life was over. Frank saved me.'

'I can't even have a canary here.'

I glanced at the window. 'I could swear I heard Sugarlips the last time we talked on the phone.'

'You weren't the only one. Somebody ratted me out. I had to find a new home for him.'

'That sucks.'

'You're telling me,' Gloria said. 'Only thing I don't like about this place.'

'People in your business?'

'No, just people. Period.'

I've had those days myself. 'Thing is, Gloria. Don't worry about Oliver in the future. We'll take care of him. But I am worried about him right now. That scene yesterday' – I swallowed hard – 'it was horrific. And it wasn't even somebody I liked very much.'

Gloria shrugged a *who did?* kind of shrug.

'Do you have any idea where Oliver is?' I asked after a moment.

Gloria's lips tightened, but she shook her head.

'I texted him, but now I'm not sure he'll get back to me.' Not if the boy was afraid people would die if he spoke to them.

'I doubt it,' was all Gloria said.

I waited a beat or two and, nothing more forthcoming, checked my phone. 'It's after nine – I should be going. I need to see Vivian's mother.'

Gloria stood and followed me to the door. 'Tell her I'm sorry. Oliver, too. I know he was trying to get hold of her.'

'I will.'

Gloria went to shut the door and then hesitated. 'I said when you first got here that Oliver was scared.'

'Yes.' I didn't want to stop her or put words in her mouth.

'He is, but . . .' She took a deep breath and then continued, the words falling over themselves. 'But I don't think it's all in his head – some magical jinx, like you say. I believe he's literally afraid that someone killed Vivian and Walter because he spoke to them.'

'About what?' I was literally begging. 'Please.'

She winced. 'I don't know. He wouldn't tell me.'

'Because he thought that would put you in danger, too,' I guessed.

'Exactly,' Gloria said.

I touched her arm. 'When you talk to him, tell him that Philip is in jail. He can't hurt anyone.'

'He knows that,' Gloria said.

'Then who's he afraid of?'

'I don't know,' she said again. 'And I'm not sure Oliver does either. But I will tell you it's somebody who is not locked up. Or that he's afraid won't stay locked up. And I can tell you one other thing – something that Oliver would never say to me.'

I waited.

'Way, Aurora, Walter, Vivian. All dead.'

'Yes.' This was not news.

'Oliver believes he is next.'

TWENTY

Oliver was afraid for his life and the lives of anyone he talked to.

But talked to about what? Just any subject? I didn't think so, but I wasn't going to get more out of Gloria, even if she knew.

Not sure where to go with all this, I kept to plan.

Hotel Morrison.

Unfortunately, Caron Egan wasn't manning the front desk at her hotel. Not surprising on a Sunday morning. The perks of ownership, though those perks were largely nonexistent when it came to coffeehouse ownership. As I said, Sarah and I routinely took home less money than we paid Amy in salary. I hoped for Caron and Bernie's sake that hotel profit margins were a little better.

Anyway, sans Caron, the desk clerk wouldn't give me Vana's room number, so I had to be satisfied simply calling her room from my cell phone over and over again. By the fourth call the poor woman at the desk who was answering my call with a cheery 'Hotel Morrison' only to be asked to connect me to Vana Shropshire's room – again – was openly glowering at me.

'You could just let the phone in her room ring for a while,' I suggested to her, since I was leaning on the opposite side of her counter.

'It can only ring six times,' she told me, 'before it goes to voicemail.'

'And I have to call back,' I said, counting the rings. 'You can see the inefficiency of—'

'Hello?' Vana's voice was groggy.

'Vana,' I said. 'This is Maggy Thorsen. I have to talk to you. It's important.'

'Maggy who?'

'Maggy Thorsen,' I repeated a little self-consciously. The desk clerk was smirking. 'You know, the coffeehouse owner?'

Nothing.

'The sheriff's fiancé?' I tried.

'Oh, yes. I just woke up, all thanks to you, and have a bit of a headache. Can I call you back later?'

I bet she had a headache. But it sure wasn't my fault. 'I'm actually downstairs. Can I come up?'

'I *told* you.' There was steel in her voice as she bit off each word. 'You woke me up. I'm not dressed, and I haven't had my coffee.'

You can't say I don't learn from my mistakes. 'Give me your room number and I'll bring up a pot,' I told her. 'Is French press OK?'

A hesitation, then: 'Actually, perfect. The room is 208.'

Score.

The Hotel Morrison lobby coffee bar specialized in pressing the brew fresh in a piston pot at your table. It provided the ceremony of making espresso drinks but was a lot faster. I had the waiter put the just boiled hot water in the pot, let it rest for thirty seconds, then add the coffee to bloom. Fifteen seconds and he stirred it, put the top on the pot and handed me the mugs to carry.

By the time I reached room 208 and the door opened, three minutes had elapsed. 'One more minute to steep,' I said, trying to hand her the mugs.

She waved me to the little kitchenette. 'I don't need a lesson in French press coffee,' she said irritably, tying up her robe.

'Good, then sit,' I said, setting the press pot and mugs on the counter. The alcohol stench by the sink almost made me gag. The woman had started early.

Moving the mugs to the table where Vana was obediently sitting, I went back for the piston pot. Slowly pressing the plunger down to trap the grounds at the bottom, I poured the strong dark brew into our mugs.

I'd barely finished before Vana had her hands wrapped around the cup like Gloria Goddard had and took a sip. 'Mmm.' She looked up. 'Now what do you want that's so important you had to wake me up?'

'It's Philip.'

'What about him?' she asked, plainly not caring.

'Why do you hate him?' I asked her, genuinely curious. 'Your daughter must have loved him enough to marry him.'

'My daughter was betrayed by a charming man who told her what she wanted to hear and then went ahead and did whatever it was he wanted to do,' she said, setting down her cup. 'I know the type.'

Uh-oh. 'Your husband?'

She laughed, a little bitterly. 'Gilbert was much older and eventually the glow of being swept away by a rich older man fades. I imagine the same is true of landing a woman who is decades younger than you. But I did right by Gilbert until the day he died. People admired me.'

'But Vivian's marriage was different?'

'She loved Philip, so his betrayals cut her deeply. She is . . . was, more sensitive than me.'

That wasn't saying much. 'Philip has been arrested.'

Vana closed her eyes, sucking in a long breath before letting it back out again and opening them. 'Then he did kill my daughter.'

'Actually, it's Walter Benson's murder he's been charged with.'

Her eyes flew open wider yet, and I could see the spider web of red veins on the white. 'Walter is dead? But why . . .' She stopped. 'Because he was the only witness, of course. He saw Philip kill Vivian.'

Walter had only seen the two arguing, but I just said, 'That's the apparent motive.'

'But then why hasn't he been charged with Vivian's murder, too? I don't understand.' She stood up, rubbing her arms. 'I stopped at the cottage yesterday afternoon. Philip makes my skin crawl with his fake concern.'

'I'm surprised you recall,' I said, a little cruelly. 'You were very drunk yesterday.'

'I . . . I . . . well, yes,' she said, sitting back down again. 'I had reason to have a few. My daughter is dead. Murdered.' She shivered.

'There's always a reason,' I said softly.

'For an alcoholic to drink, you mean.' She shivered again

and leaned over to get a coverlet from the bed, pulling it over her shoulders. 'I used to be a high-functioning alcoholic, as they call it. Nobody knew. I've slipped now, but I'll get it under control again.' She hesitated. 'Did I make a scene? At the reception, I mean?'

I grimaced. 'A bit. How much do you remember?'

'I remember having vodka and orange juice with my brunch and then going to the reception, where they served surprisingly good Prosecco. A woman with the Hermes scarf, which explained the good Prosecco. I talked to you. And Walter, I think. Did he notice I was drunk?'

'Oh, yes.' I had no intention of sparing her feelings.

Vana cringed. 'And now the man is dead, so I can't even redeem my reputation. I hope I didn't—'

'You called him upright, said you couldn't imagine him smoking joints with your parents.'

'Well, that's not too bad,' she said, seeming relieved. 'When did he . . . or when did Walter . . . how . . .?'

'How and when did he die?' I asked. 'A little later in the afternoon. A blow to the head.' I didn't give more details. 'Where were you after you left the reception?'

'I stopped at the cottage,' she said. 'I told you.'

'What time was that?'

She squinched her eyes. 'I honestly don't know. I crossed the road from the reception and saw the door open. I felt compelled to go in and scream at Philip – tell him exactly what I thought of him.'

'For how long?'

'Not long, I think,' she said. 'Like I said, it's a little hazy.'

'And then what?'

'Why, I came back here,' she said. 'Demolished the minibar.' She pointed to the door of the thing, which was ajar. Tiny empty bottles of liquor were lined up on the dresser. The woman hadn't been picky.

'How did you get back here?' I asked, picking up the trash basket and sweeping the bottles into it.

'Walked, of course,' she said. 'Or I'm sure you'd say staggered.'

'Anybody see you?'

'Maybe.' She shrugged. 'I think I farted a couple of times and thought it was terribly funny. Somebody may have heard me.'

Oy vey.

She saw my expression and rubbed her forehead. 'I know. Not a good look for a woman who prides herself on being classy.'

'But classic for an alcoholic,' I said.

She glanced at me questioningly.

'Not me, my grandfather,' I told her. 'He thought he was high-functioning, too.'

She didn't answer.

'It only makes it worse, you know.'

'What worse?'

'The depression.'

'Yes.' She sat there in silence for a moment before lifting the coffee to her lips. 'You know, this really is good. I think I prefer it to espresso drinks.'

'Don't say that,' I said automatically.

'You don't do French press at your shop?' she asked, seeming glad for the diversion.

'I promised Caron that we wouldn't, so the Morrison could have it as its own shtick,' I said.

'Well, that was stupid.'

Tell me how you really feel. 'Maybe, but Caron was my partner and I felt like I owed it to her.'

'Why? Did you leave her, or did she leave you?' Vana was eyeing me over her cup.

'I told you, we weren't partners like that.'

'Oh, I know,' she said, setting it down. 'But I also know any kind of partnership is tricky. Which is why I told Vivian and Philip that I wanted nothing to do with the shop. They could just pay me rent.'

'You told me the deed is still in your parents' names, but why?' I asked, sensing an opening to delve further. 'Your mother has been dead a year and your father . . . well, somebody told me he's been gone for years.'

'Somebody who?' she said, frowning.

'I'm not sure,' I said. 'There are a number of people at the

Manor who remember your parents. Walter, of course, and Henry Wested. Vickie LaTour, Carmen Petra.'

'Carmen?' she asked, thinking. 'Is she the redhead?'

'I don't know what color Vickie's hair was back then. But she's a redhead now and Carmen has dark hair. Carmen was the woman wearing the scarf you admired.'

'Appreciated, not admired,' Vana corrected.

Fine. I pulled out my phone and punched up the photo Vickie had shown me. 'That's your mom and dad in the middle. Walter is next to your mom, Carmen next to him. Vickie, next to your dad. Do you remember them?'

She squinted and then shrugged. 'Maybe.'

'Gianni was Carmen's maiden name. I don't know about Vickie.'

'I would only have heard first names or nicknames anyway,' Vana said, starting to open up a bit about her childhood.

I figured it was because she didn't want to talk about her drinking, but that didn't mean I couldn't take advantage of it. 'Do you remember people coming around? Friends of your folks?'

'Sure. Smoking pot, like I said to Walter. I had my first toke on a joint when I was five.' She held up a hand. 'I picked up the thing and did what I saw the adults do. My mom was horrified.'

'What about your dad?'

She tried to glance out the window, but the curtains were still pulled.

I got up and opened them. 'When did he leave?'

'Which time?' she asked. 'Pa came and went and came and went. One day he just' – she gestured to the skyline outside the window – 'stayed gone.'

Pa. As in father and also short for Paz. 'How old were you?'

'Maybe six or seven?' She shifted uncomfortably, drawing the coverlet closer. 'Why are you asking all this?'

'The baby.'

'What bab . . . Oh.' She appeared to have forgotten.

I wasn't buying it. 'A couple of these people remember your mom being pregnant in 1965. How old were you then?'

'Me? Three, I guess. I was born in 1962.'

'Would she have told you that you were having a little brother or sister?'

'I suppose so.' Her gaze was moving around the room like she was searching for an escape route.

'Then did she? Tell you, I mean.'

She swiveled to meet my eyes and I could see the child she'd been. 'Maybe. I'm not sure . . .'

'Was your mom happy about it? About the baby, I mean?'

An almost involuntary smile crossed her face. 'Mama loved babies,' she said softly.

'And she had this baby?' It was as if I was asking questions of somebody who was hypnotized or in a fugue state. It almost seemed unfair, but if Vana kept answering, I'd keep making assumptions. 'A baby boy.'

A tear rolled down her cheek. 'Joey.'

'What happened to Joey?' My voice was hoarse.

'He died.' Her fist went to her eye like the five-year-old she would have been when he died. 'He was so little. I should have been more careful.'

'Joey was sick,' I whispered, my voice breaking.

'He woke up and was crying. I just wanted to hold him.' She startled, like she'd just awakened herself.

'Oh, my God,' she said, meeting my eyes fully now. 'I think I killed him.'

'No.' I was horrified that I made her remember this thing. This sad, sad thing. 'You were a little girl and Joey was ill. It was up to your parents to take care of him, to protect him. And you.'

'I wasn't supposed to talk about him,' she said, leaning over to grip my hand as the coverlet fell off her shoulders. 'Not ever. And they . . .' Her eyes were huge. 'I don't know what they did with him.'

'I think . . .' My voice cracked, and I started again. 'I think they buried him in the backyard. Maybe they thought it was the most . . . natural.'

'They were protecting me,' she said, trying to draw herself up. 'Nobody knew what I had done. But then Pa left, and Mama was never the same. She was broken, too.'

'And you thought it was your fault,' I said, squeezing her hand. 'It wasn't.'

'I know, I know,' she said, shaking her head. 'I was little, but . . . I should have been better.'

'There's something you need to know. Something that even your mother and father might not have known.'

Now she did sit up straight and pull her shoulders back. 'What more can there possibly be? How much worse can it get?'

'Joey was born with something called *osteogenesis imperfecta.*'

'What?' It was like Vana was surfacing, clawing her way up in a way her daughter hadn't been able to. 'What are you talking about?'

'He had brittle bone disease. It's genetic. Either your mom or dad must have been a carrier.' I leaned down to retrieve my purse and pull out the article I'd printed. I flattened the papers and pushed them in front of her.

'Four types,' she read. 'How do you know what type he had? Or even that he had this at all?'

'Pavlik noticed a healing fracture on the femur we—'

'Which is why you asked me about abuse?'

'Yes,' I said. 'Once the forensic pathologist had the full skeleton, she could see multiple fractures, some healing. But also deformities of the bones and skull that were consistent with—'

'*Osteo . . .*'

'*Osteogenesis imperfecta.*'

'Imperfect bone formation.'

'Yes,' I said. 'The body has trouble producing collagen.'

'I didn't kill him.' Vana said it with genuine astonishment, trying to get used to the idea. 'But I hurt him,' she said, meeting my eyes again. 'He cried and cried and the more I tried to help him, the more he cried. I was breaking his tiny bones.'

'It's not your fault,' I said again.

Vana closed her eyes and took another deep breath, letting it out fully before saying, 'I understand. Or, at least, I'm trying to understand. It's just that I've kept this horrible guilt hidden for so long, I'm not even sure I knew it was there. It was only when you asked if my mother was happy that she was pregnant that it clicked. Because she was. And then it all went away.

Joey, my father, eventually me.'

'Did you ever talk about any of this with your mother?'

'You've seen how I am about the past,' Vana said. 'My mother was even worse. And once I left, she wanted nothing to remind her. Including me.'

'So she suffered alone,' I said.

'Would she have known if she had *osteogenesis imperfecta*?' Vana was getting the words right now.

'I only know what's in there,' I said, nodding at the papers on the table. 'But it says there's a fifty percent chance that a parent with the disease will pass it on to a child.'

'I was the lucky fifty percent then.' She frowned. 'As for my mother, I don't remember her breaking a bone or even being sick. I'm not sure about my father.'

'Like you said, there are four types of varying severity so maybe you wouldn't know if one of them had the mildest form,' I said. 'About your dad. Do you have cousins on that side? Aunts or uncles?'

Vana seemed to give that question more thought than I would have imagined necessary. 'He had a sister, I think,' she finally said.

'You never met her?'

She shook her head. 'But I remember my mother saying Pa's sister had filed a missing person report. She was irritated about it.'

'A missing person report on your dad?'

'Yes. Mama knew how he could be, but she said this sister was all upset.'

'To be fair, maybe she had reason,' I pointed out. 'He didn't come back the last time.'

'True. I don't think my mother had any family at all on her side, so she wasn't used to having to answer to anybody. I think she might have been an orphan or something. Are you trying to find information on her, too?'

'I did try,' I admitted. 'Any chance you remember her maiden name? Or was it on her death certificate?'

'I'm afraid not,' Vana said.

'Without it, I can't even find a marriage license. Do you know where they were married?'

'Sorry,' Vana said, pushing back her chair. 'Is it important?'

'Not really,' I said. 'I was more interested in your dad because of the baby. I thought maybe he'd hurt Joey' – it was good to finally have a name – 'and taken off.'

'But instead, he just took off.'

'It must have been an awful time for all of you,' I said, getting up. 'If you want to see if you can find him, you should start with that missing person report. Track down his sister and go from there.'

'Good idea,' she said, walking me to the door. 'But maybe not right away.'

I got that. 'By the way.' I turned back as I stepped into the hallway. 'Did Oliver ever talk to you?'

'Oliver?'

'Oliver Benson, Way's son. He wanted me to pass on his condolences.'

'Oh,' Vana said, a little surprised. 'Yes, I think he left a message.'

'But you didn't see him?'

'No,' she said, and the door closed.

I should have known that, I told myself as I took the hall to the hotel's elevators. Vana's still alive.

TWENTY-ONE

True to my word, I reported back to Sarah. It being Sunday, the group of seniors that frequented the lunch counter at Goddard's Pharmacy, before it fell down, had descended upon Uncommon Grounds. Self-dubbed the Goddard Gang, the gang members chatted incessantly, drank a lot and paid very little. And what little they did pay, they groused about. Still, we were happy to have them. Without commuter trains, Sunday was a quiet day and the gang made it viable for us to be open. Though we did still close at three.

It was just past one now and the Goddard Gang was gone.

'You didn't warn Vana not to invite Oliver, the portender of doom, across her threshold?' Sarah asked, taking a swipe at a jam smear on a table.

'I think it's vampires you're not supposed to invite in.' I gathered up an empty juice bottle, two cups and a plate and stacked the dishes on the counter. 'But no,' I said, turning with the bottle. 'I am worried about Oliver. He—'

Sarah had already moved on. 'This business with the baby is horrible,' she said, sinking into a chair at the table she'd been wiping. '*Osteogenesis imperfecta*. Poor Baby Doe—'

'Joey,' I corrected, crossing toward the condiment cart by the door.

'Joey,' she said. 'Poor Vana.'

I tried to stuff the bottle in the bin of recyclables under the cart.

'Just leave it next to it,' Sarah said. 'You can empty the bin later.'

'I' could, could I? Nonetheless, I did what I was told and, grabbing the rag to finish wiping the table between us, sat down across from her.

'All that time, Vana believed she killed her baby brother and ripped apart her family,' Sarah said. 'How do you live with that?'

'Repress it,' I said. 'Which is just what she did. Paz and Harmony didn't help her deal with it when it happened, of course. They all just pretended Joey never existed. She didn't even get to mourn him.'

'None of them did, I guess,' Sarah said. 'But you can kind of understand it. They really did think she'd hurt him. They were trying to protect her.'

'A three or four-year-old would hardly be put in jail for an accident,' I said. 'And if they'd taken Joey to a hospital, they'd have known about the brittle bone disease.'

'I'm not so sure back then,' Sarah said. 'It's more likely they'd take one look at the broken bones, new and old, and assume abuse.'

'Like we did,' I admitted. 'Then they'd have taken Vana into protective custody and locked up Paz and Harmony for child abuse.'

'As screwed-up as it turned out,' Sarah said, 'I guess it could have been worse.'

'Worse than burying your child in the backyard?' But I understood what she was saying. 'They also probably had no record of Joey's birth at home, so no way of even proving that he was theirs.'

'It was easier to just pretend he never existed.' She gave a little shake of her head.

'It's all so sad,' I acknowledged. 'But at least now Vana can bury her little brother. Maybe that will give her some peace.'

'She's also burying her daughter,' Sarah reminded me.

I picked up my phone. 'I'm going to tell Vana to call Pavlik. For her own good, it's best he hear all this from her.'

'He doesn't know any of it?'

'You're the first person I've told,' I said. 'Like I promised.'

'Then for your own good, I'd take the time to explain it all to him. Before Vana cold-calls him.'

She had a point. 'So much for our epicenter of evil,' I said, setting down the phone.

'You're giving up on your theory that the discovery of the baby's—'

'Joey,' I said again.

An annoyed grimace for my trouble. 'That the discovery of Joey's body, Vivian's drowning and Walter's bludgeoning were connected?'

I sighed and stood up. 'Just saying it like that, it sounds unlikely. Not even a consistent method.'

'But maybe a consistent motive?' Sarah suggested, as I went to slide the blue recycling basket out from under the condiment cart.

'If so, that motive is to cover up something,' I said. 'I thought that "something" was Joey's death. But that kind of went up in smoke when—'

'Don't forget the juice bottle.'

'Got it,' I said, snagging the thing. 'Can you open the door for me?'

'If you shove the bottle in the basket, you'll have a free hand.'

'Please.'

With a put-upon groan, she got up and pushed open the door. 'Dump that stuff in the bin and when you get back I'll have the garbage for you to take out.'

Gee, thanks. I walked down the porch steps toward the concrete apron where the commercial-sized blue recycle bin and green garbage bins stood waiting for their Monday pickup by the city. The clinking of the bottles in my basket reminded me of the ones lined up in Vana's hotel room. All alcohol, not juice, of course. The woman had a real problem and if she really had been a 'high-functioning' alcoholic, she had taken a tumble from that to crude drunk.

The thought of the elegant woman farting and laughing her way down the street after the reception . . . I shook my head, absent-mindedly flipping open a bin. The stench told me I'd gotten the garbage bin, rather than recycle, so I hastily closed the lid and moved on.

But my hand froze as I went to open the next.

Stench.

The alcohol smell from Vana's sink this morning was fresh booze, not stale from the night before. Believe me, as the granddaughter of an alcoholic, I knew the difference. That's why I'd thought she'd 'started early'. But there were no glasses in the sink and, though there were plenty of empty minibar bottles she could have downed directly, the smell seemed to be emanating from the sink itself. Hard liquor of any or many types, poured down the drain. Not wine.

Which raised the question of the half-full bottle of Sangiovese from the restaurant. There was no sign of it in Vana's room, not that it necessarily meant anything. She could have finished the bottle Wednesday night after being dropped off by Vivian and before she knew her daughter was dead. Or certainly, if not then, on Thursday. The empty bottle would have been cleared out by housekeeping the next day.

But we had only Vana's word it had been there in the first place. Or that she'd drunk everything in the minibar rather than pouring it down the drain while I was on my way up to the room.

In fact, we had only Vana's word that she had fallen to sloppy drunk from the high-functioning alcoholic she'd been all her life.

What had Philip said? When he went into the front room to pick up his keys and phone to go to the store, Vana was already there. She'd even admitted that she'd screamed at him when he'd appeared.

But . . . what if the screaming drunk act was just a cover-up for being caught there? What if Vana wasn't as drunk as she'd pretended?

If Vana had found Philip's phone in the kitchen and sent Walter the message luring him to the shed, it would explain the enormous stupidity of Philip not getting rid of that message. He didn't realize it was there. It would also explain the feeble attempt to deep-six Walter's.

I thought again of Vana 'staggering' back to the hotel from the cottage after the confrontation with Philip. The Hotel Morrison was just a few blocks down Brookhill Road or, if Vana had preferred a quieter route, up Junction Road past Uncommon Grounds to Elm, and then east. She—

'Are you going to stand there with your hand on the lid forever?' Sarah's voice demanded.

Another 'stench' made me wrinkle my nose. This, though, emanated from the bag of trash my partner had just smacked me with.

'Stop it,' I told her. 'I'm trying to work something out.'

'What? How to open the damned bin? It'll be tomorrow and the garbage truck will have come and gone before—' She opened the brown garbage bin and tossed in the bag, then went to open the blue.

I slapped her hand. 'I want to.'

'What?' Sarah stepped back and folded her arms. 'Help yourself.'

I did just that, flipping back the top.

And there, under an empty water bottle and used paper towels, I found a Sangiovese-soaked Luc's Ristorante to-go bag.

TWENTY-TWO

'Yes, yes, thanks, Luc. Eleven fifty-seven. Right.'

The wine-soaked bag with the broken remains of the Sangiovese bottle inside was sitting on a paper towel on the table between Sarah and me, time and date-stamped receipt still stapled to the top of the bag. Next to it were the nitrile gloves I'd worn to retrieve it from the bin.

I ended the call. 'Luc spoke with his valet and confirmed that Vivian was driving the Lexus when she and Vana left the restaurant.'

'There goes your theory,' Sarah said, getting up with a grunt.

'Not quite,' I said. 'I then asked Luc to check with the attendant in the booth of the parking lot across the street. That's what took so long. The woman saw a dark-colored sedan stop halfway down the block and the occupants get out and switch sides. She specifically remembered because she wasn't sure either of them was capable of driving. She was going to offer to keep the car in her lot and call them an Uber, but they took off before she could.'

'Wow.' Sarah sat back down a little dazed. 'I didn't think you were going to pull that off.'

'Me neither, at first. The valet was so sure.'

'Have you called Pavlik?'

'Not yet. I'm still trying to piece it together. This' – I pointed to the bottle – 'proves that Vana walked past here that night. The only reason to do that rather than walk straight down Brookhill Road is not to be seen.'

'And you've also proved she was driving the car.'

'Why not just keep the bottle, though? Take it to the hotel?'

'Because it was already broken. She couldn't walk into a respectable hotel lobby with that mess.' I cocked my head to study the red wine-soaked bag. 'Is that blood?' I pointed, but did not touch.

'Or tomato sauce,' Sarah said, leaning in to look more closely. 'Whichever, it's thicker than wine.'

And redder than creek water. 'Vivian had a contusion on her forehead.'

'Like Walter?'

'No, this was more a bruise than a gash, caused by something that just broke the skin.'

'Like a bottle.'

'Or the windshield or something in the car as it went into the water. If it was the Sangiovese bottle, they won't find glass from it in the car because it's all in there.' I nodded at the bag.

'But the wine soaked through the bag,' Sarah said. 'Maybe they'll find that on Vivian.'

'She was in the water for a good hour.' I shook my head. 'No, I think if we hadn't found this bottle, there would have been no way of proving Vivian was struck. The proof will be on this bag, not in the car.'

'Thank you.'

I glanced uncertainly at her. 'For what?'

'For the "we found". It was you who found it.'

'Just throwing you a bone.' I patted her hand.

She knocked it away. 'I know.'

I grinned. 'I guess this certainly rules out accident.'

'Ya think?' Sarah asked sarcastically. 'I don't see Vana driving Vivian home, conking her with a bottle and then absent-mindedly letting the car roll into the water. You?'

'No,' I said. 'Could somebody else have hit Vivian with the bottle and disposed of it after Vana left?'

'Philip came out and argued with her, like Walter said,' Sarah posited for the sake of argument. 'Maybe Vivian had the bottle, swung it at him, and he took it off her and beaned her?'

'Good try,' I said, appreciatively. 'Except for one thing I'm not sure you know.'

'There are many things I haven't known,' Sarah said sourly. 'Give.'

'I told Pavlik they'd taken the rest of the Sangiovese home with them. It wasn't in the car and when they asked Vana, she said she took it with her when Vivian dropped her off.'

'Two lies, both of which are going to bite her in the butt. Vivian didn't drop her off and here's the bottle. So how does Walter fit in?'

'He saw Vana on the parking apron of the cottage and knew she'd lied.'

'And blackmailed her,' Sarah said. 'Do you think part of the deal was that Walter would implicate Philip?'

'Maybe,' I said, thinking about it. 'Vana certainly disliked him and he's the logical patsy.' The spouse. Always the go-to in a murder investigation.

'So Walter calls the police and tells them he saw Philip arguing with Vivian wearing a robe. Kind of a weird offhand detail.'

'I think that detail was on purpose. Vana was wearing a skirt with her Louboutins that night.'

Sarah hesitated for a second and then nodded. 'If somebody else saw them, he'd be covered for thinking a woman was a man?'

'Exactly. There are windows facing in that direction, as evidenced by Sophie spotting the headlights in the creek. But Vana's animosity toward Philip aside, why implicate him or anybody at all? The initial assumption was that Vivian's death was an accident. Why not leave it that way?'

'He saw Vana wielding that' – she nodded at the wine bottle – 'and she, obviously, knew what she'd done.'

'They were afraid the autopsy would turn up something.'

'And didn't want to be left holding the bag.' She grinned. 'So to speak.'

'Even so, why did Walter get involved at all? Why not turn Vana in or, alternatively, turn a blind eye to the whole thing?'

'He's a Benson,' Sarah said dryly. 'This was a money-making opportunity. Walter blackmails Vana and gets rid of Philip, all in one fell swoop.'

I sat up straight. 'You're saying it wasn't just Vana who wanted Philip out of the way. The Koeppler property could have been the price Walter demanded.'

'Exactly.' Sarah was visibly delighted by the way things were falling together. 'Walter gets back what he considers

Benson property in the first place and, with Philip in jail and Vana under his thumb, nobody can kick up a fuss.'

'But Walter is the one who got his father to settle with the Koepplers,' I pointed out.

'Says Walter.'

True. Though Carmen believed Walter had a soft spot for Harmony. With Paz long gone and presumably Walter's marriage over, maybe he had hoped to score some points with Harmony. Or maybe the man actually had a heart and simply wanted to make sure the 'hippy-dippy' was taken care of. Nah. 'I'd love to get a look at Walter's cell phone to see if he called Vana first or vice-versa.'

'Why would Vana call him?'

'She knew he'd seen her?'

'It's possible,' Sarah said. 'But I think it's more likely the other way around. He contacted her.'

I had to agree. 'Pavlik will have Walter's cell phone. And can get Vana's.' I slid my own phone out and went to push '1' on speed dial.

'Two,' Sarah corrected. 'One is pizza delivery.'

'I changed it,' I told her as Pavlik's phone rang out. 'And my priorities. Damn, it's gone to voicemail.'

'Try Kelly Anthony?'

'I think not,' I said. 'I'm pretty proud of this one and I'd like to lay it all out for Pavlik.'

'I bet you would.'

Hee, hee, hee. 'Stop.'

'Fine.' She seemed disappointed. 'Back to blackmail, though. How would Walter have gotten hold of Vana? Did he have her cell phone number?'

'I don't think so. He did give her his card when they first met, but she didn't reciprocate that I saw.'

'Then maybe you're right and she called him.'

'Or,' I said, raising a finger, 'he could have called her at the hotel.'

'He knew where she was staying then?' She rolled her eyes. 'What am I saying? Only game in town.'

'In Brookhills certainly. Though she could have booked a short-term rental.'

'But she didn't.'

'No. And she said something to Vivian in Walter's presence about going back to the Morrison, as I recall.'

'What are you doing?'

I had my phone again. 'Calling the hotel. Can you get me something to write on?'

'You're going to ask for a guest's phone records? I don't think even Caron will give you those?'

'I don't need—' I interrupted myself. 'Hi, I'm a guest and trying to pick up my voicemails remotely? I'm afraid I've forgotten how.'

Sarah slid a torn napkin and blue marker in front of me.

'Then I just punch in star and the room number? Uh-huh.' I was listening. 'Yes, 208. Shropshire. Thank you for doing that.'

I waited, enjoying Sarah's astonished yet admiring look.

'Three old messages,' I repeated for her benefit. Punching them up, I listened to all three and then went back to replay the first, scribbling on the napkin before ending the call.

'What? What?' Sarah demanded.

'First one was from Walter Benson at seven thirty-five the morning after Vivian's death. He says he knows what happened but has her best interests in mind. Then he leaves his number and says to text him where and when they can meet.'

'Why didn't you play it for me?' Sarah said, pouting a bit.

'I . . . well, I'm sorry. I didn't think of it. I wrote it down though.' I shoved over the napkin.

'Like I can read that,' she said, referring to the smeared ink.

'You gave me a wet napkin,' I told her, picking it up to see that the blue had transferred to the tabletop.

'Paper towel,' she said, nodding at the towel under the bottle. It had a hunk torn out of it. 'And it was just damp with wine.'

'Anyway,' I said, leaning back in the seat. 'There was something in Walter's tone as he left the message. I can't quite put my finger on it, but—'

'I could help, if I'd heard it.'

'I know, I know.'

'And the others?'

'Others?'

'Other messages,' Sarah said. 'You said there were three.'

'Two from Oliver Benson, saying he was sorry about Vivian. That he hadn't known her long but wished he had.'

'He called twice?' Sarah asked. 'That seems niceness overkill. Even for Oliver.'

I frowned. 'I thought so, too. The first one was yesterday, but he called again last night saying he needed to talk to her.'

'Is that the ta-da?' Sarah asked.

'Ta-da?' It was like we had a language barrier.

'Your ta-da moment, when you keep the information from me and then—'

'Ta-da!' I said. 'But no, it's not. Vana told me Oliver had left a message. And he came by the cottage yesterday afternoon, looking for her.'

'When you found Walter,' Sarah said. 'Was the second phone message after that?'

'Yes,' I said, mulling it over. 'I hope he's OK. This idea that the deaths of Vivian and Walter might have something to do with him is disturbing.'

'You think he's being paranoid or that he actually might be in danger?'

'I don't know,' I said. 'Gloria pointed out that Way, Aurora, Walter and Vivian were all dead. That Oliver thought he was nex—' I stopped.

'Next?'

'Yes.' I chewed on the inside of my cheek, thinking. 'What do Way, Aurora, Walter and Vivian all have in common?'

Exasperation. 'They're dead. You just said that.'

'OK, then what do the first three have in common?'

'Way, Aurora and Walter? They're related to Oliver, of course.'

'Exactly,' I said. 'So, what is Vivian doing in the group?' I held out both hands, palms up.

'No idea,' Sarah said dryly.

I pumped my hands up and down, palms up.

'What?'

I did it again.

Nothing.

Fine. 'Ta-da!'

'I need to see Oliver,' I told Gloria Goddard as she opened her door.

Rather than seeming confused at my abruptness, she went straight to annoyed. 'I told you I don't know where he is.' She went to pull the door closed.

I grabbed the edge of it. 'I know he's here.'

'No.'

'Yes.' I met her eyes with what passed for steely determination for me. 'Now.'

She groaned and let go, sending me flying back into the corridor.

'Just where do you imagine he is?' she asked, righting me.

'Probably your bedroom closet,' I told her. 'But there's no need for either of us to go through the indignity of a search. Tell him to come out.'

This time, a sigh. 'Oliver. Come on out, dear.'

The bedroom door creaked open. 'I wasn't in the closet,' the boy said sulkily.

'Then under the bed,' I said, gesturing toward the floral confection of pillows and throws. 'Behind the dust ruffle.'

Gloria came into the room. 'I should get rid of that. Hopelessly outdated.'

'I kind of like it,' Oliver said, brushing lint out of his hair. 'And besides you're . . .'

'Old? I know, boy. Now talk to Maggy, which is what you should have done earlier.'

Amen to that. 'When did you find out that you're related to Vivian Woodward?'

Oliver's mouth opened, closed and opened again. 'How did you know that?'

'Eric said you'd gotten into family research and done your DNA. Did it bring up Vivian as a family match?'

'Yes.' He collapsed onto the edge of the bed. 'I didn't tell even Eric because I knew he'd tell you.'

Because he's a good boy. 'You came home for spring break to meet her?'

'No, that's just it,' Oliver said. 'On the ancestry site it said she was in Boston, so I figured I'd just send her an email when we got back. When Eric told me that he had a job doing work for Philip and Vivian Woodward and they'd just moved here from Boston, I almost fell over.'

'So that's why you waited to talk to her about the supposed job until Philip was in the shower.'

'How did you know that . . . Oh.' He ducked his head. 'Eric, of course.'

'He thought you didn't like Philip for some reason. But this being a delicate subject, you wanted to speak to Vivian alone.'

'Exactly,' he said, nodding. 'She—'

'Wait.' Gloria was holding up a hand. 'How did you know that Philip was in—'

'It's OK, I'll explain later,' I told her, not wanting to disturb Oliver's rhythm. 'You went to Vivian's door, knocked and just told her?'

'Exactly,' he said again. 'I didn't know how much time I'd have.'

'To tell her "exactly" what?' Gloria burst out.

Oliver flushed. 'That she was my half-sister.'

'Way Benson is both Oliver and Vivian's father?' Sarah's mouth had dropped open about as wide as I'd ever seen it.

I gestured for her to close it, so I could continue without distraction.

She did. For a second. 'How did Way and Vana even know each other?'

'Walter was a sophomore in college when his girlfriend got pregnant with Way and they eloped. That means that Way and Vana would have been around the same age. Walter stayed in Brookhills after college. Harmony and Vana were here, too.' I shrugged.

'When did Vana leave for New York?'

'When she was eighteen. And almost immediately married an older man and got pregnant.'

'More like the other way around.'

'Exactly,' I said, echoing Oliver. 'Vivian never knew, of

course. Vana wouldn't reveal something so potentially embarrassing.'

'And Vana's husband must have been too old to count. Or too grateful.'

'Maybe. Vana told everybody Vivian was premature.'

'How did Vivian take it when Oliver told her?' Sarah asked. 'It must have been a shock.'

'You'd think, but he said she gave him a big hug and said she was excited for the two of them to talk more. That she was elated to have a younger brother.'

'Much younger,' Sarah said. 'Like twenty years?'

'Oliver was a late-in-life baby for Way and Aurora.'

'And Vivian a very early one for Way and Vana. Did Vivian tell Philip?'

'I don't think she could have, because he didn't say anything. And, believe me, he's happy to share anything that reflects poorly on Vana.'

'Who presumably knows she was pregnant by Way.'

'Presumably,' I said. 'Oliver still hasn't been able to talk to her, though he did tell Walter. That's what they were arguing about before the reception.'

'What's there to argue about? Either it's true or not. DNA doesn't lie.'

'But Oliver says Walter had no idea Way and Vana had been together. That Vana had gotten pregnant with Way's baby "out of wedlock," like Paula had with Walter's.'

'Paula?'

'Way's mother,' I told her. 'Oliver said Walter went ballistic, blaming Way.'

'Like William had blamed Walter, no doubt,' Sarah said sagely.

'Oliver pointed out that this had happened years ago, and his father was dead. There was nobody to yell at.'

'Nice. What did Walter say to that?'

'He got all quiet, and said he had to get into the reception.'

'Which is where Vana was. And still alive to blame,' Sarah said. 'Did they speak?'

'Briefly. If Vana was as drunk as she seemed, maybe he thought it would be useless to talk to her in that state.'

'Or he'd already made arrangements to meet with her in private,' Sarah pointed out. 'Before he got this new little tidbit.'

'Yes.' I got up and wandered toward the window, trying to think. A black Land Rover rolled by and I did a double take. 'Could that be Philip? They let him out?'

'Without the new evidence we have sitting here on a table, I doubt it,' Sarah said, coming to join me.

The vehicle had stopped at the corner in preparation for turning left onto Poplar Creek Road. Heading toward the Koeppler place, but I could have sworn the Land Rover remained parked on the street in front of the cottage when Philip was taken into custody. Pavlik wasn't in the habit of letting accused murderers drive themselves to the county jail.

Going to the door, I swung it open and scrambled down the porch steps and to the right before the Land Rover got out of sight.

'Where are you going?' Sarah called from the threshold.

'Just checking.' From the corner, I could see that no Land Rover was parked in front of the cottage. And the one we just saw pass was backing into the Koeppler driveway.

My phone buzzed a message as the vehicle stopped just short of the shed which was taped off again. The driver's side door opened and Vana climbed out as the rear liftgate went up. 'Now that's interesting,' I said to myself as I walked back to the shop.

'What is?' Sarah has good ears.

'It's Vana driving,' I said. 'She must have come and picked up the Land Rover. Now she's come back, pulled into the driveway and opened the rear tailgate.'

'Think she's moving into the cottage?' Sarah asked. 'Nobody else is living there. Why pay for a hotel?'

'Because Vana is Vana,' I said, taking out my phone to check the message. 'A nice hotel is more her style than a refurbished cottage is. Besides, she hates the place.'

'So she says,' Sarah said. 'Did she pull a suitcase out by any chance? She might have used the Land Rover to get it from the hotel.'

'No,' I said, considering. 'She just opened the tailgate and went toward the house.'

'Sounds like she's going then, not coming.'

But I was opening the PDF Pavlik had texted me, pinching it out so I could read the thing. 'Here's the missing person report that the sister filed.'

'For Ray Koeppler? What's the date?'

'August 16, 1967.'

'Very sixties,' Sarah said, leaning over my shoulder to see the photo on the form. 'Look at all that curly hair.'

'My grandmother would have said, "Can't tell the boys from the girls these days."' I frowned and clicked over to my own photos, landing on the one I'd taken of Carmen's ancient black-and-white.

'Is that the gang?' Sarah asked, and then pointed. 'Sure, there he is.'

'Grandma has been proved right,' I said, expanding the photo, too. 'That's Harmony. Ray is standing next to her, but his hair is pulled back.'

'Wow,' Sarah said, studying it. 'Guess it's true that spouses start looking like each other. And dogs and their owners.'

I ignored that, going back to the missing person's report. '"Reporting party's relationship to missing person: sister,"' I read.

'But you knew that. Vana told you her aunt reported Ray missing.'

'Only because she knew that I would look at the report.' I had zoomed in on the signature. 'See?'

Sarah peered at the scrawl. 'Something Koeppler. What's the first name?'

'Matty,' I said, taking the phone away to look again, just in case something had changed. 'And, if I'm not mistaken, Matty is short for Matilda.'

TWENTY-THREE

'Holy shit. You're saying Vana's parents were brother and sister?'

'I'm saying Paz and Harmony were brother and sister.' I was at the computer, pulling up the information on *osteogenesis imperfecta* again.

'Same difference, right?'

'Maybe, maybe not.' I was leaning forward to read. 'Brittle bone disease, inherited both in autosomal dominant and autosomal recessive trait.'

'Meaning?'

'I'm reading,' I said, waving her off.

'Read faster.' She busied herself, comparing the PDF and photo on my phone. 'They do look alike.'

I sat back. 'From what I can make of this, I was right that if one parent was affected and the other wasn't, half of their children would have it.'

'Joey had it, Vana does not.'

'Right,' I said. 'But Paz and Harmony . . . Can we call them Ray and Matilda?'

'Please. And I'll point out that, at least in the photos you've shown me, they seem fine. Did anybody say they broke bones a lot or anything?'

'No,' I admitted. 'But even if they were both just carriers, there's a twenty-five percent possibility that a child would be born with OI. Possibly type two, which is the most severe form.'

'The one where they don't survive birth?'

'Sometimes.' Meaning the well-intentioned hug of a big sister could be lethal.

Sarah must have been reading my mind. 'Vana was just lucky then, not to inherit it.'

'One child in four is affected, one is unaffected and the other two are carriers but don't show symptoms. Thing is,' I said, twisting to face her, 'I'm not sure Vana is Ray and Matilda's daughter.'

'It's hard to slip somebody else's kid into your partner's uterus.'

'OK,' I said, 'so maybe Vana wasn't Ray's child.'

'You're basing this on what?' Sarah said skeptically. 'Free love of the sixties?'

'Partly,' I admitted. 'I have to check something.'

Sarah just folded her arms as I picked up the phone and followed the instructions I'd gotten from the hotel desk. Then I hung up.

'What?'

'A recording. The messages have been deleted. The guest has checked out.'

Sarah's head swiveled in the direction of the cottage. 'So she is planning to stay at the house.'

'Or she's getting out of Dodge, leaving Philip as the fall guy in at least one killing,' I said, untying my apron and picking up my purse. 'I'm going to go over there.'

'And what am I supposed to do? Mind the store?'

'Please,' I said, but stopped at the door. 'And maybe call Pavlik and tell him?'

'Tell him what?' she demanded, following me out onto the porch. 'You've just unloaded a broken wine bottle and sixty years of supposition on me.'

Supposition was a good word. And I had another theory spinning around, too. One that would explain why Oliver's simple condolence call to Vana had morphed, after his grandfather's death, into more insistent attempts to talk to her.

In fact, if I were right, this new supposition could be the key to understanding everything. 'I need to talk to Vana.'

Sarah grabbed my arm. 'She might already have killed her daughter and her blackmailer.'

When you put it that way . . . 'Call Pavlik quickly.'

When I turned down the driveway, I walked right past the cottage to the back of the Land Rover. Suitcase, as we'd suspected. But there was also a cardboard box. I'd just reached into the box when I heard Vana behind me.

'Maggy, what are you doing here?'

'I was wondering the same about you,' I said, reclosing the box and stepping back. The woman was wearing a neat navy pants suit and had another bag with her. 'Actually, when I saw the Land Rover pass by the shop, I thought Philip might have been released.'

'Then you must be terribly disappointed,' she said, sliding the bag in next to the box. 'I'm taking advantage of his absence to gather Vivian's things.'

'Are you going to drive back?' I asked. 'New York is nearly a thousand-mile drive.'

'The drive will help me clear my head,' she said, stepping back from the vehicle. 'I have a lot to think about. And to thank you for, I think.'

I wasn't so sure. 'I'm glad you have some sort of closure about Joey,' I said. 'But what about the deaths of Vivian and Walter? Can you just leave all that behind?'

'I've gotten very good at closing a chapter and moving on,' she said. 'I've done it since I was four, as you know.'

'I do know. I found the missing person report on your dad,' I said, stepping over the still-unplaced parking blocks and rebar spikes to lift the crime tape and peer into the shed. Walter's body was gone, of course, as well as the murder weapon. A rusty red stain on the floor extended nearly to the childish handprint. 'Is that yours?'

'My handprint?' she asked. 'Yes.'

'This shed was started about the time of that photo I showed you. You can see the stud wall being built to the one side. I mistook it for the cottage.'

'Interesting.'

I thought so. 'And it was probably finished, finally, about the time Paz went missing. Is that why you added this?' I was tracing the peace sign in the concrete with my finger. 'Paz means peace. As in rest in peace.'

'I'm not sure you should be touching things,' she said. 'The police won't like it.'

'Oh, they have my fingerprints on file,' I said. 'And my DNA probably. What about yours?'

'Mine?'

'It's all so interesting these days, isn't it? DNA is everywhere. Eventually, Joey's bones could be DNA'd. Maybe they will even indicate the truth about Ray and Matilda.'

She'd gone white. 'What truth?'

'That the two of them were brother and sister, of course,' I said. 'How long did you know?'

She hesitated, as if to lie, and then seemed to think better of it.

'Not until my mother died,' she said, leaning against the Land Rover like she needed the support. 'There was a letter in her things.'

'To you?'

She laughed. 'Yes, to me. Can you believe it? The woman couldn't talk to me, but she sure could write a letter. Not bring herself to mail it, of course.'

'Did you ever suspect? Before that, I mean?'

'I'm not sure. She was Mama, he was Pa. They used endearments when they spoke to each other – dear, sweetie and the like. It's not like they called each other "Sister" and "Brother".' She lifted her shoulders and dropped them. 'Who was to know?'

'Did you ever ask? Even after your father was gone?'

'Of course not,' she said. 'It was one of many things one did not speak of.'

You had to wonder what they did talk about. 'How did you feel about your parents when you read the letter?'

'Feel?' She looked up, her eyes intense. 'I *felt* like they were freaks. And that they made me a freak. I wished I'd never been born. But as it turns out, it was Joey who really paid for what they did.'

'By inheriting brittle bone disease?' I bobbed my head in acknowledgement. 'I suppose their relationship made it more likely.'

'And I, in turn, loved my brother to death.' She gave a humorless laugh.

'This aunt of yours – your father's sister who supposedly filed the missing person report – did you invent her in case I saw it was signed by Matty Koeppler?'

'By his *sister*, Matty Koeppler,' she said bitingly. 'All

Harmony had to do was put "wife" where it asked for relationship. But she was simple – more a child than I ever was. I
think she must have thought they'd put her in jail if she lied
on an official form.' She shook her head. 'Makes you wonder
if they weren't the first to inter-marry in the family.'

'Carmen referred to Harmony as hippy-dippy. That the
men, like Walter, wanted to take care of her.'

'Walter,' she said. 'He was a little odd himself. Always
hanging around, bringing Way by.'

'Way?'

She studied my face. 'Know about that, too, don't you?'

'That Way was Vivian's father?' I asked. 'Yes. Did your
mother know Paz was dead when she filed the missing person
report? Or did she find out later?'

'File a fraudulent report? Please. Not unless some man had
talked her into it.' She shook her head. 'Vivian must have
gotten that from her.'

'Gotten what?'

'A misplaced self-righteous streak coupled with a daddy
complex, of course.'

'Daddy complex?'

'Letting a man tell you what to do. Virtually choosing
that man because you want to be told.' She raised her chin.
'My mother and Paz. Vivian and Philip. Not me. I married an
older man and used him, not the other way around. Nobody
tells me anything.'

But I had to tell her something. 'I found the bottle, Vana.'

Her head jerked up, though she tried to control it. 'What bottle?'

'The smashed Sangiovese bottle from Luc's. It was in the
recycle bin at Uncommon Grounds.'

'That's odd.' Frowning, Vana lifted the crime scene tape
and stepped closer as if we were literally going to put our
heads together and figure this one out. 'I suppose it must have
been in the car and thrown away in the confusion afterwards?
I don't know why it would be in your trash, though.'

'Me neither,' I said, playing along. 'And the entire paper
bag wasn't wet. Just the bottom, soaked with wine when the
bottle broke. The receipt taped to the top of the bag was
perfectly dry and legible.'

'Then perhaps Vivian took it out of the car and threw it . . .' She gasped, her hand going to her mouth. 'Philip – could he have hit her with the bottle and then disposed of it where it wouldn't be traced back to him?'

A life playing make-believe had held her in good stead. 'You told investigators that you took the wine into the hotel when Vivian dropped you off. But neither part of that was true.'

Interestingly, she ignored the first part. 'You can ask the valet at the restaurant who was driving easily enough. It was Vivian.'

Gotcha. 'I did ask, and the valet confirmed that. But a block down the street you decided you were soberer than Vivian and should drive. The parking attendant in the lot across the street saw you change seats.'

'We changed back when we got to my hotel, of course.'

It actually was the perfect counter. I hadn't thought of that. I'd need to bluff my way through. 'Good try. But the traffic cam shows the Lexus didn't even stop at the hotel.'

There were no traffic cameras in Brookhills, but she bought it. 'Fine, I admit it. I drove Vivian home and started back to the hotel with the wine and dropped it. I couldn't carry the bag back wet and stinking of wine, so I dropped it in your recycle bin. Sue me.'

'Meanwhile, Philip and Vivian were arguing back at the car.'

'Apparently.'

'Walter lied,' I told her. 'He never saw Philip out there.'

'Why would he lie?' she demanded.

'Because he was trying to protect you.'

'That's ridiculous.' She was gazing off behind me, toward the shed. 'Walter Benson was no hero, believe me.'

'Yet he made sure your mother was able to stay on this property,' I said. 'Even standing up to his father. I wonder why that was.'

'No idea.' I'd been dismissed.

Fine. We'd move on. 'How much did Vivian know?'

'About what?' She was picking at an end of the crime tape.

Dead baby brother, father and mother who were brother and sister, missing uncle/father. All forgotten. The woman was genuinely great at re-inventing herself.

'Where shall I begin?' I said, setting my purse down on one of the rubber parking barriers. 'Wednesday night we had just found Joey's bones. You were probably devastated. And more than a little afraid. All those years of believing you had killed him. The guilt. You were drinking at dinner and it all spilled out, didn't it?'

She dropped the tape and stood stock-still.

'Didn't it?' I repeated. 'You were a child at the time. Vivian is your daughter. She would understand.'

She was staring past me toward the creek. 'It felt so good finally telling somebody. Confessing and being forgiven.'

I didn't dare interrupt.

'Vivian cried when I told her about Joey,' she whispered. 'We talked and talked. Opened another bottle of wine. Vivian loved babies, just like my mother.' She shook her head back and forth and back and forth. 'She understood, I thought.'

'Then what happened?' I asked.

'It was as we were leaving the restaurant. When I made her change drivers, she settled back in the passenger seat and said we'd have to tell the police, of course. And Philip.'

'Self-righteous, just like your mother,' I baited her.

'Yes.' She leaned forward almost eagerly. 'And defiant, like there was something bubbling under the surface.'

There was. Vivian had found out that morning that her ever-so-sanctimonious mother had a child – Vivian, herself – out of wedlock. 'Your daughter was going to tell everybody who the baby was and what had happened to him. Was she also going to blow the lid off the fact she wasn't your husband's daughter? That you had a sordid little affair and then foisted the result of that affair on the first wealthy old man you could get your claws into?'

Vana stiffened but she didn't deny it. 'I forbade her. Told her absolutely *not*.'

'It could ruin your life, after all. The one you've built so carefully for her.' I couldn't feel sorry for the woman. But I could pretend. 'Vivian should have understood that.'

'Understood?' she repeated. 'Vivian was drunk. You can't talk to a drunk.'

'You were drunk, too,' I pointed out.

'But I function at a high level, no matter how much I drink,' she said, stubbornly. 'That's why I said I would drive her home and walk back to my hotel.'

All drunks think they function. High or otherwise. 'What happened?'

'I pulled into the driveway and she was still preaching at me. Maybe I stopped the car a little close to the edge, I don't know. It was dark. I got out and Vivian got out, too, and came around the car. When I reached into the back seat to get the wine, she was right there behind me. She said I was genuine all right – a genuine slut. Can you believe that?'

Yes. 'No.'

'I straightened up and just swung the bottle back at her. I didn't mean to hit her.'

'Of course not.' I kept the sarcasm out of my voice, so she'd keep talking.

'She fell. And when I realized my little girl was dead, I panicked. I didn't know what to do.'

My little girl. Please. 'So what did you do?'

'I . . . I put her back in the car. It must not have been in park, because when I shut the door as quietly as I could, it started to roll.' She closed her eyes.

'It just rolled into the creek? And you did nothing?' I think my voice went up an octave.

'The water just closed over the car and it was gone. The night was beautiful. Peaceful, even. I . . . God help me, all I could think of was that my secrets were safe.'

My jaw was aching from the tension. 'And Vivian was already dead, after all.'

'Yes.'

'But see, that's the problem,' I told her. 'She wasn't dead. When the water started to fill the car, your daughter regained consciousness. She managed to undo her seatbelt and she fought for her life. She pounded on the windows trying to break them, claw through the upholstery if she had to. Her fingers were bloody, her nails torn off. I'm sure they didn't show you that when you identified her body.'

'No, I saw none of that,' she said, still staring toward the creek. 'If I had just known . . .'

Yeah, right. 'And Walter?'

'He must have seen me,' she whispered. 'I knew when I got his phone message that he wanted something for his silence. And I knew what kind of man he was because of what he'd done to my father.'

Ahh. 'What was that?'

Her eyes were on the shed. 'I saw the two of them arguing. The next day, Paz was gone and there was a new cement floor in the shed.' She sighed and turned back to me. 'I always wondered whether he was under there. That's why I put the peace sign there, like you said.'

Me? I was just making things up as I went. And the more horrific they were, the truer they were turning out to be.

'At the reception yesterday,' I said, 'were you as drunk as you appeared?'

'Oh, I was drunk.' She gave me a sideways smile. 'Just not too drunk. As I left the reception, I saw Philip's text about going to the store. He wanted to know if I needed anything. Sucking up, of course, probably hoping I'd give him Vivian's share of the property if he was a good son-in-law.'

'You already intended to meet Walter.'

'Yes,' she said. 'But I hadn't figured out a time or a place. Or what to do once we did meet.'

'Then you saw the cottage door open.'

'And Philip's phone was on the table in the front room. I could hear him in the bathroom.'

'It must have seemed like a sign,' I said. 'You texted Walter at the number he'd left on the voicemail at the hotel and arranged to meet at three by the shed. How did you know Philip would be gone by then?'

'He'd said to get back to him by quarter to three if I wanted anything. When he got out of the shower shortly after that, I screamed at him like a lunatic. He couldn't wait to get away from the ugly drunk.' She lifted her chin. 'If Philip hadn't left and Walter showed up at three, I would have figured something out. I always do.'

'But he did leave and Walter arrived on time.'

'Yes.' She shivered. 'The man still makes my skin crawl.'

'What did he say?'

'That he would keep my secret. Then he tried to force himself on me, can you believe it?'

Was Walter ineptly trying to hug the woman he knew to be his daughter? If so, a little preamble by way of explanation would have been good. 'What did you do?'

'I told him that I knew his secret, too. That he'd killed my father.' She lifted one of the rebar spikes, seeming to gauge its heft in her hand. 'I made him admit it.'

'He said he'd killed your father and buried him under the shed?'

'Oh, he said it was an accident. That they'd gotten into a fist fight after Joey died and my father fell and struck his head.'

So Walter had known about Joey all along. I assumed he'd kept his mouth shut to protect Vana. 'Did Walter tell you he loved your mother?'

'Of course, but she wouldn't have anything to do with him after that. The man had killed her brother.'

'The brother who had been molesting her for years. You can understand how that would make Walter feel, especially if he loved Harmony.'

'You're making excuses for a murderer,' she said.

'You're a murderer, too,' I pointed out.

'Vivian's death was an accident, just like Joey's was,' she told me. 'Nobody ever had to know.'

The peaceful surface of the water never disturbed.

'With Walter dead and Philip arrested,' Vana continued, 'I would be out of danger. Free to get on with my life.'

'But Vivian wasn't,' a voice said, and Oliver stepped out from behind the Land Rover. 'You took that from her.'

Vana whirled around. 'Who are you?'

I'd forgotten the two had never actually met. 'This is Oliver Benson.'

'I've been trying to get hold of you.' Oliver was advancing on the woman with the iron bar. 'To tell you something.'

She gestured with it. 'Move over next to Maggy.'

I shook my head, trying to warn him that it was better if we could keep Vana's attention split in opposite directions.

But Oliver's sole focus was Vana as he moved to stand next to me. 'You've already killed my half-sister and my grandfather. Are you going to kill us, too?'

'Your half-sister? Who . . .' Her hand went to her mouth. 'Of course. You're Way's son.'

'And Walter's grandson,' I said, and turned to Oliver. 'Did Walter tell you? Did he explain why he was so upset when you told him that Vivian was Way's daughter?'

'Yes,' Oliver said quietly, his face reddening. 'I wanted to tell you, but . . .'

'Family,' I said, understanding. 'But you needed to tell Vana.'

He rubbed his mouth. 'I figured she must not realize. Because if she did know and then did what she did with my father—'

'What are you two talking about?' The tip of the rebar was being waved in circles at us, like a fencing foil.

'Walter was your real father,' I told her.

'What?'

'You heard me,' I said. 'Walter was your father. You know what that means.'

'It means . . .' Her eyes were flickering, moving, like she was searching for something inside her own head. 'It means my parents weren't brother and sister.'

'Yes, it does.' Still made me queasy every time I heard it. 'But it also means that you and *Way* were brother and sister. Half, at least.'

She ran her left hand through her hair, seeming confused. 'No, I—'

'Don't you see, Vana? You committed the very same offense you hated your parents for.'

'No, no. I didn't know.' She was glancing around the yard now and for a second I thought she'd take the Land Rover and run.

'Walter was going to tell you that he was your father,' I told her. 'He'd always known, of course. He'd protected your mother all of her life and now he was going to protect you.'

By framing an innocent man. Oops.

Vana's jaw was clenched, a vein visibly pulsing at her temple. She said nothing.

'You were his daughter and you killed him,' Oliver said, disbelievingly. 'You have to feel something.'

'For Walter?' Vana was shaking her head. 'No. He knew about Vivian's death. I had to do something.'

'I know now too,' Oliver said. 'And Maggy knows. Are you going to kill us?'

Never ask a question you don't want the answer for.

'Maggy?' She was wiping the rebar spike on her pants leg. It left white gravel dust against the navy. 'She's the one who delivered the best news I've had in years. I wasn't responsible for Joey's death.'

'And yet' – I swept my hand toward the creek and shed – 'you do have a couple other deaths on your conscience.'

'That's the one good thing about believing you've taken another life for your whole existence. You get used to it.'

If 'it' was being batshit crazy. I put my hand on Oliver's arm and together we backed up, even as Vana advanced. 'We've told other people everything we know.'

'All conjecture, as I don't have to tell you,' she said, hefting the rebar. 'And if you have your phone recording in that purse of yours . . .' She snatched the bag from where I'd set it on the parking barrier with her free hand, dangling it upside down. The contents landed on the ground.

'Huh,' she said, sorting through the contents with the toe of her stylish shoe. 'Not as smart as I thought you were.'

'No phone in my pockets either,' I said, patting my jeans and my jacket. By this time, I'd hoped to hear sirens. But nothing. Either Sarah hadn't gotten hold of Pavlik or he hadn't bought what she was selling. We were on our own. 'You can't get both of us with that thing.'

'Bet your life on it?' She lifted the rebar above her head.

'Oliver Benson!' a voice called. 'You get right over here!'

Startled, Vana turned to see Gloria Goddard in the Manor parking lot across the way, waving.

Vana's attention diverted, I tugged at Oliver's arm.

The two of us turned and jumped into Poplar Creek.

TWENTY-FOUR

'Better hope that creek isn't polluted,' Sarah said, as Pavlik tucked a blanket around me.

'Damn right,' I said, giving my honey a kiss on the cheek. Pavlik, not Sarah. 'I swallowed a boatload of water.'

'Me, too,' Oliver said, as Gloria Goddard fussed over his blanket. 'You nearly drowned me.'

'I was trying to save you,' I protested.

'But I can swim. I was trying to rescue *you*.'

'You were two feet from shore,' Sarah said sourly. 'You could have just stood up.'

As it turned out, yes. 'Well, you sure took your time calling the cavalry.'

'In Sarah's defense,' Pavlik said, settling down on the back of the ambulance next to me, 'we were here. We just came in without sirens so as not to ruin any carefully constructed plan you might have.'

It was true, that when Oliver and I did finally stand up, the men and women in blue were swarming the place. 'It was Gloria who really saved the day, though.'

Gloria's face pinked up. 'Just calling Oliver home for dinner.'

'At three in the afternoon?' Oliver said, punching her in the shoulder.

'*Sunday* dinner.' She punched him back. 'No, I saw that woman threatening you from the window.'

'So, you came running down to the parking lot to save us,' Oliver said. 'That was really brave.'

The pink got redder. 'Not running and not that brave. The woman was holding a bar, not a gun. She'd have to have one hell of an arm to get me with it from across the street.'

'Still.' He kissed the top of her head. 'Thank you.'

'Yes. Thank you, Gloria.' I glanced around. 'Where is Vana?'

'On her way to the station,' Pavlik said. 'She says we have nothing on her. That it's all—'

'Conjecture?'

'Her word exactly. She says if you were smart, you would have been recording it.'

'She's right,' I said, shaking my head. 'That is one messed-up human being.'

'Her parents were brother and sister, after all,' Sarah pointed out.

'No, that's just it,' Gloria said. 'Walter was Vana's father. Oliver told me, didn't you, dear?'

'I did,' the boy said, nodding. 'My grandfather couldn't believe it when I told him that my father was also Vivian's father. He said it was like history repeating itself.'

'The baby's disease,' Sarah said. 'The brittle bone disease. Vana didn't have it because Paz wasn't her father?'

'She had a lower chance of inheriting it,' I said, 'if just her mother was affected or a carrier, rather than both parents. But we don't even know for sure that Matilda had it.'

'We don't know a lot for sure,' Sarah grumbled.

'But that's what's so crazy,' Oliver said, leaning forward so the blanket slipped off his shoulders. 'As little as we know, Vana knew even less. Yet she killed her own daughter and father to protect it.'

'Oliver is absolutely right,' I said, impressed. 'Everything that Vana had worked so hard to hide all these years – that she'd killed her brother, that her mother and father were siblings – wasn't true in the first place.'

'And yet she managed to unwittingly commit the same offense she thought her parents had,' Pavlik said.

'That she hated them for,' I added.

'Brotherly/sisterly love,' Sarah mused.

'Amen,' Gloria intoned, repositioning Oliver's blanket.

'By the way, Pavlik. I think you'll find Ray Koeppler under there.' I pointed at the shed. 'Walter and Ray had a fight and Ray supposedly hit his head and died. Walter buried him in the shed and poured the cement floor over him.' Or so the story goes.

'My grandfather is a murderer, too?' Oliver seemed too tired to be truly aghast.

'I'm sure there were mitigating circumstances,' Mrs G assured him.

'There were,' I said. 'This was after Joey died and I assume Walter wanted to protect Harmony and Vana. Keep Ray from getting Harmony pregnant again.'

'Killing him would do it,' Sarah said.

'The forensics team is going to have a field day with all this.' Pavlik groaned and stood up, holding out his hands. 'Ready to go and get into dry clothes?'

I stood. 'Mind the store for me?' I asked Sarah.

'When don't I?' she said, dryly. And then, hesitating, gave me a hug. 'Glad you're not dead.'

'Me, too,' I said.

'You, too, Oliver,' Sarah said, not wanting to be remiss. 'You know this explains something else.'

'What's that?' I asked.

'How Harmony was able to stay on that property all these years with no visible means of support.'

'I thought she was living off the land,' Oliver said.

'That only goes so far,' Sarah said. 'Somebody has to pay the taxes, minimum.'

'Walter Benson?' I asked.

'That would be my guess,' Sarah said. 'I'll check it out for you, Oliver.'

'For me?' He blinked.

'From the sounds of it, you may have a legal claim to the property,' Sarah said, and then grimaced. 'Only member of the family still alive and all.'

'Sarah,' I warned.

'What?' she protested. 'It's true. The deed was never transferred, so—'

'Enough,' I said.

'Thanks, Sarah,' Oliver said with a grin. He put an arm around Gloria. 'I think I'll stay a couple extra days before I go back to school. OK with you, Mrs G?'

'More than OK.'

They started down the drive and Pavlik and I followed.

I stopped at the back of the Land Rover. 'I am too smart.'

'Yes, you are,' Pavlik said. 'No matter what Vana Shropshire says.'

'There.' I pointed at the cardboard box.

'Evidence?' He was already pulling blue gloves out of his pocket.

'Maybe.' I shrugged, and then had to make a grab for the blanket as it slipped off my shoulders. 'But what I *know* is in there – because I put it there – is my phone. On "record". Just in case I ended up not resurfacing in the creek.'

'Cute.'

'Damn right.' I snuggled up under his arm. 'Let's go home.'